FLYING

BACKWARDS

Jennifer W. Smith

Flying Backwards

Published by Apple House Publishing Ö
ISBN: 978-0-9966954-1-1

Editing: Sue Ducharme of TextWorks
Cover Design: G. S. Prendergast

Author's Note: This is a work of fiction. Names, characters, places, and incidents are a product of the author's imagination. Locales and public names are sometimes used for atmospheric purposes. Any resemblance to actual people, living or dead, or to businesses, companies, events, institutions, or locales is completely coincidental.

Novels by Jennifer W. Smith

Contemporary Romance

Flying Backwards

Landing in Love Series

Defying Gravity

Holding Pattern

Ground Control

Turbulent Kisses

Flight Plan

Falling in Love at Christmas: Holiday Special I

Protecting my Love at Christmas: Holiday Special II

Rescuing Love at Christmas: Holiday Special III

Paranormal Romance

Broken Water Series

The Rare Pearl: Book 1

The Forsaken Pearl: Book 2

The Vanishing Pearl: Book 3

Wiccan Haus Series

Legends Mate

Join my Newsletter

You will get up-to-date information on my latest books, and how soon they are available, right to your inbox. I'll let you know when I've got book specials. Also, I love meeting my readers. I'll post author/reader events where we can meet in person. I'd be honored to sign your novel! Simply go to my website jenniferwsmith.com and sign-up for the newsletter.

Chapter One

On a typical Saturday morning, at the Clark family's house, Eleanor Clark turned down the long driveway in her Ford Escape and parked alongside her sister's Ford Explorer. The crunch of wheels on gravel announced her arrival. She grew up in this redbrick house in rural Pennsylvania, part of a "made in America" kind of family. The front shrubs were neatly trimmed and the steps swept clean. The wooden door displayed an inviting decorative wreath containing a pineapple, the official symbol of welcome.

Eleanor scooped an apron off the passenger seat and slung her bag over her shoulder as she exited the car. Polly, the family's Golden Retriever, sniffed the air from her grassy spot on the front lawn.

"Hey, girrrlll!" Polly thumped her tail at Eleanor's greeting. She generously scratched Polly on the head until her mother's raised voice drew her attention. She lifted her brows. "What now? Looks like I showed up at the wrong time." Polly panted heavily in reply, her tongue lolling.

Eleanor trudged around to the side of the house, scanning the yard for her dad, figuring he was probably out there somewhere. On weekends, if Russell Clark wasn't inside watching sports she would usually find him maintaining the yard. She heard distant clanking coming from the barn before her mother's elevated voice again drew her attention to the kitchen.

The main door stood open, allowing the cool, summer morning breezes to drift through the screen door. The standing fan already hummed in the kitchen, moving the air around. The temperature would rapidly rise on this late-August day. *With the ovens going, we girls will be sweating for sure.*

"Hello," she said as she opened the screen door, remembering to ease it closed behind her to avoid the loud bang her mother hated. The conversation between her mother, Heidi, and her older sister, Victoria, came to a halt. Eleanor's mother had an aggravated set to her lips.

Victoria ignored her sister, shook her head in disgust and blurted, "She's so irresponsible."

Eleanor guessed who she spoke of but paused in case some explanation was forthcoming. None was offered.

Seemingly defeated, Heidi waved away the comment and shrugged off her tension. With a somewhat forced grin, she greeted her daughter, "Hello, Eleanor." Already at the cupboard, she opened the door and took out a mug. "Want some coffee?" She'd selected the World's Best Mom mug and began pouring from a half-full pot before Eleanor could respond.

Victoria mustered a half-smile. "Morning, Eleanor. Did you remember your apron?"

"Coffee sounds great, Mom. Thanks." Numb to Victoria's bossy comments, Eleanor held up her apron. The lingering tension in the room raised her curiosity. "So, what's up?"

"It's Lizzy," Heidi poured cream into Eleanor's coffee.

Lizzy again? Elizabeth, the baby of the three Clark girls, was affectionately called Lizzy by everyone. Victoria and Eleanor's names were never shortened. Lizzy lived at home and attended community college on and off. She started at school again a couple of weeks ago.

"She's already blown off one of her classes. She claims she stayed up late to finish a paper, at the last minute, and then she skipped the class altogether. What is she thinking?" Heidi asked, exasperated.

Eleanor could empathize. She had followed Victoria's lead, attended a local college, and then worked and paid rent when living at home. Eleanor worked for her mother's catering business until she landed a secretarial job at a start-up software company. Victoria became a partner in their mother's business, appropriately named Clark's Catering, when she finished culinary school. She did the job effortlessly.

Not Lizzy. Their parents did everything differently when it came to her. Maybe the six-year age gap between their last two children came into play; Victoria and Eleanor were two years apart. Lizzy, a surprise baby, took being babied to a whole new level.

Eleanor not only worked a full-time job now, but she showed up many weekends helping her mother and Victoria cook, deliver, or do whatever was needed for the family catering business. Eleanor longed to go for a run instead of coming here, but she'd never leave them stranded when they needed help— even if it seemed to happen constantly. Lizzy never helped. They were all sick of it.

Lizzy strutted into the kitchen without a care in the world, her water bottle in hand. She wore sweats rolled to the knee, a tank top, and her dark hair pulled in a misshapen bun on top of her head.

Speak of the devil.

"Morning." Filling her water bottle at the refrigerator, she nonchalantly asked, "Prepping for that bridal or baby shower thing tomorrow?"

"Yes. Baby shower. It's a brunch. Mrs. Johnson's daughter is expecting. And where are you off to?" Victoria's sarcastic tone was lost on Lizzy.

"Oh yeah, I went to high school with Claire Johnson," said Lizzy. She screwed the cap onto her water bottle. "Tyler has a soccer game. I'm going for a run and heading over to the field." Tyler Peterman had been Lizzy's good friend since middle school. Tyler was secretly in love with Lizzy. Of course, everyone, even Lizzy, knew the "secret." Lizzy used his affection to her advantage a little too often. In Lizzy's defense, she remained a loyal friend to Tyler all these years.

"Do you have any schoolwork?" Heidi couldn't help but ask her wayward duckling.

"Mom!" Lizzy threw up her hands. "I have all weekend."

Heidi relented, pointing to some freshly sliced banana bread on a cutting board. "How about some breakfast?"

Nodding, Lizzy pulled ear buds out of her pocket, planted one in each ear, and then grabbed two slices of bread off the counter. She left, letting the screen door slam behind her. "Bye, Dad!"

Eleanor glanced out the window to see their dad waving from the yard. He bent over the lawnmower holding a can of gasoline.

She clenched her teeth, envious of her sister jogging away. With a wistful sigh she returned to her task.

"You should have made her stay and help. Or at least do something productive," Victoria chided.

"It's not worth the fight," Heidi sighed. "Here's your coffee, Eleanor. Let's get to work girls."

Eleanor hated the defeat in her mother's voice. Heidi, active mother of three, who once ran the PTA and church bake sales while juggling her business, seemed tired. Heidi plugged in the heavy-duty mixer and focused on making dough for the mini-scones. Victoria unloaded ingredients from a large canvas bag with the name REYNOLDS embroidered on it.

"So how's work?" Victoria asked while she twisted and secured her coffee-colored hair with a claw hairclip.

"Fine." Eleanor tried to think of something exciting to add, but managing an office was dull. There were rumors of the office relocating to Boston, but Eleanor didn't have the courage to bring up the subject. She didn't need to hear, "What are you going to do? Get a new job? Move to Boston?" She busied herself with tying her apron, but Victoria went on.

"How's Phillip?"

Eleanor braced for what was coming next.

"Any new wedding plans?"

"Phillip is fine. He's been busy. We haven't had time to plan anything." She reached for the scone recipe to review it, even though she knew it by heart.

"You've been engaged for three years. What's taking so long?"

Five years ago when she met Phillip at the software company, they'd spent late nights ordering take-out and getting to know one another better. The job had good pay and benefits, and dating Phillip made it exciting. She admired his intelligence and dedication. He was successful, kindhearted, and he loved her.

"Can't find a good caterer." Eleanor's jest got a grin from their mother, but it seemed to irritate Victoria.

"Well, I'm just saying, your eggs aren't getting any younger. Your chances of having children start to decrease after the age of thirty."

Eleanor wanted to be annoyed with her sister, but Victoria had been trying to have a baby for years. Their mother set out the measuring cups and gave Victoria a sympathetic smile.

"I'm *only* twenty-eight," Eleanor tried to keep her voice lighthearted.

"You'll be *twenty-nine* in October, it's barely two months away," Victoria snapped, but seemed to realize she'd gotten worked up. The room fell silent.

Children are the last thing on my mind right now. Big deal, so I've been engaged for three years. So I live with Phillip in a home he bought with his previously girlfriend. When I told him I wanted to get used to the big change of living together for a while before planning a wedding, he had agreed, if only to make me happy.

After a couple hours of listening to small-town gossip while she worked, Eleanor grinned when she heard familiar footsteps as her father's shoes crunched across the driveway. Then Russ's tall, broad frame filled the doorway.

"Girls." He nodded at the three women, who all paused to look up at him. Russ had been outside all morning tinkering with the lawnmower and cutting the grass as the air became hotter every hour.

"Hi, Dad," Victoria and Eleanor said in unison.

Polly followed him in and headed for her water bowl. As Russ washed his hands and forearms he asked over his shoulder, "What time's lunch?"

"Let me get you a cold drink." Heidi scooted to the refrigerator to pour her husband some lemonade. "I can fix you a sandwich. What would you like?" She rattled off his choices.

"Ham." He gave his wife a wink as she handed him the full glass. He drank his lemonade and announced, "I'll be back in five minutes." Russ told his faithful old dog to stay.

Eleanor used the interruption to make her getaway. "Well, I've got to get going." She pulled off the apron, balled it up, and crammed it into her bag.

"Do you want a sandwich? I've got plenty," Heidi waved at the array of lunchmeats and cheeses she pulled out of the refrigerator. "I can make tuna salad."

"No thanks, Mom. I told Phillip we'd have lunch before heading to the home improvement store this afternoon."

"Are you finally renovating? Where are you going to start?" Victoria considered herself a great decorator and had frequently commented to Eleanor if she did not make Phillip move them to a more suitable house (meaning one his old girlfriend did not pick out) then they should at least renovate the outdated ranch.

"Yeah, we're looking at tile for the bathroom." Their home had three bedrooms, one bathroom, an eat-in kitchen, and a living room with an attached sunroom. The house had last been remodeled in the '80s.

"Let me know if you like something and want a second opinion." When Victoria and her husband, Perry, had bought a new-construction house a few years ago, she had dragged Eleanor to numerous stores shopping for everything from can openers to furniture.

"Okay." Eleanor slung her bag over her shoulder as she headed for the door.

"Thanks for your help, and Eleanor, I made an extra loaf of banana bread for Phillip." Heidi handed the neatly wrapped bundle to her daughter. "Dinner is at six tomorrow. You're still coming?"

Eleanor nodded. "Of course. Good luck with the shower. Tell Mrs. Johnson I said congratulations."

"I will. We should be finished by three. I'm making pork chops for dinner." Heidi held the screen door open and waved to her daughter.

"Bye, Dad, see you tomorrow."

Eleanor's dad strolled across the grass, ready to eat his lunch.

"Okay, kiddo, see you tomorrow," Russ answered, never breaking his stride.

Eleanor noticed her dad bending to kiss her mother, who still held the door, waiting for him. Heidi smiled into her husband's eyes before they disappeared inside. Their romantic exchange got Eleanor thinking as she slipped into her blistering hot car. *What kind of greeting can I give Phillip when I get home?*

Eleanor parked at the local supermarket and phoned Phillip.

"Hello?" Phillip answered, sounding distracted. This meant he couldn't take his attention off his computer screen to identify who called him. *Not surprising.*

"Hey, it's me. I'm at the market. I need to pick up a few things. Want anything special for lunch?" Eleanor enjoyed the cold blast of air conditioning that met her as she walked through the store entrance, phone tucked into her shoulder.

"No. I just ate the leftover chicken and rice casserole."

"Oh, you already ate. We were supposed to eat together and then go to the home improvement store." *Does he ever listen to anything I say?* "Is there any left?"

"Sorry, pet, I finished it. I thought you'd eat at your mom's." Phillip's pet name for Eleanor was not very original; what Eleanor had once thought charming was now just irritating.

"Never mind, I'm at the market now. I'll pick something up. Just be ready to go out soon." To be fair, when he worked on the weekends it freed up her time to help her family, or go for a long run, or curl up with a good book. Sometimes it worked to her advantage.

"Got it. See you soon."

She disconnected and grabbed a basket, heading for the vegetables. She selected a healthy variety for a hearty salad. She whizzed down a few aisles collecting some staple items before heading for the frozen pizza. Tonight would be salad, pizza, and a movie, a typical Saturday night.

As Eleanor waited in line at the checkout, her mind drifted. She imagined arriving at home and giving Phillip a long passionate kiss that would lead to peeling each other's clothes off while they stumbled their way to the bedroom. He had been working a lot, and they seemed to be in a rut. Maybe a brief delay before getting to the store would be a nice distraction. Eleanor's heart was not really into shopping for tile.

She tried to spice up their minimal love life. A few nights ago she surprised Phillip by joining him in the shower. She had caught him off guard, and he mumbled, "I'll be done in a minute and it's all yours."

"What's your rush?" she purred, wrapping her arms around his neck and moving in for a tantalizing kiss.

"Oh…oh, this is unexpected." He kissed her for a moment before saying, "I'll see you in the bedroom then. Just let me finish rinsing off."

She paused briefly, and coyly tried again. "I thought maybe we could have some fun in here?"

"Na, let's just go to the bedroom."

Eleanor blinked, returning to reality as the cashier asked her if she wanted paper or plastic for the groceries.

Eleanor pulled her vehicle into the carport. She had blasted the air conditioning the whole ten-mile ride home.

Phillip appeared at the car door, his hair damp. "Need help?"

She figured he'd jumped in the shower after hanging up with her. He looked cool in his light-blue polo shirt and khaki shorts. Unconsciously, she tucked a stray lock of hair behind her ear. She thought she must look a sight after sweating all morning in her mother's kitchen.

"Hi! Sure, there are a few bags. Mom made you banana bread," she said, opening the rear door, revealing the paper bags and the bread. Phillip bent slightly to kiss her before retrieving the bags. They entered through a tiny mudroom, where Eleanor hung her purse on a peg and kicked off her flip-flops.

"Sure is steamy today." The house didn't have central air conditioning and she grumbled at the stuffiness. In the kitchen, she poured a glass of lemonade.

Phillip unloaded the bags on the counter. "Want these in the fridge?" He pointed to the vegetables. At Eleanor's nod he piled the various items on the shelves. She sipped and watched him as he placed the frozen pizza in the freezer, the canned beans in the cupboard, and sponges under the sink. He paused. "You look tired. Do you still want to go out?"

Now is my chance. I need to put my seductive scheme into action, give him a passionate kiss... She paused only a moment before she said, "I'm fine. Just hungry, I guess." Turning away, she reached for a loaf of bread to make a sandwich. Whether she could not face being turned down or she just didn't want to be with him, she didn't know. *What is happening to me?* She fought the lump in her throat, trying not to cry. *You are being ridiculous.* She shook off her melancholy.

Chapter Two

In mid-October the Clark's Catering ladies enjoyed some welcomed downtime. Eleanor reluctantly agreed to shop for tile with Victoria. Her previous outings with Phillip a couple months ago had no results. Victoria took her procrastinating sister to a tile shop in a strip mall, where she made quick work of plucking out the perfect tile combinations for Eleanor's approval. Victoria, in her element, enjoyed herself, but Eleanor couldn't ignore her nagging thoughts. *Does this really matter? Is this what I want? I just don't care about that old house!*

Victoria pointed to a coffee shop at the other end of the L-shaped plaza. "I need some caffeine." As they moved in that direction Victoria's cell phone rang. She dug through her huge designer purse and held up her index finger to Eleanor. "Clark's Catering, Victoria speaking."

Eleanor slowed to a stop in front of a travel agency office, lured by the various exotic posters advertising a tropical destination, a Mediterranean cruise, and a tour of London, Paris, and Rome. Eleanor had always wanted to go to Rome and Paris. In fact, in high school she came very close to going on a senior class trip to Paris. However, that year her dad's union went on strike, and with the expense of Victoria's college tuition and twelve-year-old Lizzy's braces, the costs were too much for the Clark family budget.

Rome: classical architecture built by the ancient Romans, the bountiful fountains…and the food…she could almost taste the cheesy eggplant parmesan she imagined. She always dreamed of traveling.

Her daydream drew her in deeper… She glimpsed across the Piazza di Trevi into his dark sexy eyes. The man's teeth flashed white against his sun-kissed skin and his sensual smile made her heart pound. This hunky stranger came straight for her.

Victoria's voice jolted Eleanor. "Sorry, it was the Cooper bride with a question about the beef medallions. Of course, we can get grass-fed beef. Everyone wants it these days. Oh, you'll love her colors, dark orange and purple. Different, huh?"

"Yeah." Eleanor stared longingly at the poster of Rome, her hunky Italian's smiling face fading away. "Yeah, can't wait to see that combo."

Lattes in hand, they sat outside at one of the café's two bistro tables. "So, Eleanor, what's up with you lately? You seem so glum. Is it because you turned twenty-nine? Getting older sucks! Sorry I was on your case about your eggs a while ago."

Eleanor replied nonchalantly, "No, I don't care about that." This restlessness she felt worried her, but how could she talk about it with Victoria when she didn't even know herself why it was happening? Worse yet, what could she do about it?

Her birthday had been another confirmation something was amiss. She looked forward to a fun night out at Champ's Billiards with her sisters and the guys. They'd gotten a table, ordered food, and then shot pool while listening to a live local band. Eleanor sat off to the side where she could watch the band and still see Perry boast good-naturedly after every shot. The band dialed it down to a classic Journey song. The whole bar sang and swayed to the melancholy lyrics. It was her night, her birthday celebration–why didn't she feel the joy they did? The thought had sobered her.

Promptly at midnight her sisters yelled out birthday wishes, which prompted others around the bar to respond in kind. Phillip walked up to her, smiling. "Happy Birthday, pet." He leaned in to kiss her, and she practically held her breath. Time seemed suspended.

Let this kiss be magical.

She received a smoochie kiss, and then Phillip retreated. Forcing a smile, her heart sank. The epiphany, the revelation there was *no* magic between them, buzzed through her. *I can't live like this and feel like this anymore.*

Victoria peered over her coffee cup at her sister, concerned. "Seriously, what is going on with you, Eleanor?"

Eleanor sat facing the travel agency, feeling wistful. "I think I need a vacation."

"Don't we all," Victoria muttered into her cup.

"I just wish I could go somewhere really far away." *Far away, escape my life... my stale relationship, boring job and demanding family.*

"Well, if you got married, you could honeymoon somewhere really far away." It made sense to Victoria, but Eleanor thought about a solo trip.

Shrugging, she changed the subject. "Right. So anyway, are you going to need help with the Cooper wedding?"

Easily distracted with anything regarding the Cooper wedding, Victoria said, "*Yes* we can use your help."

"Well, you can count on me." *I'm not going anywhere.*

Eleanor had vowed to do something about her life but wondered how exactly she was going to accomplish it. She did not have to wait long for the metaphorical ball to get rolling. The Monday evening after her birthday, Phillip sat looking at her across their dinner table. She noticed his excitement.

"I have something to tell you," he said intently. "You know those rumors about the company moving to Boston. Well, we had a meeting today, and it's true."

Eleanor didn't respond, so Phillip went on. "Now I know this would be a big change for us. You'd still have your position if we want to think about making this move." No matter how much he wanted to go, he offered her the option for them to stay in Pennsylvania. She never lived outside of York County, even when she attended college. Boston seemed far, but it's not what bothered her.

"When is this happening?" True, not new or shocking news; there had been rumors, but the idea proved life altering.

"By the first of the year. They've already signed a lease."

Neither of them had touched the food on their plates.

"What do you want to do?" Eleanor asked, but she already knew his answer. His work was his life. And his work was moving to Boston.

"This would be an amazing opportunity for me. Open so many doors." He added sincerely, "You'll be my wife, Eleanor. I want you to be happy with whatever we decide together."

Wow, what can I say? Any time not spent with her and her family, he spent working on his projects. A good wife would support her husband. *This is a no-brainer. How can I say no?* She joked. "Do you think we'll pick up a Boston accent?"

He blew out the breath he held and chuckled. "I promise we'll make this work. We'll get a place with plenty of extra room for your family to come and stay. It will be great. Oh, and we can definitely have the wedding here near town."

Oh yeah, came the afterthought, *the wedding and my family.* She felt a little numb.

Eleanor convinced Phillip to wait a bit before telling her family. She thought they needed to figure out more details first. He readily agreed, just thrilled she'd said yes.

For the rest of the week, she went through the motions at work. Phillip worked late several nights, excited to finalize his projects before the big move.

The other office girl, Laura, who was not relocating, scanned the job ads and left them open on the lunchroom table. For the fun of it Eleanor thumbed through them. *What else could I do besides office work? Maybe I could pursue something more interesting once we settle in Boston.* She only meant to get some ideas. In black and white, she read an ad for Meade Airlines hosting an open interview and seeking to hire flight attendants. The interviews were being held next Wednesday at a hotel in downtown Philadelphia.

Hmm...I could travel to exotic places. I could go far away and start a new and exciting life, be someone else... Wait! I have a life, she reminded herself. *I am starting a new and exciting life in Boston. I'm going to plan a big wedding and be married to Phillip for the rest of my life.* Still, she could not help herself from daydreaming of the possibilities of what could be, a daunting thought for a small-town girl, but Eleanor could not get the idea out of her head.

The following Wednesday morning, the day of the open interviews with Meade Airlines, Eleanor had taken a shower, but she stayed in the bedroom, stalling. When she looked at herself in the mirror, she recalled her promise to herself to live a better life. Could she miss this opportunity to interview with an airline? *No!* Finally she came into the kitchen and saw Phillip already dressed and munching on the last spoonful of his granola.

"I'm not feeling well. It's my stomach. Maybe I caught a stomach bug." Eleanor flattened her hand over her belly and offered a pathetic look.

"Sorry, pet. I'll tell Laura. She can run things today." Phillip placed his bowl in the sink. "I hope you feel better." He gave her a peck on the forehead, gathered his things, and left.

Eleanor's stomach was upset because of nerves not a stomach bug. She dashed to their bedroom and retrieved a gray suit from the back of her closet. Quickly she changed, carefully applied makeup, and added some tasteful accessories. She smoothed her long ponytail into a neat bun, ready for the interview in Philadelphia. If she left now, she would beat the traffic.

The GPS guided her to the hotel in record time. *What am I doing here? Am I even flight attendant material?* Eleanor suspected she appeared average-looking, not as striking as Victoria or as pretty as Lizzy. She studied her refection in the rearview mirror. *Do I have what they are looking for? Do I have what it takes?*

She entered with trepidation and followed the WELCOME TO MEADE AIRLINES signs to a ballroom. The upholstered chairs were set up theater-style. People filed in and sat down. Scooting into a row, she did the same. She sat up straight, adjusting the fit of her suit jacket, and glanced around. The others were mostly younger and underdressed. Eleanor considered her age, wondering if it would count against her. There were only a handful of candidates who appeared older. She waited for the general introduction to begin. Eleanor's nervousness slipped away as her excitement began to build.

Wow, if I get this job...the possibilities! She tried to contain the anticipation. *I shouldn't be here...* She hated lying to Phillip, but telling him about this interview would just confuse things. *I probably won't even get this job.*

"Attention, everyone, let's get started." All eyes turned to the tall Latin beauty whose accent seemed as exotic as she looked. "Welcome, on behalf of Meade Airlines. My name is Maria Sanchez, and this is my associate William Grant. We'd like to talk to you first about the airline and our program and then break off for individual interviews." William worked his way down the aisle, passing out envelopes stamped with the airline logo.

Maria gave a brief history of the airline and the current hub locations. The job required employees to live in one of the hub cities. New flight attendants would be on call and if summoned would have to report to the airport within four hours. This meant their bags had to be packed and ready. She described the schedule as on-call days and scheduled days off each week. A scheduler would contact flight attendants about a trip, ranging anywhere from one day up to four days. After completing the monthly work-hour quota, flight attendants would be off until the new month started.

William discussed the hourly pay rate and the potential add-on incomes, like per diem, flying the lead position, and other roles that didn't make sense to Eleanor yet. She learned about a mandatory six-week training session at the Pittsburgh Training Center. Meade Airlines would provide a free airline ticket to Pittsburgh, cover the hotel room and transportation to and from the hotel to the training center. No paid salary during training. Meals were not covered.

"This is the first round in the interviewing process. We will notify you by mail if you will be called for a second interview. There are up to four rounds of personal interviews. Good luck. On behalf of Meade Airlines we thank you for coming out today." Maria smiled and moved to one of four interview tables. Two Meade Airlines employees sat at each table. Before Eleanor knew it, she sat in front of Carl and Suzanne for round one.

"Welcome. I'm Suzanne, this is Carl, and you are…?" A pen was poised above her clipboard, her face friendly and persona professional.

"Eleanor…*Nora* Clark. You can call me Nora." She'd never before introduced herself as Nora. Everyone called her Eleanor, but she'd never particularly liked her name. Her mother had wanted authentic names, so she had named each of her daughters after an English queen: Queen Victoria, Queen Eleanor, and Queen Elizabeth. Eleanor could never imagine Victoria as Vicky or Tori. But *Nora* somehow suited her new mindset. Nora's confidence rose, and she was pleased with herself for yet another subtle change.

"Nora, what interested you in coming to this interview today?" Suzanne assumed the lead. Carl sat ramrod straight, his gaze sweeping over her.

Nora held her breath for the briefest moment, and in that moment, her truest feelings were finally released. "I'm ready for a journey, and this could be the doorway to it."

"Tell me more." Suzanne and Carl exchanged knowing glances. "Are you currently employed?"

"Yes, I have an office manager position at a software company. However, as of the first of the year the company will be relocating." The authentic excuse for seeking new employment gave Nora relief.

"Oh, are you opposed to relocating? With this job you'd need to live within sixty miles of the base assigned to you."

"No, relocating is exactly what I need. I also feel like a career change is in order," she assured.

"What experiences would make you a good candidate for our airline?"

"In my current job, I'm constantly involved with customer service issues, which has taught me to work with others during stressful situations." Suzanne nodded approvingly, and Nora continued. "Also, my family runs a successful catering company, and I've worked all aspects, from cooking, to serving, to customer relations to budgeting to dealing with every incident— you name it and I've done it. I worked with my family part-time through high school and college and then full-time for a couple years until I landed my current job. I still help out as often as I can, though it's run by my mother and older sister." Undeniably, she'd made a good fit in her family's business. Heidi and Victoria had talked about her becoming a future partner, but Nora never felt like she could be a partner. It just didn't feel right.

Suzanne silently read from the clipboard neatly holding Nora's paperwork. "I see you speak French. We have an international program."

Smiling, she nodded. *My two years of French in college and four years in high school might finally pay off. It's been awhile since I've spoken the language, but I could easily brush up on it.* Nora hadn't even thought about domestic versus international travel. "I'd be interested in the international program."

Suzanne made notes while Carl spoke up. "As you know you'd be required to attend six weeks of unpaid training. You'd have a roommate, but the room would be paid for. Is this something that would work for you?"

Roommate, no problem. Do I have enough money to float me for six weeks? Yes. She had no student loans. And Phillip paid the mortgage and utilities. She had put money in the bank for years. "It won't be a problem."

Suzanne and Carl asked a few more questions and concluded the interview. Carl slid an envelope across the table and paused, his dark fingertips resting on it. "Now, you were told you'd be mailed a letter stating whether or not you've got a second interview. However, we are allowed at our discretion to give out a few envelopes for further interviews. We feel you are a great candidate. Most people are not cut out for the demanding schedule of a flight attendant. You seem mature, friendly, and customer service savvy. And it's definitely a bonus you can speak a foreign language. So congratulations–you'll have a second interview. Please don't open this until you're outside because not everyone will be receiving one. It will give you instructions about who to contact. Thanks, Nora, have a fantastic day."

Wow! Nora couldn't believe it. She was a *great candidate*. "Thank you." She slipped the envelope into her purse and stood to shake their hands.

Nora sat in her car, holding the envelope. *I can't believe I just did that. And I can't believe I've got a second interview.* Shaking, she opened and read the letter congratulating her. It instructed her to call the listed contact within the time stated and schedule an appointment to meet at the Philadelphia airport. *Okay, what am I going to do now? What am I going to tell Phillip? How am I going to explain this?* Well, first of all she needed to get home before Phillip called to check on her. Nora's head pounded by the time she got home with too much to think about. The phone rang as Nora returned her gray suit to the closet.

"Hey, pet, how are you feeling?"

She could tell Phillip was in his car. "Much better. It must have been something I ate. Are you finally going for lunch?" The digital clock on the nightstand displayed 2:30 p.m.

"Yes, I'm headed to the grocery store for a deli sandwich. Do you need anything for your stomach?"

"Um…maybe you can bring some ginger ale home later." Guilt consumed her, twisting in her stomach. She'd never been the sneaky type. "I think I'm going to nap for a bit." She could use some ibuprofen too. *I deserve to feel sick. I'm a ratfink for lying.*

Chapter Three

The pineapple wreath on the Clark's front door had been switched for one with a witch riding a broomstick. Pumpkins and various gourds lined the steps in preparation for Halloween tomorrow. Nora entered through the kitchen door, shutting it quickly and shaking off the cold. *It's time to start wearing my coat again. This sweatshirt isn't keeping the chill away.* In the deserted kitchen a large bowl filled with assorted mini candy bars sat on the island.

Score!

After plucking a couple of her favorite treats and stuffing them into her hoody pocket, Nora followed the sound of the television into the family room.

"Hi, Dad, are the Steelers playing?" A Pittsburgh fan, Russ had grown up in the city and never missed a game. Frequently Perry watched the games with his father-in-law while Victoria and Heidi cooked or shopped or visited friends. But today Russ watched by himself.

"Hey, kiddo! They play at four." Russ sat in his favorite leather chair holding a glass of dark beer, a can of peanuts within his reach. Polly raised her head at Nora's voice and thumped her tail. The dog rolled to expose her belly. Nora earned a doggy grin by scratching Polly's ribs.

"Where's Mom?"

"She's around," Russ said.

With a sigh Nora rose and headed for the stairs. She paused at the top of the steps, listening for her mother. All was quiet. She crossed the hall and stood at the threshold of her childhood bedroom. It remained as she left it four years ago when she moved. This room summed up her happy childhood. Her stereo rested on her one-drawer nightstand, and the CDs were neatly stacked in a basket below. The books she read were still nestled in the bookshelves, and an old poster of her favorite boy band hung on the wall. She spent nights in this old room from time to time when she stayed late to help prep for a catering job, if the weather was bad, or Phillip traveled during the week for work. She liked hanging out with her family and sharing weekend dinners. This house was so homey. Always tidy and clean. It always smelled of baked goods and fresh linens. She crossed over to the bed and sat, looking around while she pulled a Kit-Kat bar out of her pocket.

Nora bent over, reaching between her legs, and felt around for a shoe box under her bed. It made a scrapping sound as she slid it out across the wood floor. In the box, among other things, were some headphones. She placed them around her neck and guided the box back with her sneakered foot. There was a CD already in the player; before pressing PLAY she adjusted the headphones and plugged them in. Cranking the music, she laid back on the bed. She closed her eyes, losing herself in the melody.

Nora experienced a weird "someone is watching you" feeling. When she opened her eyes she saw her mother standing in the doorway, her shoulder propped against the doorjamb. Nora squeaked in surprise. She bolted upright, pressing one hand over her pounding heart and pulling off her headphones with the other. "Mom, you scared me!" She reached over to silence the music vibrating from the headphones.

Heidi chuckled. "Yes, I see. I thought I heard someone up here. I was attempting to organize my bedroom closet." Heidi noted her daughter's humorless smile and walked in to sit beside her on the quilt covered bed. "What is it, Eleanor? What has been bothering you? You've been glum for some time now."

"Glum" was the word Victoria had used not so long ago to describe her too. *My family sees me as glum!*

Nora traced the pattern in the quilt with her fingertip while she pulled her thoughts together. "MMM...the company I work for is relocating." She peeked at her mother's concerned face. "To Boston," she added. At Heidi's raised eyebrows she went on, "Yeah, so it's a huge deal for Phillip. A great opportunity. Of course, I'd still have a job there with him if I wanted it."

"If you wanted it? But?"

"It's a huge opportunity," Nora repeated in a higher pitched voice. Her mother's silence begged her to continue. "I just...I just...don't want to go with him." *There–I said it.* A weight lifted from her shoulders.

"Well, honey, relocating isn't bad. Boston's not so far."

"No! It's not that. I don't want to be with him. I don't want to marry him!" she blurted. Fists balled, tears filled her eyes as she looked to her mother for guidance.

"Oh, I see." Heidi reached for her daughter's hand, loosening her balled fingers. "It's okay. It is going to be okay. You've felt this way a long time, haven't you?" Nora nodded, biting her upper lip. "You've been the one holding off the wedding plans?" Another nod. "Does Phillip know any of this?"

Nora slowly shook her head; she closed her eyes, squeezing out teardrops.

Heidi repeated, "It will be okay. Honey, it is better you realized this now, before you got married." She squeezed Nora's hand. "When is the relocation to Boston taking place?"

"January." Nora sniffed and wiped her tears away with the sleeve of her sweatshirt.

"Honey, you need to tell him. Phillip will be all right. You will be all right. We will get you through this," Heidi said. "Today. You'll tell him today. Then you'll come home to stay with us for a while. Can you do that?"

Heidi's rational instructions gave Nora the courage she needed.

"Yes. Thanks, Mom." As they embraced, Heidi stroked Nora's long hair with her soothing touch.

"Don't worry. You can always work with us until you find something else." Heidi's motherly instincts kicked in, attempting to solve all of Nora's problems.

"Actually..." Nora straightened, sniffling. "You might not believe this, but, on a whim, I went on an interview. I got a second interview and...I was hired." Nora's eyes sparkled with excitement and remnant tears.

"Wow. Does Phillip know about that?"

"He doesn't know." At Heidi's raised eyebrows Nora continued, "I kind of lied. I said I was sick and drove to Philly for the interview. A week later I happened to already have a personal day planned because of a dentist appointment, plus I was planning to make the final tile selections, but I canceled my dentist appointment and went to the second interview. Phillip worked late that night and never asked about either my dentist appointment or the tile, so I didn't say anything."

"You lied?"

Nora heard the surprise in her mother's voice and confirmed with a nod. She had always been a no frills, no surprises, kind of person, and yet what she had done and was planning to do broke her mold. "No one knows."

"Who did you interview for?"

"Meade Airlines. I'm going to be an international flight attendant." Nora pressed her lips together to control her grin. The enthusiasm over a new start drowned out any feelings of guilt or sorrow at the break she would have to make here.

"I can't believe it–a flight attendant," Heidi mused.

At her mother's sudden change in expression, Nora chuckled, especially knowing she had the reputation as the most reserved of the Clark girls, the good-natured middle child who went along with her demanding siblings. She had never been the adventurous type, and she'd stayed close by her family–they were her comfort zone. This new drive was like an awakening in her neurons, turning on switches that had been dormant.

"When do you start? Won't you have to move?" Heidi asked.

Nora heard the distress in her mother's questions. "After I attend several weeks of training in Pittsburgh, then yes, after I officially pass, I get assigned to a base–hopefully Philly. It's the closest to you and Dad."

"Your Aunt Lynn lives outside of Pittsburgh. We've never been close, but I could give her a call. She could check in on you."

"Mom, I don't need to be checked on. This is not summer camp. And besides, Dad hasn't talked to his sister since last Christmas."

"You'd have some family nearby is all."

"Mom, I know this seems crazy." Nora inhaled a deep breath, her excitement wavering. To her mentor, she asked, "Mom, am I crazy? Should I do this?" Doubt wedged its way in.

"Eleanor, you need to decide what is right for you. Your father and I will support whatever you decide."

Insecurity resurfacing, Nora needed her mother's steadfast support. "I want to do this. I want to see the world and change my life. I feel bad about Phillip, but I don't think it's fair to stay with him if I can't give him one hundred percent of myself."

"He loves you. He will be heartbroken," Heidi warned. "I know you feel bad about it, and I feel sorry for him too, but you are right."

Nora's heart wrenched at her mother's warning. But it was time for her and Phillip to move forward, although in different directions. They planned to tell Nora's parents tomorrow at Sunday dinner that they had given up on renovations and decided to put the house on the market. The FOR SALE sign would be going up next week.

"Do you want to talk to your dad before you leave?"

Nora shook her head. Why mess up his pleasure in watching the game? "Let me talk to Phillip first. I'll come home later."

"Okay, honey, we'll be waiting for you."

Phillip assembled a sandwich when Nora walked in the kitchen. "Hey, pet, want salami and cheese?"

"Hi." She forced a brief smile. "No thanks, I'm not hungry."

"How was the game?" Normally Nora watched football with her dad and usually filled up on snacks.

"Steelers play at four." She reached around him to the cabinet and took out a mug; she filled it with tap water and put it in the microwave. "I'll sit and have some tea while you eat."

Nora listened to Phillip's plans for the move to Boston. Between mouthfuls, he filled her in on some great townhouses he had seen online, areas with great restaurants. He even mentioned them taking a vacation on nearby Cape Cod.

"Phillip, we need to talk." The pit of Nora's stomach burned.

In reaction to the gravity in her voice he paused with the last bite of his sandwich midway to his mouth. She rushed on before she chickened out. "I don't want to go to Boston with you."

"We talked about this, Eleanor. You agreed the change would be good. It really is a great opportunity for us." He dropped the forgotten bite on his plate and pushed it away.

"Phillip, I want *you* to go to Boston. I...don't want to go." Nora placed her hand over her heart and with anguish, "I don't want to marry you and I'm moving in with my parents. I'm so sorry." She struggled to keep her tears in check, but they threatened to spill over.

"What? Where is this coming from? Wow..." Phillip slumped in his chair.

He seemed to wrack his brain for answers. "Eleanor, I love you. We don't have to move. I'll get a different job. We can stay here and work this out. I promise."

His declaration did not change her mind. "No, it's not the move. I care about you, but I'm not in love with you anymore. You deserve someone who can love you completely. I've felt this way for a while now. This move will make a clean break for us." She could hardly stand to see the lost look on his face. "I know this seems like it's coming from out of nowhere, but this hasn't been working for some time. Haven't you noticed?"

"Is there someone else?"

"No! Honestly, no." She touched his sleeve. "Phillip, go to Boston. Make a new life for yourself. You deserve it."

He pulled his arm out of her reach. He shut down.

"I'm going to go pack a few things and go. I think this is best for both of us," she said quietly, hoping her words sunk in as she slipped away to the bedroom. She yanked a duffle bag down from the top shelf of her closet and set it on the bed. In less than ten minutes the bag overflowed with her garments. With her arms loaded, she braved the hallway. Phillip stood at the sink in the kitchen drying his lunch plate. "I'll come by for the rest of my things this week. I'm going to give a week's notice at work on Monday too." He would not turn to look at her. "I'm sorry, Phillip." She wanted to say more, but she already told him how she felt.

He nodded and grunted, "Mmhmm."

She left, leaving Phillip still standing with his back to her. Tears rolled down her cheeks because she had selfishly hurt someone who loved her. Was there a way to break the news any better? No matter how guilt-ridden and sad she felt, she still knew this was the right thing to do. Her relationship was over with Phillip. The flame had burned out.

Monday morning, Nora gave her notice at the office. Everyone seemed shocked, but they thankfully kept questions and comments to a minimum. She had a knot in her stomach as she waited for Phillip to arrive. When he did, he walked straight to his office and would not even look in her direction. The rest of the week went pretty much the same way. Friday afternoon she knocked on his office door.

"Sorry to disturb you." She closed the door behind her. He gave her a tight-lipped nod. "I just wanted to let you know I am heading over to the house now to pick up the last of my things–if it's okay with you."

Phillip cleared his throat. "Yeah, fine." He shuffled some papers around. "I have some things here to catch up on, so I'll be home late anyway."

Nora paused, trying to think of another way to express her regret, yet knowing he wouldn't forgive her.

He gave her a pleading look.

"Okay. Well then, I'll leave the key under the mat." Their eyes locked. It felt final for them both.

The tears on her cheeks dried by the time she pulled into the carport. A FOR SALE sign sat on the lawn, confirming he was leaving town. She carried in a few cardboard boxes from the car. The bedroom was a good place to start. Clothes, shoes, some books, a yoga mat, and some small hand weights went into various boxes.

Nora walked around the living room looking at framed photos of her and Phillip. One photo was taken at a friend's birthday party and another at the lake. She passed them by and picked up a photo of herself with her parents and Lizzy at Lizzy's high school graduation. She collected the photo and one of her with Polly wearing matching Santa hats. Nora shook her head, realizing nothing else was hers to take. They had bought things like sheets, towels, and some dishes together, but she did not want or care about them. She never wanted to spend time in this house and never cared about fixing the place up.

At the kitchen cupboard she retrieved her favorite mug and noticed the ring holder on the windowsill. She glanced at the engagement ring on her finger, a beautiful round stone in a simple platinum setting. Sliding it off her finger, she placed it in the holder. She couldn't keep it. *Phillip will notice it when he gets home.*

She slipped the mug into a box and loaded her car. Placing the house key under the mat, she drove away, feeling freed.

Nora returned to her parent's house and her family rallied around her. Dad hugged her, Mother fretted over her comfort, Victoria uttered sage advice, and Lizzy became her snuggly sofa companion. It had been one emotional day, one emotional work week.

As the leaves fell, the cold November wind kicked up. Since moving out of Phillip's house, Nora went on long daily runs, attended Tyler's games with Lizzy, and brushed up on her French skills. The family gathered to celebrate Thanksgiving, though Nora felt the negative space traditionally filled by Phillip. The Thanksgiving feast was an all-out affair, but Nora ate little. She lost some weight, perhaps due to mounting anxiety while she waited for training to start in January. This break in her routine, at times, made her doubt her choices. *What if this doesn't work out and I end up alone?* When these thoughts entered her head, she pushed–no, shoved–them out of her mind. Still the apprehension returned and pressed heavily on her.

Nora hadn't heard from Phillip, but heard his house had sold in six days. Lizzy mentioned she saw a moving truck there a few weeks before Christmas. He was probably in Boston by now. Nora wished the best for him. She realized even though the thought of being single was a little intimidating, something within her was changing, opening to new possibilities. The gears of ambition and desire were turning, building her anticipation for what was to come.

The packet from Meade Airlines arrived with all the information she needed for her training. Finally the day had come. She survived an emotional good-bye before she drove to the airport, on her way to Pittsburgh and a new life.

Chapter Four

Nora's plane landed in Pittsburgh as a blanket of snow fell on the town, and the cold temperatures kept most of it on the ground. The snow let up as she boarded the hotel's shuttle van and smiled at the five passengers. She wondered if they were in the flight attendant program too.

Two girls sat across from her, chatting. One of the girls wore a skirt and cardigan sweater set. A wool coat and scarf were folded on the seat beside her. The second girl was petite, and she had dark, wavy hair past her shoulders.

"Sure is cold here. We get some cooler days in the mountains in North Carolina, but not this cold," sweater set commented. She slipped her scarf around her neck to ward off the chill.

"Yes, cold, but look at the snow. It's pretty. I've never seen snow for real. I was *hoping* it would snow. We're from Miami." wavy hair girl pointed to herself with her index finger, then to a guy in the back with her thumb. She spoke rapidly and loudly. She dressed in fitted tan pants with some spandex in the fiber blend, and the short, leather jacket did not seem like it kept her warm.

"You might not think it's so pretty after six weeks of it," jeered the guy who never looked away from the frozen landscape.

"Oh, shut up, Miguel. What do you know about snow?" she retorted over her shoulder and rolled her dark eyes. "That's my cousin, Miguel, who has never seen snow either." He made no further comment.

"Are you two headed for flight attendant training?" asked a girl with strawberry blonde hair who sat two seats over from Nora.

"Yes, we are," said sweater set. "Are you?"

"Yeah, my name is Bree Royce. I flew in from Washington, DC." She smiled at everyone, because everyone's attention was on her. Bree was striking. She had a pale porcelain complexion, and the hue of her blue eyes appeared almost turquoise. Her smile framed straight, gleaming-white, movie-star teeth.

"Nice to meet you, Bree. I'm Rebecca, from North Carolina. And this is Jackie and her cousin Miguel from Florida. We all met on our last flight up here before changing planes. We were all in the same row. Can you believe it?"

"Hi, I'm Nora Clark. I'm going to training too. I'm from here. Well, eastern Pennsylvania."

They all exchanged nods and smiles. Then all eyes rested on the last passenger, who sat in the second to last row, curled up, facing out the window. The girl wore a hoody sweatshirt and baggie dress pants. She had glanced over when Bree spoke, and then her gaze darted back to the drab view of fields, trees, and overcast skies as the bus drove them to the city limits. She straightened and stretched before she half smiled. "Hi, I'm Brittney." She waved. "From Florida too."

They made small talk for a while. None mentioned how nervous they were, even though they traveled from afar and would face obstacles that could have two possible outcomes: they made it or they went home.

The bus stopped at a basic block-style hotel, with no embellishments. The dated lobby offered alcove seating and an entrance to a pub-style restaurant. *I'm expected to pay for my meals during my stay, so I hoped the pub food is decent.*

Miguel breezed by them, got his key from the front desk, and disappeared into an elevator. Nora wondered about his aloof personality and how he would interact with passengers in the friendly skies. Jackie and Rebecca stepped up to the front desk next and were assigned the same room. Nora and Bree signed in and were paired together. This total stranger, Bree, was going to be Nora's roommate for six weeks.

"Let's check it out." Bree handed Nora her key card.

As they headed toward the elevators, Nora noticed Brittney getting her room assignment. Nora glanced from Bree's Coach purse and matching designer luggage to Brittney's backpack slung over her shoulder and the faded blue duffle bag at her feet. *Hmm, this is going to be an interesting six weeks.*

Their room was basic, minimal and clean, and had two double beds, a mini fridge, and a microwave. Outside the bathroom was an additional sink and mirror, which would be helpful when the girls got ready at the same time in the morning. The closet was large enough for the two of them, and they each got three drawers in the dresser. Bree claimed the bed by the window. They unpacked their bags.

The packet mailed to Nora gave instructions for the types of clothing, shoes, and even jewelry allowed to be worn during training. Meade Airlines requested business-casual dress. Nora shopped for a few suitable items like the collared shirts and navy shoes specified. She needed a swimsuit for water-emergency training. She invested in a navy pencil skirt, pantyhose, and three pairs of dress pants. Stress made her anxious, so she worked out more consistently to help deal with her escalating emotions. She wasn't disappointed when this resulted in a smaller dress size. For the first time, she'd made it through the food-crazy holidays and lost weight.

"So, Bree, tell me about yourself. You're from Washington, DC?"

"Yes, DC and Potomac, Maryland." She pulled out one lovely garment after another. "Mr. Royce, my dad, is in DC, and Mrs. Royce, my mom, has the house in the suburbs. They're divorced."

"What made you decide to do this?" It seemed like Bree led a pretty plush life from the quality of her stuff.

"Mostly to get away from *them*. I wanted to do something for myself, something that didn't involve either of them helping me. Plus, this job just seems fun and free."

Yes, *free*. Freedom was exactly what Nora felt. Even though breaking up with Phillip was heart-wrenching, she felt as if a huge weight had lifted from her shoulders. She couldn't waste the rest of her life in a doomed relationship, void of passion and shared companionship. And she loved her family dearly but didn't want to be involved with the family business any longer. She owed it to herself to overcome her timid, obliging ways and seek fulfillment in life–free to go, literally, where the wind would take her. "You said it! Freedom–I can't wait to start traveling. I feel like I've been trapped in a small town my whole life." Nora handed Bree six of the twelve hangers provided. They both felt the mutual connection of a budding friendship.

"Really." Bree looked as if she considered her new roommate for a moment. "Where do you want to go first?"

"I'm in the international program, so any of Meade's European destinations will be great. Also, I am looking forward to using the flight benefits to travel when I'm not working. First stop–Italy. It's always been on my list of places to visit." She worked at the buttons on the shirt she'd just put on a hanger.

"Italy is amazing. You will definitely love it. I spent a summer there just after college. Mr. Royce has a golf buddy who owns a vineyard in Tuscany, and we got to stay in his villa for two months." She paused for a moment. "International flight attendant–I should have applied for that." Bree slid a cream-color silk blouse onto her hanger. Nora imagined it was a one-of-a-kind designer item, unlike her cotton-polyester blend. Bree folded the matching camisole and placed it in the drawer next to her dainty lace bras and panties.

"Do you speak Italian?" Nora asked.

"I speak some Italian. My roommate in college was from Sicily and talked nonstop on the phone to her family in Italian. She spoke half-English, half-Italian the rest of the time." Bree chuckled. "I got pretty good at understanding the language during my summer in Italy. I dated a guy there who only spoke Italian." Bree sighed dramatically. "Yeah, we spent a lot of time together," she giggled, but didn't elaborate. "So, how about you? Do you speak any languages?"

"Oui, I speak French." Nora confided she'd worked hard to brush up the past couple of months.

The girls got to know each other better while they finished unpacking. Nora stashed her cotton bras and underwear quickly in the dresser drawer. She lined up her shoes in the closet. She brought sneakers for the gym, a pair of ankle boots, and the required navy shoes. She lined her three pairs next to Bree's dozen sets of fashionable footwear. Nora dug in her bag and pulled out her slippers to add to her side, although the tattered addition didn't increase the appeal of her collection.

Unpacking finished, Nora phoned home to report she'd made it to Pittsburgh. The call was brief because Meade Airlines was hosting a welcome reception in one of the hotel's ballrooms; it was starting soon.

The small ballroom, divided by a floating fabric wall, filled in fast. Nora and Bree each accepted a glass of wine offered at the makeshift bar and grabbed one of the last empty tables. Nora glanced at Bree in anticipation. Bree sipped white wine, her regal posture made her stand out among the otherwise ordinary group.

Nora's gaze searched the room for the few familiar faces from the shuttle bus. Jackie and Rebecca sat across the room at a table with two other girls. Miguel loomed nearby. She guessed around one hundred people were squeezed in attendance.

Maria Sanchez walked in. Nora recognized her from the initial open interview session. Maria stood next to a table piled high with large, thick envelopes. She welcomed the group and wasted no time covering the upcoming itinerary. Monday through Friday, shuttle buses would transport everyone to the training facility. Classes would typically run from 8:00 a.m. to 5:00 p.m., with an hour lunch break. She reminded them they were responsible for buying their own lunches. The training facility had a cafeteria, and there was a sandwich shop within walking distance. In addition on Saturday mornings they would have training, and the shuttle buses would take them to various facilities for specialized drills. Sundays were free.

"You will be divided up into five groups. There will be a morning lesson in the classrooms, followed by an afternoon exam covering the morning's lesson." She explained more on how the scoring worked. Two retake exams during the entire training program were allowed if trainees scored below 80 percent. If someone failed to meet this requirement, he or she would automatically be sent home.

Nora worried the fantasy career she dreamed of could be over almost before it began. *Are the exams tricky?* Over her shoulder someone whispered, "I heard rumors that *half* the trainees went home last year."

Bree gave Nora a reassuring smile.

Maria continued, "After the daily exams you will move to other types of training. During the following weeks, you are required to accomplish various tasks inside the mock airplane cabins. Each trainee is required to reach the overhead bins and close them, arm and disarm the aircraft doors, lift out the forty-pound emergency window, and buckle themselves correctly into the flight attendant jump seats."

Nora's stomach fluttered with excitement. *This is really happening!*

"Please come collect an envelope. All details will be available to you. I will be around to answer any further questions." Maria became quickly surrounded by eager trainees.

The first Monday morning, after Bree and Nora grabbed coffee and a muffin from the hotel's continental breakfast bar, they boarded the transport van. Arriving at the training facility, they wished each other good luck; they were not assigned to the same class.

Nora and her classmates sat at tables facing a whiteboard with the names CHAD and STACY neatly written across it. Nora sensed the enthusiastic energy in the room.

Chad welcomed the class. "Stacy and I are flight attendants as well as your trainers. The first lesson is on airline terminology."

Nora took detailed notes. Chad seemed easygoing and he remained on topic while energetic Stacy often added side stories she found amusing.

Nora and Bree met at lunch and discussed the morning lesson, reviewing their notes over cafeteria plastic clamshell salads. After lunch the trainees took their first written exam. Nora was nervous, but she stayed focused. In the afternoon they lectured about uniforms and appearance standards. Every aspect of the uniform was discussed, from avoiding overstuffed, bulging pockets to collars required to lay flat. No detail was left out. On the subject of earrings: only one matching set of earrings could be worn at one time. Various shapes were not authorized, including dangling or hoop earrings more than one inch in diameter. No ear cuffs, nose rings, novelty shapes, or earrings with moving parts were permitted. Nora decided her diamond CZ studs would be a safe choice. She thought of Bree, knowing her diamonds were real.

As Stacy covered personal hygiene, she remarked the obvious statements had to be made, like wearing deodorant and maintaining dental care. Nora turned to a fellow trainee, and they silently raised their eyebrows at each other.

Hair color and length were discussed. "Only natural hair colors are permitted, and hair hanging past your shoulders must to be tied up."

Nora considered her own lack of hairstyle, always worn straight and long. *Perhaps it's time for a change.*

The next topics were nails, shoes, stockings, and tasteful makeup application. Nora owned very little makeup and often didn't wear any. She definitely needed tips. *Hmm. Bree wore makeup that enhanced her luminous eyes and shimmered on her slightly pouty lips.* Nora made a mental note to take a crash course in beauty from her.

Stacy somberly stated, "Sorry guys, but due to budget cuts the airline won't be giving you all personal makeovers as specified in their packets." Later Nora heard some trainees were disappointed. Makeovers were usually a highlight of "Barbie boot camp."

Nora earned an 85 percent on her first exam. Relief washed over her. The next day, Chad covered bag storage for the crew on board, checking cabin supplies, cabin inspections, and other details. She took detailed notes during the morning sessions and looked them over during lunch before the exam. This became her routine to prepare for exams.

On Wednesday, boarding, approach, and arrival procedures were explained. Both Nora and Bree were now scoring higher on the exams. Thursday afternoon, they filed into a warehouse area housing the mock jets. Partial planes were cut open in sections for training purposes. The aircraft qualifications began. Nora breezed through the physical requirements and service training without problems.

By Friday, twenty-three of the one hundred and twenty-eight trainees had gone home. Whether they failed exams or left on their own Nora didn't know. Stress seemed to settle in on the whole group. When someone did not pass the makeup exam given the following morning, that person was immediately taken to the hotel to pack and driven directly to the airport. He or she was simply gone when the rest of the group returned to the hotel. No good-byes. It was unsettling.

One week down. Five more to go.

Nora dressed casually for Saturday's first-aid training. She became certified in CPR and learned how to use an AED, a.k.a. automated external defibrillator. Nora and Miguel were paired during the morning exercises. During Nora's first impression of Miguel, he seemed standoffish. But during the exercises she finally got a chance to talk with him, and although quiet at first, he started to open up.

"I'm trying to overcome my shyness," he confided. "I'm making an effort to be friendly and I've made some friends."

Based on the stories she heard so far, she realized most of the people in training were overcoming something. This kind of new career could be the ultimate fresh start.

To celebrate the completion of their first week, Nora, Bree, Rebecca, Jackie, Miguel, and Chris, Miguel's roommate, walked half a mile to the nearest shopping plaza, to a Chinese restaurant. The night was beautiful, clear but cold. The friends sat around a circular table and ordered fancy umbrella drinks. They chatted about how intense the training had been and how strict the compliance rules were.

Rebecca commented, "I'm getting my hair cut shorter so I don't have to pin it up."

"I noticed a salon in this strip mall," Jackie offered.

"Yes, I saw it too." Rebecca fiddled with a loose bobby pin. "I'm thinking I'll walk over tomorrow for a cut."

Nora chimed in. "I want to do something new with my hair too. I'll walk over with you." Nora liked Rebecca's southern charm. As she looked around the table at her new friends, she was amazed these strangers from different states were now gathered together and bonding, forming friendships.

The next day, Sunday, the stylist at the salon told them they were only open on Sundays when Meade held flight attendant training; it apparently drummed up substantial business. Rebecca looked great with her new bob cut. Nora had six inches cut off her hair, however it still touched the middle of her back, and the stylist added long layers, which gave it some fullness. Still too long by airline standards to wear down, she experimented with a coiled bun at the nape of her neck.

Nora discovered Sunday was laundry day. Everyone had waited to do laundry and there were only two machines in the building! From that day on, Nora and Bree decided to do their wash during the week around dinnertime, when the trainees were off in search of food. On their weekly laundry night they ordered takeout salads from the local pizza place.

Sundays, their only days off, soon became Nora's weekly call-home day. She chose the time when the family generally got together. Her mom had sent a care package to the hotel, and the homemade goodies made her miss her mom even more. She wondered how she and Victoria were getting along without her help, but she couldn't bring herself to ask. It was their business, she reminded herself.

The first part of the second week covered first class and coach services. The trainees practiced manipulating carts and drinks in the mock cabins. In first class, Nora would also be responsible for getting the pilots their drinks and dinners, as well as the passengers. In the coach cabin, she discovered pushing and locking those heavy carts was trickier than it looked.

Later in the second week, the exams became more difficult, including memorizing the six terms for turbulence and their definitions, which seemed too similar to Nora to distinguish. Even trickier were the classes on transporting medical goods and their various labels. Chad informed them they might receive coolers containing contents like eyeballs. Like kids in the fourth grade, the trainees made faces in response.

Nora's scores ranged from 85s to 95s. Stress continued to expand among the trainees. Fourteen more people went home.

After two weeks, Nora and her friends agreed they needed a night out on the town. Bree helped Nora apply makeup from her vast collection of products. Nora took extra time blowing out her new hairstyle and curling the ends. Bree lent her a low-cut black shirt.

"Wow, I wish I could fill it out like that." Bree feigned jealousy, glancing down at her reed-thin frame.

"I don't know… It's kind of tight…and revealing." Nora eyed herself in the mirror. She had a hard time admitting how sexy she looked.

One of the trainees lived nearby and drove his sports utility vehicle to training. Everyone piled in and he drove the gang downtown. Nora glimpsed the wild side of certain trainees at the club, their actions later leading to hookups. Several guys hit on her, but she attributed it to being in Bree's company, after all, Bree was the head-turner. Nora did find one guy attractive, but she didn't pursue him.

In the third week, the exams covered airport codes and US and international geography. They briefly reviewed time zones and the twenty-four-hour clock convention. In the physical training session, Nora learned how to put out a fire with an extinguisher. She opened an aircraft window for evacuation purposes and loudly chanted instructions for how to climb through and slide off the wing. She evacuated several different styles of aircraft using a deployed slide. They practiced with some trainees wearing signs around their neck: BLIND PERSON, HOLDING AN INFANT, and others to prepare the trainees for all possible situations. The instructors taught them the evacuation procedures and successfully instilled the significance of how critical their job might be. Flight attendants did not just serve drinks and hand out pillows; they could save lives. Nora felt empowered.

During one evacuation drill, it was Nora's turn to be in the mock flight attendant jump seat. Other trainees sat in the passenger seats and stared at her. At the right moment, she would be responsible for leading the passengers during an emergency. Nora inhaled deeply and rehearsed her memorized commands. The trainer turned off all the overhead lights, leaving only the emergency lights illuminated, giving off an eerie glow. The trainer began to speak in the silent cabin. "You have prepped the cabin for an impending emergency landing. It is night. You have instructed your passengers to cross their arms in front of them and lean forward in the brace position. The captain gives the signal and you chant, "Brace for landing!" Once you recover from a jarring crash landing, what do you do? What if the emergency lights have malfunctioned and flicked off? What if you are in total darkness? You are in charge–what do you do next?" Nora and the other trainees felt the gravity of the scene the trainer had established. After a moment of stunned silence, Nora started calling out the next sequence of commands. The drills were repeated several more times.

The next day–running hijacking drills–was emotionally difficult. The shadow of airplane terrorism in 2001 lingered in everyone's mind.

The fourth week covered trip scheduling, which functioned on a seniority-based system. Stacy warned the senior flight attendants always picked the best trips, and new employees got what was left–if there were any trips left. If you were junior and didn't get a trip, then you were on call in case a senior attendant cancelled a trip for any reason.

Saturday the group trained at the facility's Olympic-sized pool. A few trainees claimed they couldn't swim. Swimming was not a requirement, so they stayed in the shallow end and didn't get their hair wet. Nora jumped into the pool, slipped on a life vest, and manually inflated it. Next, trainees worked together to inflate a raft in the pool, climb inside (Nora needed a hoist from a couple guys to slip over the jumbo edge), and set up its built-in tent cover. She had no idea she would learn survival techniques to become a flight attendant. She felt pumped she'd overcome so many obstacles in such a short period of time. She could not be happier this was her new life.

Sunday morning, Bree came out of the bathroom after her shower with her hair wrapped in a towel turban on her head. She was smearing lotion up and down her arms when she saw tears in Nora's eyes.

"What's wrong?" Bree joined her on the edge of the bed.

Nora smiled at her friend's genuine concern. "Nothing's wrong. I just hung up with my sister, Victoria. I'm going to be an auntie. She's been trying for so long to get pregnant and has wanted to be a mom since we were kids." Nora sniffed at the memory of her sister hogging the baby dolls. "It's funny. I thought my big sister had the perfect life. In high school Victoria was captain of the varsity cheerleading squad, and she dated Perry Reynolds, the quarterback. Of course the dream couple reigned as homecoming king and queen. They got married the summer after she graduated from the Pennsylvania School of Culinary Arts. They had a big wedding at the country club and honeymooned in the Poconos." Nora's pause was reflective. "But she couldn't seem to get the one thing she's always wanted—a baby."

"Aww, that's so nice. I don't have any siblings. I envy you."

"Yeah." Nora sighed, "I just wish I could be there."

"I'm sure your sister understands."

Nora shrugged, hating missing out.

"It must be nice to have a big loving family. I'm just a pawn to my divorced parents. At age twelve they sent me to a private boarding school, and I spent many summers in England with family friends. I was lucky if they showed up for my tennis matches or horseback riding events."

Nora told Bree her story–why she left and who she left. Bree raised her eyebrows when she heard Nora had been engaged, but she was sympathetic. When Nora spoke about family obligations, Bree understood.

"I've often sacrificed what I wanted in order to keep the peace between my parents," Bree said.

The girls shared the fears they'd face if they didn't make it through training. They both had so much riding on this opportunity to make a fresh start. They'd become the friend the other could lean on.

For the first time since high school, Nora had connected with someone outside of her family unit.

The last two weeks of training went quickly. Sixty-two trainees had gone home by then, about half of the group who started. The most nerve-wracking aspect of the training that came next was working a *real* flight with *real* passengers, many of whom leered at her TRAINEE badge. Nora had been tense as she boarded and settled passengers and checked equipment. She was social and friendly with the other flight attendants, but she did not share how she rushed to the oppressively small washroom and vomited. The anxiety flushed with the blue toilet-bowl solution, and she returned with a smile plastered onto her face. *Fake it until you make it.*

Nora remained as one of the sixty-six graduating trainees. Brittney, who rode on the bus the first day with Nora, went home the second week. Miguel's roommate Chris went home the third week. Others Nora had befriended were gone. But Bree, Rebecca, Jackie, and Miguel had made it to this day. She could not think of an alternative possibility if she had not made it. How embarrassing it would be to fail "Barbie boot camp," as some had joked.

Bree applied finishing touches to her makeup. Nora slipped on her shoes and watched her for a moment, admiring the flight attendant uniform she wore. *Bree would look good in a paper bag, but the uniform gives her an essence of respect and authority. Do I project that?* Adjusting the polyester dress, Nora double-checked her appearance in the mirror. Smoothing her hair into a bun at the nape of her neck had quickly become her style, and she wore it so today. She felt professional and assertive, proud of herself for succeeding when so many had already gone home.

Nora held a sheet of paper containing departure details, she said, "We should head down soon. They want our luggage in Ballroom B, before the ceremony, which is in Ballroom A."

Within the hour Nora would get her base assignment, determining where she was going to live, making her anxious. Her choices had narrowed down to Philadelphia, Washington, or Boston, as those were Meade's international bases. *Not Boston. Phillip will be there.*

"I'm ready," Bree declared. She had twice the number of suitcases as Nora. Luckily for her, Meade allowed unlimited bags on the flight home.

"I can't believe we're done. Do you think we'll end up in the same city?"

"I hope so! Then we can get a place together." Bree surveyed her pile of luggage. "I think we need a bellhop."

The ceremony went swiftly. The wings they would wear during all future flights were pinned to their uniforms. Afterwards everyone ran around to find out who was assigned to which base. Nora and Bree both got Philadelphia and hugged enthusiastically.

Meade gave the new employees one week to get their affairs in order; they needed to be on base and on call by then.

"I'm calling Mr. Royce right now so he can get us set up in Philly." Bree dug out her cell phone. "Since I made it through flight attendant training all on my own it's okay if Mr. Royce helps with one last thing."

Rebecca ran over, waving her orders. "I got Philly. What did you get?" It turned out the majority of new flight attendants would be based in Philadelphia, due to added flights there. Even Jackie and Miguel were joining them in the City of Brotherly Love.

Nora called her parents. They were thrilled with the good news.

Chapter Five

In March, Nora returned to her parents' house a new woman, with a new career and a fresh outlook on life. Her mother remarked, "I can tell you made the right decision just from the way you carry yourself. A mother knows her daughter."

After Victoria filled Nora in on her pregnancy so far, she then wanted to know more about her sister's future plans. Nora smiled at Victoria's compulsion to give her advice whether she wanted it or not.

Lizzy just wanted to know if she could fly for free. Nora explained she could request a buddy pass, a free pass for a fellow companion who traveled on standby along with her.

No one spoke of Phillip, who was long gone in Boston by now. She did wonder about him. *Did he move into the townhouse he told me about?* Nora could not bring herself to ask. It was over, and she did not want to look back.

Nora unpacked and repacked. By midweek, Nora was ready to make the move to Philadelphia. She could not believe the airline only allowed employees *one week* to find a place to live in a new city. New employees were expected to be packed, moved, and ready to work within that time. She never would have managed the feat of finding a place to live so fast without Bree? Bree's father, not only got them into a townhouse, but he got them in immediately. When she asked Bree how he did it, Bree only commented, "I don't know. He gets me whatever I need."

Nora packed her bags into her car and kissed her family good-bye once again. She promised this time it wouldn't be as long as six weeks before she visited again. Being away from her family for so long had been hard for them all.

Their townhouse, an authentic Philadelphian brownstone, was not far from trendy South Street, and shops, bars, and restaurants were within walking distance. When Nora met Mr. Royce he insisted the girls would not be paying for the place.

"You girls aren't going to start out making much money. Save it," he said, holding up his hand against protest. "It's the least I can do for my little girl." There was no arguing with him. Nora was starting to understand how challenging it was for Bree to get away from *Them*. Bree's father was overbearing, but he came through for his daughter. "You can't fight City Hall," Bree said in defeat, and her father nodded and chuckled.

The narrow brownstone's front door opened into a living/dining room combination with the stairwell along the right wall. The modern kitchen had a door that led onto a small deck and patio surrounded by a fence. Bree occupied the larger bedroom on the second floor with a private bath. Nora's bedroom was smaller, and she had to use the hallway bathroom. Conveniently a washer and dryer were located in the upstairs hallway.

Mr. Royce treated the girls to dinner. Before he left, he gave Bree a credit card and told her to buy whatever she needed for the house. The girls went shopping for essentials and splurged on a high-end television.

A week went by before she got her first assigned trip. After she dressed in her pressed uniform, she gazed in the mirror, overwhelmed with pride. *I did it. I am a flight attendant. And I'm off to London.*

Nora drove to the airport, recalling all she had learned in her six-week crash course. She made her way to the gate; the gate-agent gave her access to the jet-bridge. When she got to the plane, the pilots were making their preflight checks. The lead flight attendant introduced herself and eyed Nora suspiciously.

"Hi. I'm Nora. This is my first working flight." She remembered how embarrassing wearing the TRAINEE badge had been on her training flight. The smirks from passengers had been unnerving. With long inhales and exhales she calmed her nerves. *No emergency visits to the washroom!*

"You'll be in the coach cabin. The jump seat is just behind first class. Do you remember what equipment you need to check?" The lead flight attendant was stern but polite.

"Yes, I'll go do that right now." Nora's hands felt clammy; she discreetly wiped them on her uniform. The other flight attendants arrived, and thankfully were much friendlier. One of them walked Nora through all the checks, showed her where to stash her bags, and gave her tips. Nora smiled as the passengers filed on, assisting them as needed. Before she knew it the hectic boarding process ended and she buckled into the jump seat. The helpful colleague buckled in beside her. She sat backwards, facing the passengers. She bounced along as the plane taxied onto the runway. Over the continuous exhale of the air vents she could hear the plane engines rev. The jet sped up and lifted off the ground. The seatbelt pressed against her chest as momentum pushed her forward. *Here we go!* She was flying backwards, up, up, up into the sky.

The first trip went off without a hitch. The flight left Philadelphia in the evening and arrived in London in the morning. Working with the time change was challenging, but worth it. The other flight attendants told her to stay awake, fight the urge to nap, until evening when traveling to Europe; it was the best way to enjoy a layover. Exhausted, she followed their suggestion and it paid off. A city bus tour and some shopping filled her day. The weather was cool and drizzly, so she invested in a lightweight raincoat. There was little space in her company-issued luggage for souvenirs. She wondered how Bree would manage to travel so lightly.

On the returning flight she was careful not to burn her fingers on the hot food trays again as she had on the way over. During training, the trays had been room temperature and empty. Double-checking each supply cabinet latch to make sure it was fastened properly, she recalled the story Stacy told in training about the time she'd left a cabinet unlatched during takeoff and paper cups had launched out, rolling all over the galley and into the aisle.

When Nora returned to Philadelphia, she met Bree's mother. Mrs. Royce checked into a high-end boutique hotel downtown, and she stayed for a few weeks. While visiting her daughter,

Mrs. Royce hired an interior designer to furnish the house. Although the choices were shown to the girls, Bree's mom made all the final selections, insisting the girls would like her preferences after installation. Workers came and went all three weeks. The painters were the first to arrive. Furniture delivered and drapes installed. Nora returned home from a three-day trip to inspect the finishing touches—kitchen counter stools, hanging artwork, area rugs, and pots and pans. The house looked amazing. Although both girls were grateful, they were glad to see her leave.

Nora's parents and sister Lizzy drove to Philadelphia one Saturday in early April to check out the townhouse and spend the day with Nora. Bree, on standby, had been called away on a trip. Heidi was especially disappointed they were not meeting Nora's new friend. Nora promised to bring Bree home for a visit. Over dinner Nora shared travel stories, beaming to be around her family again. She had already been to London and Paris, and she was leaving for Madrid the next day.

"The first thing I do is sign up for a city bus tour," Nora said as she cut into her steak. "A flight attendant friend who's been flying for a few years told me that's a good way to start in every new city. It gives a good overview. Then with each returning visit, I can tour buildings or museums or whatever caught my interest on the city tour." As she chewed her meat she watched the three heads bob in agreement. Nora didn't miss the impressed glances her parents exchanged or the excited wonder in Lizzy's praise.

Nora and Bree settled into their new routines once they finally had the place all to themselves and thrilled when they had the same days off. Since their trips often overlapped they got into the habit of leaving a notebook on the counter to write notes to each other. It came in handy when one of them was unable to call because she was in-flight or the time difference was crazy. Typically, notes would read something like: *Help yourself to the leftover Chinese food–just got it last night… A repairman will be here sometime on Tuesday to fix the loose board on the back step… Sorry I ate the last yogurt—didn't have time to go to the store. I owe you.*

As months passed, Nora's confidence in her job skills grew. She mastered the scheduling system and enjoyed the long overseas layovers in Paris, Madrid, and Frankfurt. She swiftly learned she could work the bulk of her monthly quota of eighty hours early in the month by signing up for back-to-back trips. Each overseas trip averaged more than forty hours. So, she could time out after two trips as long as she had the required rest time in between, a minimum of twenty-four hours. To time out meant she would *not* be on call for the remainder of the month; she could enjoy some free time.

Nora planned to use her flight benefits to see destinations of her choice after timing out; additional discounts were available to flight attendants at hotels and some restaurants. Although the overall pay wasn't much, the free-flight benefit couldn't be beat. She could finally see the world–or at least the destinations Meade flew to.

By late April Nora timed out and decided Rome would be her first adventure. After researching hotels, bus routes, and places of interest, she decided on a hotel off the beaten path but within walking distance to a city-tour-bus stop. She did not want to blow all her income on one trip because she had big plans to visit as many places as she could, within reason. Nora hoped to travel with Bree, but Bree didn't get the chance to time out early enough in the month. Disappointed she was not going with her friend, she could not miss out on her small window of opportunity. In a week, she would be on call again.

Chapter Six

Nora checked into her budget lodgings at the Hotel Grande in Rome. "Grande" seemed a misrepresentation for the modest hotel. Familiarizing herself with the area would be a great start; she would take a stroll and keep an eye out for a café to have lunch. The dark-haired girl at the tiny lobby desk handed Nora a map, circled a few sites, and gave her directions to the bus stop. Off to explore, she felt a little jittery, but exhilarated at making extraordinary things happen in her life. *I can't believe I'm actually in Italy–all by myself!* She let go of her safety net, pushing herself, and embracing the unknown. She would be just fine.

Nora, lost in her thoughts, realized she had not arrived at her piazza destination. She unfolded her map and began to retrace her steps. The narrowing residential alley didn't seem right. As she turned, she was suddenly knocked backwards; she toppled to the ground. With a painful yank her bag was pulled free from her arm. The thief dashed away before she even saw him. She twisted around, yelling, "Heeeeyyyy!" only to see the pumping legs of his form retreating down the alley. She shook with panic as she thought, *Oh no, my wallet's in there...my money and ID!*

Nora blinked away frustrated tears several times before she saw a brawny man reach out and knock her assailant to the ground with one swift punch to his face. He reached down and pulled the guy up by the front of his hooded sweatshirt, twisting his fist for a thorough hold before he sent a second blow to his chin, dropping the assailant to his knees. The guy dropped Nora's bag and mumbled something in Italian. The larger man shoved the attacker away, pointing and warning him in menacing Italian. The hooded guy scrambled up into a staggering run and was soon again at top speed, dashing from sight down another alleyway.

Nora sat on the ground, stunned. Her rescuer scooped up her bag and jogged over. Squatting at her side, he questioned her in Italian. She had no idea what he asked her. Despite her ordeal, she could only focus on the attractive stranger. She stared at his handsome face framed by dark wavy hair combed back and curling around his ears, resting just above his broad shoulders. Thick eyebrows framed hooded, dark eyes. The broad face balanced with generous lips... *Oh, his lips.*

"Miss?"

Nora snapped out of the trance. "Oh! Oh, thank you so much." She stood, but winced in pain, grabbing her hip, which had taken the brunt of her fall. *That's going to leave a huge bruise.*

He cupped her elbow with his large hand to help steady her.

"Are you okay, miss?" he said in English, his voice deep, smooth and heavily accented.

"Yes, thank you. Just bruised, I think." She blushed and accepted her bag. He bent to retrieve her map giving her the opportunity to notice the muscles rippling under his T-shirt when he reached down. He dressed in sweatpants and sneakers. *Perhaps heading out for a run. He's in amazing shape.*

He handed her the map. "Do you need help finding your way? You are American?"

"Yes, I'm from America and I'm lost. I got turned around somehow. I'm Nora, by the way." She held out her hand. "Nora Clark. I can't thank you enough."

"Hello, Nora. It's a pleasure to meet you." He clasped her hand. It's pull like a warm magnet drawing her to him. "I am sorry we met under these circumstances. This is a nice neighborhood, but these young kids will find every opportunity to prey on tourists. Please excuse the violence. I'd like to think a good scare, without police involvement, might make the boy think twice next time. His mama will want to know why his face is so bruised, eh. You should carry your bag like this..." He let go of her hand and lifted the bag's long strap over her head. "Across your body." As he murmured the word "body," his heavy-lidded eyes slowly shifted down her torso.

Nora's voice chirped. "Could I buy you a cup of coffee? It's the least I can do…"

"Antonio." He wore a knowing, crooked smile.

"Antonio," she repeated. Maybe her heightened senses lingered after the attack, but she was hyperaware of his all-consuming presence, and her pulse raced.

He dragged the side of his index finger over his bottom lip, considering her. "How about dinner? And I will be taking you, to make up for what has happened to you in my city."

Nora's eyes widened in surprise. "You don't have to do that. I mean, it's really nice of you. Um, I'd love to." She cleared her throat, "I'm staying at Hotel Grande."

"Then I will pick you up at eight o'clock at your hotel. May I walk with you to the end of this street?"

"Yes, that would be nice."

Antonio directed Nora to the corner where she had become turned around. They chatted about the city until they reached the corner, and Nora headed in her original direction. Antonio tucked in ear buds and jogged away in the other direction. She could not resist peeking over her shoulder. Broad shoulders swayed as his body moved in rhythm. As he retreated he did not look back, so Nora allowed her gaze to linger.

Wow! What just happened! Here I am, thinking I'm so adventurous, and I'm knocked on my ass and my bag is stolen— only to be returned to me by a gorgeous man! And I dared to ask him out for coffee! Which now is dinner… Oh my! Nora swallowed hard. *I've got to call Bree.*

"Hey, Nora, how's Italy?" Bree sounded glad to hear from her.

Nora heard her take a sip, probably her morning latte, realizing it was still quite early in Philly.

"Bree! You won't believe what just happened!" Nora didn't leave out a single detail. "So I'm going to see him tonight for dinner. What do you think?"

"I'm glad you are all right. Antonio sounds like a knight in shining armor. And gorgeous too! How the hell did you get so lucky? I'd totally do him." She laughed, but then said more seriously, "Nora, you should do him. You deserve it. Go for it, girl!"

"What? *No*! Bree, he's a stranger." Nora tried to sound offended.

"Well, you'll get a feel for him over dinner. Then see how it goes." Nora heard her take another sip. "But you better call me and tell me what happens," she admonished in a stern voice.

"I have nothing to wear." Nora nibbled on her fingernail.

"You didn't bring anything? Go buy something sexy. A short dress, with a clingy bust line. You have great boobs–tease the man a little. After all, he did a heroic deed for you."

Nora stifled a laugh with her palm. "I didn't know you admired me so," she said in a high, delicate tone. And they both burst into laughter.

"I gotta go. I'm meeting up with Rebecca. We're going shopping and then out to lunch. We both have another trip tomorrow. Wish I was with you in Italy. Ciao, bella."

"Okay. Tell Rebecca hi for me. Talk to you later." Nora hung up with a heavy sigh wishing Bree were there to go shopping with her. She had packed the matching lacy bra and panties she'd purchased on one of her shopping trips with Bree. Bree spent gads of money on unmentionables and professed wearing sexy underwear empowered a woman. Nora only felt uncomfortable and itchy.

A nearby church bell tolled the eight o'clock hour when Antonio met Nora sitting on a bench outside of Hotel Grande. "Good evening, Nora."

She stood. "Hello, Antonio."

He approached and then kept right on coming, until he stood very close to her. As he clasped both her hands in his, his head dipped to the left and his lips gently brushed her cheek. Slowly his dark head swiveled to the other cheek, where his lips sent a tingle down her spine. She tried not to visibly tremor at the sensual touch. She'd forgotten the Italian custom of kissing both cheeks, and her heart hammered as the scent of his skin and cologne assaulted her senses.

"Nora, you are beautiful." His gaze slowly accessed and admired her every curve. The new dress was the darkest shade of ruby red, a fitted, over-one-shoulder wrap that clung to her curvy frame.

Nora registered the approval in Antonio's eyes. "Thank you. You cleaned up well, yourself." *And yes, you are just as spectacular-looking as I remember. There is no hero effect here, just plain old attraction.*

He released one of her hands, holding the other possessively in his grasp. They didn't walk far to the restaurant and were soon seated in a quiet corner. The short, somewhat round proprietor greeted Antonio with a vigorous pump of a handshake. He turned to Nora with a broken, "Welcome…welcome." There were smiles all around. Antonio was also friends with the waiter; apparently he ate here frequently. Nora liked what she'd seen so far. Someone with bad intentions would not take her to a place where he was well known.

"May I order for us?" He tapped his wineglass with his finger. "They have excellent wine here. It's mine." He smiled genuinely.

"Yours? How so?" Intrigued, she leaned in.

"My uncle owns a vineyard. I do marketing and distribution for him. Would you like to try my favorite?"

"Yes, please. I have to confess I don't know much about Italian wines."

Antonio nodded to their waiter across the way while pointing to his glass. With a corresponding nod, the waiter disappeared. *Indeed, they know Antonio well.* He did not live too far from here, according to Nora's calculations. He had been emerging from an enclosed courtyard when he stopped her attacker earlier. They indirectly walked in that direction on their way to dinner.

"Well, I hope you enjoy this one. Did you get a chance to see the city today? I hope you weren't too deterred after this morning's ordeal."

"Yes, I was fine. Thanks to you. I just held onto my bag a little tighter and paid more attention to my surroundings. I even got in some shopping."

As he leaned his elbow on the table, eyes slowly yo-yoing down her torso, he slid the side of his index finger over his bottom lip, back and forth. Slowly. Mesmerized by his slightly open mouth, and seeing his bottom teeth and tongue, her tongue went dry.

Damn, that habit is sexy.

Antonio sprawled, draping his arm over the chair when the waiter appeared. The two men spoke in Italian while the waiter poured the wine. He left the bottle and flashed Nora a smile before leaving them alone.

Nora had arranged her hair up in a twist, a clip holding it in place, and a warm breeze tickled her neck. She raised her glass and said, "To you, Antonio, for being my hero today."

Antonio rewarded her heartfelt toast with an amused smile. "I don't know about a hero, but I always did like Superman when I was a boy." He chuckled, and she joined in.

After her first sip, he smiled with delight at her "Mmm." With the second sip, the warmth of the alcohol spread through her. "It's delicious."

"Shall I recommend a dinner selection?" he asked as he gestured to the waiter across the room. Nora nodded. And after the waiter left with their order, Antonio asked, "So—what brings you to Italy?"

"I'm just seeing the world. I've always wanted to visit Italy, so here I am." She deliberately sounded vague, waiting for the right time to tell him what she did for a living.

"And you are traveling alone? No companions?"

From his doubtful expression, she gathered it seemed odd to him.

"I came alone this time. As a flight attendant, I can travel when and where I want. My schedule doesn't always match up with my girlfriend's schedule."

"You're a flight attendant?" When she told guys she was a flight attendant, their eyes would predictably glaze over as they conjured up some fantasy about the Mile-High Club. And there it was on Antonio's face. *Hook, line, and sinker.*

"Mmhmm." Nora nonchalantly swallowed another sip of her wine, waiting for his wondering thoughts to return. She politely answered his questions: "What airline do you work for?" "How long have you been flying?" "How often can you come visit me?"

Wait. What?

"Well, this wine is definitely worth another visit," she flirted.

Nora enjoyed the rest of the evening eating delicious food and chatting easily as they got to know one another.

"How long are you here for?"

Today was Monday. Saturday, she timed out and left Sunday evening. She slept a little on the overnight flight, but sleeping on a plane was an art form. This morning she forced herself to stay awake after she checked into her hotel, but she was now getting sleepy. Nora stifled a yawn. "Excuse me. I'm still on East Coast time. I'm hoping to get a flight on Thursday. I can only fly standby."

"How would you like to drive out to the vineyard with me tomorrow? I need to drop off something for my uncle. It would be a good opportunity to see the countryside. It is beautiful this time of year."

He wants to spend the whole day with me. Oh I like you Antonio. Really like you. The fact I would run off into the countryside with a stranger is just crazy. But..."I'd like that," she said, trying not to reveal her eagerness. "Is it far?"

"It's a little over an hour. If we leave at two o'clock, I can give you a tour of the vineyard. Aunt Maria will fix us a meal. She would not let us leave without eating," he laughed, but she could tell he was fond of his aunt.

They walked toward her hotel, stopping before they crossed the narrow street. "Nora, I enjoyed your company very much." Already clasping her hand, he drew her close and brought it to his lips, branding a kiss across her knuckles. "I look forward to tomorrow. Get a good night's sleep." He released her, yet his sultry gaze held her captive. And there was a promise in those dark eyes.

Get a good night's sleep indeed. She thanked him again for dinner and for everything he'd done for her. "See you tomorrow," she said breathily, and retreated into her hotel.

Nora slipped into a nightshirt and called Bree to report on the dinner, informing her nothing had happened–so far. Bree sounded disappointed for the lack of juicy details but pleasantly surprised about a second date.

When Nora hung up she catalogued how her life had transformed drastically. *I can't believe I had the guts to go to the interview and take this job. I've never really left home before and now here I am in Italy, touring by myself. True, I was accosted and almost mugged.* She shuddered. *But luckily I made it through unscathed. It only made me be more aware.* Nora thought of her life before being a flight attendant. *I chose not to become a partner in the family catering business, yet I gave up much of my free time to help them with the business. Why couldn't I just say no?* Nora entered the bathroom and pulled out her toiletry bag, her thoughts continuing. *I knew at the time I took that office job it was going to be a temporary thing. But I stayed at that unfulfilling job for years to be closer to Phillip. Poor Phillip. He wasn't a bad guy, he was just not the right guy. Phillip kept me tethered to a life I was slowly drowning in. But I've changed all that. I cut those ties, and I feel elated I'm allowing myself to freely choose what is best for me.*

Nora washed and dried her face and applied moisturizer, gazing at her refection in the mirror and thinking of Antonio. *I guess Antonio thinks I'm attractive since he asked me out.* She examined her flawless skin, her well-balanced features, and the delicate arch of her eyebrows. She shrugged.

Nora slept well, but her erotic dreams were laced with a dark-eyed man. It was funny how the poster of Rome long ago when she was tile shopping with her sister had prompted her daydream of a dark-eyed Italian man. It seemed as if her fantasy was coming true.

Chapter Seven

The next morning Nora boarded the city bus to Piazza di Trevi to see the Trevi Fountain. According to legend, if you threw three coins into the fountain with your right hand, over your left shoulder, the first coin would guarantee your return to Rome; the second would lead to a new romance; the third would lead to marriage. Nora dug in her pocket for coins. Heart pumping, she wildly sent the coins flying over her left shoulder. *This is crazy— but what the hell!*

She continued sightseeing until noon and then maneuvered the constricted streets to her hotel to shower before meeting Antonio. She stood in the warm sunshine dressed in blue pinstriped shorts, an airy peach blouse, and cute sandals. Her sunglasses held her loose hair away from her face. A compact, sporty car purred to the curb, and Antonio jumped out. He greeted her with a double kiss, and she drank in the aroma of his cologne. He wore linen pants and a lightweight shirt.

Antonio cupped the silky strands of Nora's hair and ran them through his fingers. "You have lovely hair." It was in a haphazard bun when he saved her, and she wore it up at dinner last night. She desperately wanted to reach out and touch his hair, too. *Oh, to run my fingers through it, and then grip it in fistfuls and pull him down to me...* But she smiled sweetly and thanked him as they strolled toward the car.

Antonio navigated the traffic and pointed out city sights. Nora relished having her own, *very handsome*, personal tour guide. When he mentioned the Trevi Fountain and its legend, she tried not to blush. *I'll never admit I ran over there this very morning, like a silly tourist, to throw my coins in.* As they left the congestion of the city behind, Nora thought the countryside was postcard perfect. Antonio shared information about his family and the business, clearly proud. The sound of his deeply accented voice was tremendously sexy, and she was content to just relax and listen to him. She spoke a little about her own family. The mention of her family's catering business quickly led to an interesting conversation about food and wine pairings.

They stopped at a market just outside the city, where Antonio purchased his Aunt Marie's favorite Italian lemon cookies. Nora purchased a small bouquet of flowers to offer the hostess. The sports car hugged the road as it passed vast vineyards.

"I want to show you the vines before we reach the villa," he said, pulling over. Nora grinned as he collected her hand and guided her up the sloping hill to the grape vines. He gave her a tutorial about the growing process, passionately explaining how important each step affected the wine making process. She smiled and nodded enthusiastically, his captive audience, but found herself daydreaming about his hands on her body.

"Shall we go to the villa? Have I bored you?" He pulled her close and wrapped his arm around her shoulder.

"Are you kidding? This place is amazing. It's breathtaking here. I can see why you love it." With an inhale his chest puffed with pride and his smile broadened. He bent down and kissed her with his full, firm lips. A kiss soft and sensual. Lingering. As their kiss ended, he smiled wickedly.

She held her breath and waited.

"My aunt will be expecting us."

He's playing with me, taunting me, testing me…teasing me.

"We should go then." *It's just a kiss.*

Antonio's arm remained around her shoulder as they returned to the car. At the passenger side door, he pressed his body against hers, sandwiching her between his hard body and the car. He cupped her chin and ran his thumb over her bottom lip, his face inches from hers. When his tongue slid out and replaced his thumb, she trembled. The seductive lick became a full, sensual kiss.

When the taste of him filled her mouth she was glad the car door held her up, because her knees were weak. Yes, she felt weak in the knees. She clutched his waist and then ran her palms up and down his muscled ribcage. She clung to him. *If only we weren't on the side of the road in the middle of nowhere—I'm about to burst!*

Eventually he pulled away with apparent effort, a low grumble in his throat. Once their bodies were no longer touching, they simply regarded each other for a few moments, each aware of what the other wanted. He smirked before he backed away. She reached behind her for the door handle, got in, and clamped her legs together, trying not to squirm in her seat. That tingling he caused deep down in her core was expanding.

As they continued the drive, Antonio continued in his easy manner describing the property. Parking at the villa, he called out the window to a man carrying a case of wine bottles. The man crossing the lawn smiled and yelled hello.

"That's my cousin Paolo. He is one of six boys. I have lots of cousins."

The country villa had a sweeping row of arched doorways that opened into a large central courtyard. The balcony above was framed with wide marble balustrades. The russet clay tiles on the rooftops baked in the sunshine.

Paolo placed his case down and yelled, "Antonio, Christina! How are you?"

As they approached his cousin, Antonio said, "Paolo, this is Nora."

"Nora, it is nice to meet you. I thought you'd brought Christina. They look alike from far away."

Antonio inspected her and nodded. "Yeah, I can see it." That was all he said on the subject of Christina, and Nora wondered why. The two men embraced, and then Antonio ushered her toward the house. The villa stayed surprisingly cool inside, despite the warm afternoon sun. Aunt Maria, who appeared in the kitchen doorframe, wiped her hands on her apron and opened her arms to him when she saw Antonio. The petite woman, her dark hair shot through with gray, placed a slim hand on Antonio's cheek before they exchanged a double kiss.

Aunt Maria spotted the box Antonio was carrying. "Are those lemon cookies?" At his sheepish smile, she replied, "Such a sweet boy. And who might we have here?" She shifted her gaze to Antonio's guest.

"This is Nora. She's from America."

Soft-spoken Maria welcomed Nora in English. Nora could not believe this tiny woman had given birth to seven sons.

"It's nice to meet you. These are for you." Nora handed Maria the bouquet.

Maria thanked her and then led them into the kitchen, where all manner of food was being prepared. Lovely dark-eyed women of various ages were introduced as cousins and nieces. Antonio seemed relaxed and socialized with the additional family members who crowded in to join them. There were fourteen in all, including two children belonging to one of his many cousins. They enjoyed a delicious meal with several wine pairings out in the courtyard. Though rapid Italian was spoken most of the time, everyone was polite to Nora. The sun descended as they said their good-byes and headed back to Rome.

When they approached the city Antonio invited her to his place for a nightcap. It was early still so she agreed. Nora had not asked who Christina was, and Antonio never said, but it plagued her. If Christina was a girlfriend, surely there would be some clue at his place. Maybe she was an associate? Or a friend? Another cousin?

The walk-up apartment had a pleasant view of a historic piazza. While he poured them wine, she scanned the neat and orderly space. She sat on a sofa, facing double doors that opened to a modest balcony. He handed her a glass and opened the balcony doors. A cooling night breeze floated in as she sipped her wine. The din of the distant city wafted in. He turned on some mood music and joined her.

"Thank you, Antonio, for today. I had a nice time. Your family is so sweet. It makes me miss mine." She feasted on his brandy-colored eyes framed by dark, lavish lashes. Many times throughout the day she imagined what would happen when they were alone. *You are so out of my league, yet here you are, with me...* She reached out to run her thumb over his lush lips.

He caught her hand and kissed her palm and then each fingertip. He slid her middle finger all the way into his mouth, sending a fire bolt to her belly. The hot and wet sensation only magnified when he slowly drew it in and out. She moaned out loud. He stopped and took the wine glass from her hand, stretching past her to place it on the end table. He was an inch from her, but he did not touch her body before he slipped into his seat and dragged her on top of him.

"Antonio…" She paused and searched his eyes. "Do you have a girlfriend?" She hated to ruin the mood, but she didn't want to be involved in someone's cheating relationship. She had to know about Christina. The nagging feeling wouldn't leave.

"I have a lot of girlfriends," he purred as he caressed her behind and more, making her bite her lip. And despite the baseball-sized bruise on her hip from yesterday's fall, she felt no discomfort, only building pleasure.

"I mean…Christina. Is she your…girlfriend?"

He slowed his stroking.

Maybe I really don't want to know. Oh, why did I pick this moment to ask?

"Christina was my girlfriend at one time. Now we are just friends who see each other from time to time," he replied nonchalantly.

Nora translated that to casual sex. Friends with benefits. *Maybe I could do that. I don't need another complicated relationship right now. Bree had said, "Go for it, Nora. You deserved it." I may not have indulged in casual sex in the past, but it would be a step toward moving on after Phillip. And there is no finer man than the one who lay underneath me now. Beside I probably will never see Antonio again after this.*

He watched the play of emotions cross her face and seemed to recognize his cue when her eyes darkened with desire and her breath quickened. He shifted his hips, emphasizing his need, and she lowered her mouth to his. *You are an amazing kisser. I could simply kiss you the entire night.*

He caressed her thigh and slid his fingers under her shorts. He poked and stroked her until she sat up panting. That muscle she hadn't used in a while was throbbing now.

"Let's go into my bedroom." He shifted her so he could stand, and he pulled her up from the sofa, leading her into the dimly lit room.

He unbuttoned the top buttons on his shirt and pulled it over his head. Where her hands had been touching a few minutes before, her eyes were now feasting. He had a washboard stomach, and wisps of dark hair sprouted from his chest. Nora thought him out of her league, but a man like him wanting her, made her feel so sexy and powerful. Of course she wanted him—her body screamed for him—but the question that stalled her movement was...should she? She'd only known him for two days. What about her morals? What about wanting new and exciting experiences? He would be a new and exciting experience—yes, she wanted to *experience* what he offered. She slowly unbuttoned her blouse. He shuffled toward the bed, never taking his eyes off her. He switched on the lamp.

She shrugged out of her blouse and let it slip to the floor. Her shorts came off next. She could feel a blush rush up her neck at his approving wolfish smile. He stood at the edge of the bed and opened the nightstand drawer, pulling out a square packet. Nora licked her lips in anticipation.

He reached for her, running his palms up her arms to her shoulders as his dark head nuzzled her neck and he ran his tongue along her collarbone. With a ragged breath she gave into him. *No more doubt from this moment on—just pleasure.* Nora slid her fingers into his thick, wavy hair and pulled his head back while she seared him with kisses along his jaw and nibbled his earlobe. She meant to give as much pleasure as she received.

After Antonio rolled off of her, Nora stretched like a satisfied cat. She had never experienced lovemaking like *that* before! She had needed this, even if it tipped her moral compass and made her feel naughty. Yes, she would return to Rome and visit Antonio often. She could have a friend like him with benefits. *So many benefits.* She stayed the night, though she did not get much sleep. They enjoyed each other again before falling asleep, and he woke her early for another round.

Antonio went out for an early morning run and was showering when she rolled out of bed.

"I'm going to the hotel. I need to shower," she said from the bathroom doorway.

Antonio stepped out of the shower stall, toweling his chest. "I can turn the water on and wash your back if you'd like to shower here."

He's so sexy!

Nora would've considered it if she wasn't so sore down there. She hadn't been with anyone since Phillip. Sadly, she needed a reprieve, and suddenly, she felt self-conscious and sticky.

"I think some clean clothes and a toothbrush would be good."

"I have extra toothbrushes. You could wear my T-shirt–or nothing at all." He secured the towel around his waist.

Extra toothbrushes! Condoms in his nightstand! Lots of girlfriends! Suddenly Nora felt buyer's remorse.

"I want to see you tonight. It's your last night here. I'll take you to dinner." He reached for her.

Forget buyer's remorse. He is worth it. Not only was his body god-like, he was a nice guy, although his one fault was the "lots of girlfriends" thing. *But,* she reminded herself, *I'm in Italy just enjoying my vacation. It's not like I'm looking for a relationship. Antonio is the right guy at the right time, and I'm going to enjoy every minute with him.*

"I can't wait." She allowed him to kiss her until she reluctantly pulled away.

Antonio had some work to attend to, and Nora wanted to see more of the city, so they agreed to meet at seven o'clock. This time he drove them to a very romantic restaurant on a hilltop overlooking the city. As they finished the last of their wine, Antonio held her hand. He leaned in, his eyes roaming over her. "Will you visit me again, Nora?"

"I can try to get an overnight in Rome next month. I'd have between thirty-six and forty-eight hours of free time before the return flight. We could meet up."

"I'll pick you up at the airport, and you can stay with me." He lowered his hand under the table and ran it up her thigh. "Would you like that?"

She caught her lower lip between her teeth. Their eyes locked, and at her tiny nod he leaned closer and kissed her.

Later at his place Antonio begged her to spend the night, kissing her senseless until she agreed. In the morning they walked to a café for coffee on the way to her hotel. He left her in the lobby insisting he'd return to drive her to the airport after she'd showered and packed. Antonio kissed her long and hard before she got out of his car. She was going to miss him, especially his touch.

Nora sighed with contentment as the aircraft made its steady climb to forty thousand feet, leaving Italy–and Antonio–behind.

Chapter Eight

In Philadelphia, when Nora told Bree all about her torrid time with the sexy Italian stud, she couldn't stop the red blush that reached the roots of her hair. They sat on the sofa with their feet drawn under them.

"I *cannot* believe all that happened!" Bree said. They giggled like schoolgirls. Bree held her breath, trying to control her laugher before she took a long swallow of wine. "I need to go back to Italy."

Nora shrugged and shook her head. "Tell me more about that guy you said you met at the club. Are you still seeing him?"

"Yeah. Tyrone. You'll meet him soon, I guess," she replied vaguely. Bree did not seem like she wanted to talk about Tyrone. She waved a dismissive hand and changed the subject. "When are you driving out to see your parents?"

"Well, I leave tomorrow night for Paris. When I return from France I'm driving over to stay with my parents overnight. I feel bad that I haven't been home to see them as much as I thought I would. You're welcome to join me. You know my mom is an amazing cook, right? And she made me promise to bring you with me at some point. Can you come?"

"If I'm not flying, I'll definitely join you."

Days later, Nora drove Bree to York County. Her family gave Bree a warm welcome. Beautiful and gracious Bree impressed everyone she met. Nora caught her family exchanging glances that implied, "Wow, isn't she something?"

"You really have changed—look at you. How much weight have you lost?" Heidi fussed over her daughter at first, but as the night went on she was content just to have Nora under her roof again. "Eleanor, we are so happy to *finally* meet Bree," Heidi, chided.

Bree raised her brows at the name Eleanor; she'd only known her friend as Nora. Nora's parents and sisters had been just as surprised when they had heard their Eleanor had a nickname.

Before settling in for the night, Nora sat on the guest bed while Bree stood and brushed her hair. "Your family is so nice. And so...normal. It's like a Norman Rockwell painting here."

"What?" Nora laughed at her friend's assessment. "Your mom and dad are nice too."

Bree pulled a face. "You don't have to say that just because you're my friend. Mr. and Mrs. Royce are ridiculous and overbearing. And you know that's true." She pointed her hair brush at Nora, daring her to say otherwise.

"Whatever. *You* are ridiculous." Nora yawned dragging herself up. "I'll see you in the morning."

Nora and Bree returned to Philly the next day, did laundry, and repacked their flight bags. Bree was off on an Albany/Orlando roundtrip. Nora jetted off to Helsinki.

Bree complained, "These East Coast cities suck. I wish I was going with you. Maybe I should look into the international flight program."

Nora encouraged her to do so.

After Helsinki, Nora's final trip in May was to Rome, the City of Eternal Love. Nora's heart pounded as she phoned Antonio to tell him she was returning to his city. He picked her up at the airport and took her to lunch. They spent the rest of the afternoon in his apartment rediscovering each other. They walked to dinner at a nearby restaurant, where they ate on the patio, enjoying the warm night. When they returned to his bed, they pleased each other throughout the night and in the morning. It seemed she couldn't get enough of him. Nora took a nap in the afternoon before she had to get ready to leave for the airport.

Nora strode through the airport in her uniform, wheeling her luggage slightly behind her so she could easily move through the crowds. In every airport, she felt the stares, and got smiles and nods from gentlemen. It was still hard to believe she attracted such attention. But today, after the torrid time she spent with Antonio, she felt sexy wearing her hot pink panties under her conservative skirt. Bree had said something about sexy underwear once, and now Nora knew what she meant.

On a warm night in early June, Nora answered the door in her stylish dress from Italy, the one she wore on her first date with Antonio. Bree arranged a night out on the town with Nora, Rebecca, Jackie, and Miguel.

"Hey guys, it's great to see you." Nora hugged her friends.

Hanging out together proved tricky because of their various trip schedules, so tonight was a rare occasion. Rebecca came by the most often. They didn't see Jackie as much, and this was the first time they convinced Miguel to join them.

Over pre-club drinks in the townhouse Rebecca apologized to her friends, "I'm transferring to the North Carolina base. It's been tough making Philadelphia my home." Rebecca shared an apartment with two roommates who were best friends, and Rebecca previously mentioned she felt like a third wheel. "I'll really miss you all, but I can always fly in for a visit."

"Well, we better get to the club to make the most of your time left," said Jackie.

The guy Bree dated, Tyrone, was meeting them at the nightclub. Though the girls lived together, Nora and Bree would sometimes not see each other for a couple weeks at a time, so Nora hadn't yet met the elusive Tyrone. But she had overheard some disturbing phone calls. She heard Bree say things like, "No! I wasn't out with another guy!" Or, "Yeah, I can find my own ride." Or, "I'm not going to say anything." Or, "No one knows." Nora decided not to ask Bree about the calls until she met Tyrone, although what she heard left Nora wondering what kind of guy he was. She had a funny feeling it would prove to be an interesting evening.

They each shared crazy stories from their flights as they walked to the local hotspot. At the club they met up with Sergei and Alexei, the Russian pilots who flew for a freight airline and lived across the street from Nora and Bree. Just after the girls moved in Sergei had noticed Bree outside her townhouse wearing her uniform. They struck up a conversation and the four of them had been friends ever since. On occasion Sergei and

Alexei had joined the girls for pizza and a movie, but usually the four of them hung out on the stoop on nights when the weather was nice and their schedules happened to sync. Even Rebecca had joined them a couple of times. Nora introduced the pilots to Jackie and Miguel when they arrived. Jackie and Miguel stood near the dance floor, watching the dancers. The Russian guys were not much for dancing so they hung out at the bar. Nora thought they were both really nice guys, and she was thankful to have a good group of friends. In her old life she only hung out with Phillip or her family. *I've been missing out!*

From the dance floor, Nora smiled across the room at Sergei and could not help but notice how he kept a watchful eye on her. Nora found the pulse of the music primal and intoxicating and she bounced along with the crowd feeling free. When several guys made a move, trying to dance with her, she acted as if she were interested for a minute, flirting with her eyes and tossing her hair, then she'd slip into the crowd with a little wave good-bye. Oh, the look on those boys faces! Just when they thought they had her... she slyly smiled, feeling powerful and naughty, completely out of character. When had she become a vixen? In this moment, she did not care. Since her time with Antonio she felt something awaken within her, and she wanted to explore just what that was. Before him, she had never been anyone's object of desire. Phillip hadn't *desired* her or pursued her like he wanted to sexually devour her.

The song ended and Nora returned to her circle of friends. Suddenly, a tune motivated quiet Miguel to show off his moves on the dance floor. The crowd parted; his old-school break-dance moves had the dancers cheering him on. Nora and Bree exchanged surprised glances.

"Wow—he's amazing! And he's overcome his shyness." Nora yelled to Jackie, who wore an all-knowing smile.

"Miguel and I spent a lot of time on the Miami scene in the clubs."

They all felt loose and friendly after drinking for several hours. Even Rebecca, their Southern Christian girl, grooved with a beer in her hand.

The drama started when Tyrone made an appearance around midnight. He arrived with a gang of friends, who dominated one side of the bar. When Bree introduced Nora to him, Tyrone barely gave her a glance. "What's up," he murmured into his drink.

Bree, all smiles, said, "Hey, babe, do you want to join us on the dance floor?" Trying to entice Tyrone to join her friends, Bree exchanged mini hand waves with Rebecca, who was grooving with some guy on the dance floor. Tyrone's eyes cut across the crowded floor, then returned to Bree.

"Naw…And you stay here with me." Bree stayed next to him, but he turned away and ignored her while he talked to his fellas. Nora could tell it bothered her friend, but Bree pretended everything was fine.

The next song cued up. "Let's dance–I love this song!" Nora grabbed Bree's hand, only to have Tyrone clamp it.

"She's sittin' wit' me." He smiled, but it did not reach his eyes. "You go ahead though, it being your favorite song and all."

"Yes! Go! I haven't seen Tyrone all night," Bree urged. Nora slid her hand out of the sandwich. *What an asshole. Why is Bree with this guy?* Clearly Bree was uncomfortable and not hiding it well.

"Okay," Nora chirped and walked away. What was she going to do–argue with Tyrone in the deafening, packed club?

Nora joined Sergei and Alexei at the bar, dancing forgotten. "I need a drink."

"Some vodka?" Sergei teased.

"I'll do a shot," she announced. Tyrone had a sobering effect, and Nora wasn't ready to be sober.

Sergei's loud, deep voice with its heavy Russian accent caught the bartender's attention. "Three shots of vodka–top shelf." Sergei's voice always caused heads to turn. Though he was a tall, well-muscled, formidable type, his pale blue eyes sparkled when he laughed. Nora really liked him. She'd seen him angry a couple times and hoped to always remain on his good side. He could appear quite menacing when he wanted to. Sergei had kept the corner of his eye on her all night. She knew his eyes lingered a little longer when she moved on the dance floor.

"What's going on? That sleazeball with Bree–did he upset you?"

Nora sat on the stool he gave up for her, and her face softened. He was perceptive too, and she appreciated Sergei could tell she was upset. "That's Bree's boyfriend." She glared down the bar at them. Tyrone and Bree were now in a heated argument. When Sergei called her name Nora blinked out of her trance, not knowing how long she'd been watching them. He handed her the shot of vodka.

The three of them raised their glasses, calling the famous Russian toast "Nostrovia!" in unison. Three heads tilted back, taking their shots, and then three glasses clanked on the bar. Sergei and Alexei chuckled at the face Nora made. Someone called her name and she twisted around to see Jackie, Miguel, and Rebecca standing near Bree, as close as they could get in the crowd. Rebecca was pointing frantically toward Bree and Tyrone. Tyrone's gang was already heading out the door, though he still argued with Bree, standing over her and yelling in her face.

"What the hell!" Red spots flashed in Nora's eyes as she watched her friend being berated by some loser boyfriend. Everything happened fast.

"Get the tab, we're leaving," Sergei said to Alexei over Nora's head.

She shoved her way down the packed bar. "Excuse me! Excuse me!" *These drunk bastards won't move.* She wasn't very big, but her bony elbows helped her open a path.

By the time she reached Rebecca, Rebecca was frantic. "Nora, don't let Bree go with him." Nora saw Bree following Tyrone out the door and rushed to follow them. Outside, Bree pleaded with Tyrone.

"I swear, babe, he never touched me." Bree followed him like a puppy. Nora had never seen her like this. *Why is she with this loser? She could have anyone.*

"Why are you a lying bitch? I saw it with my own eyes," he accused.

"Bree!" Nora yelled. An electric-orange muscle car pulled up to the curb. The door swung open, and Tyrone moved toward it. "Bree, let's go home," Nora suggested as she reached Bree's side.

Suddenly Tyrone turned around and shot Nora a warning look. He'd already taken several steps toward the car, leaving Bree standing there, but after Nora staked her claim, Tyrone seemed to have acquired a renewed interest in Bree. "Bree, get in the car."

Bree regarded at him, clearly confused.

"I said get in the car, bitch."

"I don't think so," Sergei's heavily accented voice bellowed. He followed Nora through the crowd and out the door. She hadn't even noticed but now her heart skipped a beat. *Thank God for Sergei.*

Three of Tyrone's buddies stepped from the tricked-out vehicle. Tyrone acted cocky until Alexei, who was three inches taller than Sergei, jogged out of the bar and asked, "Is there trouble?" The hulking duo presented a threatening front. Nora knew boxing was one of their hobbies. As a result Alexei's face was all angles, and Sergei's nose was crooked.

"No trouble," Tyrone said to the Russians, backing away as his friends slid into the car. He spit at the ground in Bree's direction and said to her, "You ain't worth no trouble, bitch." The car pulled from the curb before Tyrone could shut the door all the way.

Nora exhaled a long sigh, not realizing she'd been holding her breath. Relief washed over her. "Thank god you didn't leave with that guy, Bree." Rebecca, Jackie, and Miguel came out of the club just then, their concern evident.

"What happened?" Rebecca ran up and hugged Bree. "Are you all right?"

Bree caught her top lip between her teeth, unable to speak. Nora assured her, "Everything's fine now. We're going home."

The group walked in silence to the townhouse. Reaching their street, Jackie spoke up. "We're going to take off. Miguel didn't drink much so he's going to drive us home. Want a ride, Rebecca?" Rebecca nodded, and the three of them crossed the street to head toward their car.

"Okay. I'll call you tomorrow," Nora yelled in farewell. Bree kept walking, her arms tightly folded over her chest.

When they reached the brownstone, Sergei and Alexei stopped on the sidewalk. Bree, who remained silent the whole time, ran up the steps and slammed the door behind her.

Nora thanked them again. "What would I have done if you were not there? What could I have done?" Nora sat on the stoop. Sergei joined her.

Alexei said, "Anytime you need us, Nora, we're just across the street. Good night."

"Night," they replied at the same time.

"Geez, Sergei, I can't believe that guy." Nora gritted her teeth.

"You were pretty brave, standing up to that punk. I've never seen you so angry. How were you planning on stopping him?" Sergei tugged on a wavy lock of Nora's hair.

She shrugged, unable to think of an answer. "I don't know. Honestly, I'm really glad you were there." Distracted, she wrestled with finding a solution for this problem. "Ahh." She released some frustration. "I don't understand any of this. I've been working so much... I didn't know this was going on with Tyrone. Bree never really talked about him. Oh..." She suddenly remembered the phone calls. "I'm an idiot!" She placed both her hands on her head and shook it. "I've got to go talk to her." She placed her hand on his bicep. It was so large her whole hand and fingers lay flat without her fingers curling. "Thank you for following me out of the club. I don't know what I would have done without you and Alexei."

Sergei had been leaning against the upper stair tread. He sat forward and placed one hand on the small of her back. The other skimmed her knee and began easing upward before resting it on her bare skin.

An alarm went off in Nora's brain. She braced her hands against his chest, stalling him. "Sergei, I..." she faltered, unsure what to say. She stopped the kiss he was ready to give her. Antonio's face flashed before her eyes, but she scolded herself, *No commitments—just having fun!* She considered the possibility of kissing Sergei, but the timing was all wrong. "I need to go inside. I'm sorry."

"You are a good friend to her, Nora." With his face so close to hers, she could smell the vodka on his breath.

"So are you," she whispered, searching his eyes for a clue to what he ultimately wanted. Sergei grunted in agreement, lifted himself off the stoop, and walked toward his brownstone across the street.

He was going to kiss me! And she didn't think she'd mind kissing him, but she would have to think about that later. Right now, she needed to talk to Bree. She scrambled up the steps, slipped inside, and locked the door.

Nora knocked on the bedroom door. "Bree, can I come in?"

"I'm going to sleep."

Nora barged in anyway. "Please talk to me. Are you okay? What is going on? Why are you seeing that guy?" Nora blurted as she crossed the room and sat at the end of Bree's bed.

Bree had the covers pulled up to her chin. "I don't know. He was all right for a while. He's not usually like that."

"Why were you arguing?" Watching Tyrone yelling in Bree's face had made Nora's blood boil.

"Oh, that." She waved her hand. "Tyrone thought some guy next to me grabbed my ass, but he didn't. He acts crazy when he gets jealous."

"He was a jerk the whole time. Bree, you deserve to be with someone better than that loser. Please tell me you won't see him again. You're not planning on seeing him again, are you?" Nora knew she could not tell her friend what to do, so she was reduced to pleading.

Bree shook her head, and Nora felt relieved. Nora had the impression that Bree's fondness for bad boys had to do with her family life. Previously Bree had confessed she'd dated guys that drove her parents crazy. There had been an older musician and then some guy with questionable tattoos. Her parents' divorce seemed to have exacted a toll on Bree's choices for healthy relationships.

"Thanks, Nora, for looking out for me." Bree's chest softly convulsed, and humiliated tears spilled.

Nora tucked Bree into bed she slipped from the room. She scrubbed her face clean, slipped on a T-shirt, and snuggled under her grandmother's quilt with a heavy sigh. She worried about her friend and was dismayed she had been right about Tyrone.

Unable to stew on the situation any longer her thoughts returned to her Russian neighbor.

Sergei... He'd wanted to kiss me tonight. He's always been sweet to me. She'd sensed he liked her, but she hadn't expected him to actually make a move on her. He was good-looking in a rugged sort of way. Not like Antonio. Antonio was hunky and sensual. How was it possible she had two men interested in her? She needed to see Antonio again–to be in his arms. She planned on picking up a trip to Rome at the end of this month. Yes, as soon as she could–she had to see him again.

The morning after the Tyrone incident, Bree confessed her insecurities to Nora about the guys she dated. "I choose them for all the wrong reasons, it's like I get a high when I feel like they are aloof or dangerous... It's a challenge to get them to date me." Bree spooned yogurt into her mouth. "I'm so stupid." She dug for another serving.

Nora asked the tough question. "What are you going to do about it?"

Bree poked around in her yogurt cup as she considered her options. "Okay, I know what you are thinking, and you're right," she finally answered. "I'm turning over a new leaf. I'm done dating assholes," she pledged.

"You better be." Nora toughened her voice. "You deserve better."

Choked with emotion, Bree nodded at her friend's fierce devotion.

Chapter Nine

Nora's next trip took her to Vienna. After completing the food and beverage service on her Austrian-bound flight, Nora had some time to herself. She sat pondering the love interests in her life.

Antonio... He was passionate. He commanded her body to want him with one glance from his dark eyes. She liked how his possessive hands were always on her–his arm slung over her shoulder, his hand at the small of her back as he guided her beside him, caressing her shoulders and thighs as they sat side by side at cafes. Their relationship was physical, and it was okay if that's all it was. And anyway, it was too early to think about it becoming more than that.

Nora's thoughts shuffled to the next man on her radar. *Sergei...* She hadn't seen him since he almost kissed her. Was *she* interested in *him*? She considered several of his good points. She loved his accent. He was attractive and a nice guy, who seemed especially sweet to her. Not only did he have a good job, but he lived in America (big plus), and obviously really liked her. Those were good points to consider.

Vienna was beautiful and clean, and the people were friendly. Nora paired up with two flight attendants she'd flown over with who were nice enough to take her around on her first visit. Nora couldn't stop taking pictures of the charming old-world city. Her companions took her to their favorite restaurant for dinner, where Nora tried Wiener schnitzel, very thin veal slices, breaded and deep-fried. *Who doesn't like anything that is deep-fried?* That night in her hotel room she called her parents. There was a six-hour time difference, so it was still afternoon in her hometown.

"You're in Austria?" Heidi asked. "She's in Vienna, Austria," she repeated to Victoria. "Victoria and I are preparing for this weekend's wedding function."

"Did you get the photos I texted you?" Nora sent trip photos to her mom when she got the chance. It helped to ward off her guilt since she hadn't been home in weeks.

"Oh, yes. Your dad and I have enjoyed them. How are you?" Heidi asked.

"Great. Everything has been going well. How is everyone there?" The conversation felt a little too formal. She missed her family. Nora could picture them in the kitchen, and wished she were there right now. Seeing the world was a dream come true, but there was nothing like spending time with your family–the people you loved, the people who loved you. A wave of homesickness washed over her.

"Everyone is fine here. Victoria is going to text you some pictures of the Miller wedding. It was an elegant event–wait until you see their cake." Heidi chatted for a few more minutes. Then Victoria got on the line to beam that pregnancy was agreeing with her.

"I'm so happy for you Victoria. I promise I'm coming home soon." At Nora's stifled yawn, Victoria assured her they were busy with a deadline and she should get some sleep.

Immediately following her Vienna trip, Nora picked up a trip to Germany. She then returned to Philadelphia for a few days before she would leave for Rome. She hadn't seen Bree or Sergei for over a week. Bree wasn't home when she entered the townhouse mid-morning. Nora surmised Bree was probably at the gym. She went upstairs to do laundry and repack her suitcase. The suitcase had its own bench in her room and was constantly being unpacked and restocked, always ready to go at a moment's notice. Chores done, Nora headed down the stairs. Bree opened the front door when she reached the last step.

"Hi!" Nora's cheerful voice cried, "Boy, it's been a long week."

The girls settled in on the couch to catch up. Bree chugged a bottle of water, her gym clothes an indication where she'd been this morning. She had Nora's undivided attention when she said, "Wait until I fill you in on yet another incident with Tyrone."

After redoing her blonde ponytail, she began, "I sent Tyrone a text after his stunt at the club and ended things. But when I returned from my trip earlier in the week, Tyrone came by, banging on their door and threatening me if I didn't answer."

Nora squeezed her balled fists.

"Once again Sergei came to my rescue. Not only did Sergei flatten Tyrone with one punch, but apparently Sergei knows someone who knows someone that Tyrone gets his drugs from. Let's just say he won't be bothering me anymore."

"Drugs?" Nora raised her eyebrows.

"Don't worry, it was all him. I don't do that shit."

"Wow. Well, it's a good thing Sergei's our neighbor." Nora got up to hunt around in the kitchen for something to eat. "I'm glad Sergei was around. I hated leaving you here alone."

"Yeah, he is so sweet. He even spent the night."

Nora's head snapped up. "Sergei spent the night?"

Bree took another swig from her water bottle and joined Nora in the kitchen.

"Yeeaaah–on the couch, so I would feel safe." Bree sent Nora a look. "It's not like that." She wrinkled her nose. "He's not my type."

"Right." Nora felt foolish suggesting there could be something between Bree and Sergei. Though men were consistently attracted to Bree, Sergei only seemed to have eyes for Nora. Apparently Bree was not Sergei's type either.

Nora's came up empty-handed after rummaging in the refrigerator and cabinets. "What do you want for dinner?"

"I don't know. I'm so tired of take-out. Do you feel like cooking?" Bree asked hopefully. Bree did not cook, even though her mother had set up their kitchen as if a chef lived there. Nora was not a trained chef, but she could cook.

"How about I run down to the market? I'll make some baked chicken, rice, and green beans."

"I love you," Bree said with emphasis before she headed upstairs to take a shower.

Nora chuckled, grabbed her purse, and headed out the door. She hoped to avoid Sergei for now. She didn't want things to be weird between them. Tomorrow night she would be on her way to see Antonio. Glancing around, relief washed over her as Sergei was nowhere in sight.

In the third week in June, Nora was bound for Antonio's arms again. It was the third time she visited him in the two months since she met him. He picked her up at the airport, and they had barely closed the door of her hotel room before he was tugging off her clothes. After an hour of lovemaking, Nora's sweat-drenched body felt satisfied and relaxed, but Antonio was insatiable. She was drifting off when she felt his hot wet tongue circling her bellybutton. She reached down and clutched his unruly dark hair.

"Oh, let me rest, Antonio. I've been up all night."

"Okay. A little nap, then I'll take you to lunch." He rolled from the bed, bent to retrieve his pants, and pulled a cell phone from his pocket. Nora's heavy lids pumped several times before they closed, catching a last look at his splendid physique. She drifted into a restful slumber.

The street noise woke Nora. Rolling from the bed, the tangled sheet slipped free, and she stood nude, stretching. Dark eyes fixed on her, Antonio remained still as a statue, until he blinked. He sat naked at the desk, where he had been scrolling through e-mails on his phone. Suddenly embarrassed, she mumbled, "I need a shower." She padded to the bathroom and turned on the faucet. Stepping under the refreshing water, she lifted her face, smoothing her hair.

When she opened her eyes, Antonio was posed like a predator in the doorway. His forearms braced against the doorjamb; she observed the steady rise and fall of his chest. There was only a small glass shower wall between them. He strutted toward her and slipped into the shower, the space clearly made for one person. She felt confined as his large body overwhelmed the tight interior. Her backside flattened against the glass, and her long hair plastered itself to the wet surface. Cupping the back of her neck, he held her still while his tongue plundered her mouth.

His hungry kisses caused her to easily forget about the constricted space. Still holding her neck, he pivoted her torso so she faced the glass wall, and she rested her forehead there. Behind her his knee wedged between her legs, causing her to widen her stance. *Oh no, not again.* But he made her inner protest rapidly fade.

His primal lovemaking left her somewhat sore. They had enjoyed each other again after their lunch outing, and they ordered dinner in, giving them time to play all evening. When Antonio slipped off to work the next day, Nora was glad for the reprieve. She met up with the other flight attendants from her crew and joined them for a day of exploration. There were endless sites to visit in the city of Rome.

Antonio picked her up later, and as they drove to dinner she told him about her day. He easily reached her knee in his sports car, but his caresses crept further up her leg. Over authentic fare and glasses of wine, Antonio talked mostly about the vineyard. Then, keeping his voice low and seductive, he detailed what he was going to do to her when they were alone again. Nora glanced around, praying no one overheard his outrageous declarations. She redirected the conversation. "Your family's vineyard is incredible. You're fortunate to have a big, close family. I admire that," she said sincerely.

Antonio puffed with pride. "You are a keeper." He lifted her hand to his mouth and gave it a wolfish bite. She swatted at him playfully. "Our vineyards are our legacy. Our children's children will run them. I am confident."

"Are you planning on having any of those children?" She pictured dark-eyed little boys and girls running around with their mischievous cousins.

"Of course. Eventually I'll marry an Italian woman, and she will bear me many children." He drank from his wine glass.

This was news to Nora. He wanted many children, but *he wanted to marry an Italian woman.* Nora was clearly not that woman. What the hell was "You are a keeper" about?

At the slight change in her demeanor, Antonio added, "I would like for you to remain my special companion–my desire, my heart."

"Antonio, what are you asking me?" Nora's stomach knotted.

"I want us to remain as we are. You bring me great pleasure. I hope I give you the same." He kissed her knuckles, but she slipped her hand from his grasp.

"There's someone else, isn't there?" Her voice rose. *He's definitely trying to tell me something. I should've known there was someone else. Is it that Christina girl? What are you hiding?* Panic flooded her.

He glanced around, lowering his voice, clearly hoping she would follow suit. "I've been engaged for a long time to someone who has the same feelings about marriage as I do. She is interested in a platonic arrangement for now, but eventually, in time, we will marry and have children. This is how the vineyards will be passed down to our families. I have always been comfortable living a more open lifestyle. And I want you to be a part of that lifestyle." He spoke as if this was a common custom. Nora felt sick and insulted.

"Like a *mistress*?" Nora was appalled. How could this be happening? These were modern times. How had this gotten so weird? *I should have known this was too good to be true.* "I don't want to be 'the other woman.' Is it Christina?"

"No, not Christina–she is just an old girlfriend, like I told you." He tried to reclaim her hand. "No... Nora, *you* are *the* woman. Believe me. *She* is the other woman. She has family obligations, like me. Our families have history. We have an arrangement. Our marriage won't even take place for many years. And besides, she has other lifestyle interests as well."

"Lifestyle interests? What are you talking about?" Nora glanced around, thinking maybe she would flee, but something kept her glued to her seat. *Maybe curiosity?*

"She prefers women," he stated as a matter of fact. "And she has a long-time partner. Her family wants her to have children and live a 'normal Italian life'. We are very traditional people. I've offered her that life in exchange for my own freedom, so to speak."

Nora wanted to remain calm, but her heart was jumping in her chest. "I...I don't think I can do that. I don't know what to say." It seemed sudden he was bringing up an arrangement. Nora hadn't thought about where this relationship would go. There was no denying the physical pull they felt toward each other. She had told herself this was for fun and it would run its course. It was too soon for Antonio to be telling her his feelings for her. *His heart...what does that mean?* Sure, he was being honest–better to know his intentions sooner than later–but on the other hand, this was pressure. This meant labeling it.

"Know this, Nora." He leaned in. "I want to keep seeing you. I just want you to know about me. I am no deceiver of women. I can see us sharing something amazing together." When he looked at her like that, with those alluring eyes and his sensual smile, all she wanted to do was take him to her hotel room and forget about what he'd just said. She did not want to label it. Her erratic heartbeat slowed.

"Antonio," Nora whispered, stopping his words. "All I know is right now, tonight, I just want to be with you." She surmised this would probably be her last night with Antonio.

In the hotel room Antonio wasted no time paying very special attention to every detail, showing her she made the right decision. However after their lovemaking, which felt like *lovemaking* and not the raw, marathon sex she usually shared with him, he had pulled her close, snoring softly into her hair. Wrapped in the heat of his body, slick and satisfied, Nora knew this was their last time. She fingered his silky black hair, loving the way it curled around his ears. This image, she would store away as a sweet memory.

Nora dissected her relationship with Antonio as she drove home from the airport. At first she reveled in the element of excitement that came just from being seen with him. She had that "Yeah, he's with me" smugness when other girls gave her curious looks. And, true, he satisfied her physically, more than anyone she'd known. However, his sudden proclamation had unquestionably tainted the fairytale. She said good-bye to him with a heavy heart all the same.

At mid-day Nora easily found a parking spot across the street from her brownstone in front of Sergei's place. Lifting her crew bag from the trunk, she heard a familiar voice laced with a Russian accent.

"Hello, Nora." Sergei walked up with a grocery bag in hand. Guilt immediately swamped Nora for avoiding him. Especially after he stood up to Tyrone for Bree–twice!

"Hey, Sergei, how have you been?" She set her luggage on the sidewalk and locked her vehicle.

"I've been good. Working a lot. I have a few days off now. How about you?"

"Yeah, I'm timed out. I could use some downtime." Nora searched his pale-blue eyes, wondering if he'd bring up their intimate moment. There was no sign of awkwardness in his laid-back demeanor. Nora continued. "Hey! Bree told me what you did about Tyrone when he came banging on our door. Thanks for taking care of that situation."

"Mmm. That punk won't bother her again."

"That guy's a jerk." She still couldn't get her head around what Bree saw in him. "But *you* are awesome, Sergei. We should have you over for dinner—to thank you."

"I would love to have dinner with *you*." He grinned. His intention was not lost on her.

"*And* Bree!" She laughed as his smile broadened. "All right, I'm off." Nora slid the handle of her luggage up and headed across the street.

"How about tonight?" he called. Nora turned and drooped her head forward, emphasizing how tired she was. "I will cook for you guys," he offered, and she raised her eyebrows. "I was planning on making beef stroganoff–authentic Russian meal." He held up the plastic grocery bag.

Nora narrowed her eyes. "You cook? It's not from a can or anything like that?"

"You wound me." He placed his hand over his heart. "It is my grandmother's recipe."

"Really, you intrigue me. What time do you want us over? Bree told me she should be home by three." Nora could not pass up a home-cooked meal, especially since she'd been traveling almost constantly all month. Besides, having an authentic Russian meal would be fantastic. *Who knew Sergei could cook? Another plus for him!*

"Seven." Sergei sounded delighted Nora found his cooking talent appealing. "I'll get started right away and let the meat simmer for as long as possible."

"I'll bring wine," she said. Nora rolled her bag across the street and carried it up the stairs. "See you later. Thanks," she shouted before disappearing into the house.

Nora quickly unpacked and crawled into her bed, dog-tired. She awoke to the sound of her cell phone ringing. "Hello?"

"Hey. I'm bummed," Bree announced. "After my flight was delayed half the morning, it's now canceled due to a mechanical issue. They are putting us up in Orlando tonight. So I won't be home until tomorrow morning."

She sounded annoyed, a surprise, because Bree was usually happy to hang out in Orlando, where the weather was usually sunny.

"It's been pouring here all day."

Oh, that explains it. "Sorry, Bree. We'll plan something for tomorrow when you get back." Nora noticed the time. She had been asleep for almost two hours. "I'm just jumping in the shower, so I'll talk to you tomorrow."

Nora hung up and dashed for the bathroom. She wanted enough time to walk down to the specialty wine shop a few blocks away. She'd promised Sergei she'd bring wine.

Sergei opened the door and saw Nora was alone.

"It's only me tonight. Bree is stuck in Orlando." She took a deep breath as she entered his house. "Oh, it smells so good in here." *That smell does not come from a can!* She followed Sergei to the kitchen. His townhouse shared the same setup as hers across the street. She hadn't been inside before now; she immediately noticed how tidy and clean it was given two guys lived there. The furniture was minimal. There was a large canvas featuring boxing gloves on the living room wall, artfully done.

Sergei lifted the lid off the pot; Nora's mouth watered. "Wow, I can't wait to taste that." She smiled at him. "I went to Zoe's and got some red." She held up a big bottle of red wine.

Sergei opened a kitchen drawer and hunted around for a corkscrew. "Ah, here it is." He made fast work of opening the bottle and spent a couple minutes hunting down stemmed wine glasses.

As he poured two glasses, Nora listened for evidence of his roommate. "Where is Alexei?"

"He went to visit some friends in DC for a few days." He handed her a glass. "So it is just the two of us."

Nora took a long swallow while she thought of what to say. "Sergei, what happened before... You know, that night we all went out...when you–"

"When I wanted to kiss you," he finished.

Okay, it's out there now. How do I feel about it?

"It is all right. Bree told me you are seeing someone else. I didn't know. I am sorry if I made you uncomfortable."

Oh, she told him about Antonio! What did she tell him? "Yes, I have been seeing someone, but it's not serious. I'm not sure if I'll see him again." Nora swallowed another sip feeling she had to fib. If she claimed things with Antonio were over she might as well tell Sergei to kiss her now. She peeked at him over the rim of her wine glass. If he had been going to say something, it was interrupted when the oven timer started beeping.

"The bread!" When he opened the oven the smell of fresh bread filled the room. He pulled out the baking sheet with a towel and set it on the stove. "I did not make the bread. But I know a good bakery."

"What can I do to help?" At his suggestion Nora set the table and sliced the bread while Sergei mashed the potatoes and filled their plates. He refilled Nora's wine glass before sitting down.

Nora dug in. "So good, Sergei. I am impressed." He sipped his wine and watched her eat before he lifted his own fork. She continued. "I feel bad. I said I'd have you over for dinner, but here I am, at *your* table."

"I am glad you approve. But I must admit I only know how to make five or six recipes." He reached for a slice of bread. "Next time you can make me your favorite American recipe. I am not picky. I eat whatever."

"Okay, I'll think of something good." Nora found herself wondering about when Sergei had come to America and if he still had family in Russia. She asked him such questions over dinner.

By the time they'd done the dishes together and were relaxing on the sofa, Nora had discovered Sergei had moved to America to attend college and went on to train as a pilot. At thirty-one, he'd been flying international freight planes for nine years. His parents and a younger sister lived in Russia and had not visited the United States yet.

"My mother teaches English to school children. She studied in England at a university to further her own education. My sister, Lydia, is an English-speaking tour guide. Lydia has been asking me all the time to come here to America for a visit. My father is also a pilot. He flies supply planes in Russia. I have not been home in…" He paused to calculate. "Two years."

"I wish my airline flew to Russia. I'd love to see it."

Sergei grinned. "Not many girls make comments like that." He poured the last of the wine into Nora's glass, and she lowered her eyes. As he moved, Nora suddenly noticed a burn on the underside of his right arm, close to his elbow. She set her glass on the coffee table and reached for his arm. "You burned your arm." Nora knelt over him to get a better look. She gently twisted his arm so he could see it. The skin was red and irritated.

"Hmm, it's just a little burn. It is nothing." He lifted his head, and she was caught up in the tranquil blue of his eyes. She stretched her fingers to gently caress his square jaw. She closed her eyes and lowered her mouth to his. It was a brush of lips at first, but she deepened the kiss and concentrated on the taste of his mouth. Sergei did not touch her; it was as if he didn't dare to, not wanting to scare her away.

Nora drew back and sat on her heels. "I don't know why I did that. I'm sorry. Do you have a first-aid kit? I can treat your burn."

"Forget the burn. I told you it is nothing." He pulled her to him, but loosened his grip when she spoke.

"Maybe this isn't such a good idea. Had I known it was just going to be the two of us, I…" She started to stand. *Perhaps I am trying too hard to displace Antonio.*

"Don't go. Finish your wine. We will just talk. We are friends. I promise to keep my hands to myself."

After a pause, she said, "Okay." She felt guilty for kissing him before she even knew what she wanted. "Tell me about

Russia." Nora settled in and sipped her wine while she listened to Sergei's animated tales about the town where he grew up and its famous sights. As he spoke, she felt buzzed from the wine…and horny. Nora assumed her pupils were dilated as she felt her body awakening. *Damn Antonio for waking this beast within me.* Her gaze drifted along Sergei's torso. She could see every muscle under his tight T-shirt.

"Nora, are you okay?"

She hugged her empty wine glass to her chest, her gaze fixed on his face. She blinked slowly.

"I think I had too much wine." She had not eaten all day until Sergei served her dinner. She'd had two glasses of cabernet before dinner and one with dinner; they had finished the bottle after dinner.

"I'll walk you home." Sergei eased the glass from her and pulled her up.

"Thanks again for an amazing dinner." She bent to retrieve her sandals and the room swayed. Sergei steadied her, supporting her arm as they walked to the door. He held the door open and the warm and balmy breeze blew in. She padded barefooted across the street, carrying her sandals. He followed her. She had trouble fitting the key in the lock, and he had to take it from her. Once he opened the door, she walked in and sat on the stairs.

"I don't think I can walk up all those steps." She released the clip that held her hair and it tumbled in soft waves over her shoulder. The thin sundress strap slipped off her shoulder. Nora knew she was tempting him when she saw Sergei's jaw tighten.

"Okay, up you go." He easily swept Nora up off the step and carried her up the stairs. He paused on the landing until she pointed to which room was hers. Moonlight poured through her window. Sergei set her gently on her feet, but she kept her arms locked around his neck.

She stood on her tippy toes and tried to draw him closer, but he resisted. "You had too much to drink, Nora. I'm leaving."

"Kiss me good-bye," she whispered breathily.

He paused in the semi-darkness for several moments before his mouth touched hers. She moaned and pressed against him. Nora wanted to forget how Antonio made her feel like she was just one of his *many* girlfriends. Nora could have as *many* boyfriends as she wanted too. Sergei undoubtedly wanted her, and she was not going to stop him.

Between frantic kisses, Sergei said, "Get into bed."

Nora released him and turned to climb into bed. She swung her head at the sound of her bedroom door closing and paused in shock to hear Sergei's heavy footsteps going down the stairs. She supposed she should be grateful he hadn't taken advantage of her, but she felt rejected. Knowing she was not thinking clearly, she waited until the urge to call him passed. She settled under the sheets and was asleep in moments, although she slept fitfully that night.

Chapter Ten

June was coming to a close. Because Nora and Bree had both finished their flying requirements for the month, they finally had time to travel together. They had originally talked about visiting Paris, but Bree knew of an upcoming event that would make it worth their while to visit England. Bree's good friends, the Andrews, were hosting an annual charity event at their country estate north of London. She assured Nora it was *the* event to attend. Even celebrities turned out for the function.

"My friend Ash and I met years ago during riding competitions. Her parents are the nicest people. For all the money they have, they're always supporting causes, for the right reasons," Bree said sincerely. "Anyway, we have a place to stay at their country manor. It's not Paris, but I think it would be worth it."

"Sounds intriguing... What celebrities? How soon can we leave?"

They grinned at each other.

"I don't know. I think Ash said she knows a Spice Girl or something. Let's see if we can catch the evening flight tonight." Bree started typing on her laptop. "How early can we get to the airport?"

"As soon as the dryer stops and I can throw the clothes into my suitcase." Nora paused. "How fancy do I need to be? Will the dress I bought in Italy be okay?"

"Totally. You look hot in it. Okay, I've got it. We are leaving at 6:55 p.m. Doesn't look like a full flight. I'm putting us on standby."

Nora called and left Sergei a message. "Hey, Sergei. I wanted to let you know Bree and I will be out of town until the end of the month. We're visiting England. I owe you dinner…and an explanation. Talk to you soon."

They made it on the flight without complications. During the long trip, Nora got a chance to unload about the saga with Antonio.

"Ha! He's a piece of work!" Bree laughed at the end of Nora's tale. "A kept woman. Geez, he does sound intense."

Nora couldn't help but laugh too. "I know, *right*? It's so absurd. And *intense* is an understatement." Nora wiped tears of laughter from the corner of her eye. *Bree keeps life real, calling things for what they are.* "Anyway I don't think I'll see him again. It's too weird."

After their laughter died down, Bree made it simple. "Hey if there's no one else and he cleans your pipes—"

"Stop it," Nora giggled.

"Just saying… He's a great time. And he's far enough away not to bother you if you want to end it. Really, the ball is in your court, Nora. Always be in control of what you want."

Nora studied her friend. It was good advice–if only Bree could take it herself. After the incident with Tyrone escalated earlier in the month, Bree seemed to move on. She pledged to turn over a new leaf. Bree's toxic preference for the "bad boy" types brought her the wrong kind of attention. Her relationship with other guys she dated in the past had never ended well. Because Bree was exceptionally beautiful she tended to intimidate the average nice guy.

Nora sighed, wondering if she should mention how Sergei almost kissed her the night of the Tyrone incident and that she kissed him after he made her dinner. She came on to him when she was drunk, and he did not take advantage of her. Totally embarrassed, she did not want to mess up her friendship with Sergei. Nora decided against mentioning it. After all, nothing really happened in the end—or so she told herself.

Late June was a lovely time of year to visit England. The country air was cool and fresh. Bree's friend Ashley Andrews met the girls at the airline's drop-off section on Thursday morning.

Ashley gave Bree a long hug and turned to hug Nora. "Welcome, Nora. It is so nice to finally meet you!"

Ashley had a mop of auburn curls that bounced at her shoulders. Her pale skin was dotted with hundreds of light freckles in the cutest way and her hazel eyes sparkled with laughter.

"Where are all your bags?" Ashley put her hands up, questioning Bree in her raspy voice.

"I've learned to travel light now that I'm a flight attendant," Bree bragged.

"Never would have believed it of this one." Ashley jerked a finger in Bree's direction. Nora liked her instantly.

They drove through the countryside for an hour before they pulled up to the estate. Nora's eye's widened. "Wow, Ashley, this is beautiful. You really live here?" Nora felt a little uncomfortable to be so awestruck. *Ashley must think I'm an 'ignorant commoner',* Nora thought to herself in a British accent.

"No. Not year round. It's so far from the city. I would die of boredom if I was here all the time." She pulled the car around to the side, where there was a garage with six extended bays. She pulled into the second bay. "We used to come for several weeks each summer when my brother and I were younger. Now we mostly hold charity functions here."

They collected their bags, and Ashley showed them to their rooms. They each had their own bedroom with a private bathroom. Ashley explained the guests at Saturday evening's charity event would return to the city after the function or stay locally in town. Bree and Nora were the only overnight guests.

"My mum insisted on having lunch prepared for us. She'll return soon. She's meeting with the florist about some last-minute changes. In the meantime, I'll show you around." To Nora, she added, "If you love the outside of this place, wait until you see the inside."

Bree let her in on a secret. "There's an indoor pool!"

Ashley's mother arrived after the tour. She was warm and friendly, giving Nora a hug, saying any friend of Bree's was more than welcome. She looked like an older, taller version of Ashley.

"Thank you for having me, Mrs. Andrews. Your home is remarkable."

They enjoyed the lunch laid out by the staff, but no sooner had they finished when Mrs. Andrews excused herself to double-check every detail for the charity event. Ashley mentioned her father would join them on Saturday. This gala was strictly her mother's baby.

After lunch Ashley drove them to a neighboring estate to visit their friend Corrine Westborough. During the drive, Bree explained, "Our dads have been friends since college. We used to vacation here when I was little and that's when I met Ash and Corrine. We were nine. I learned to ride horses and eventually competed, along with Ash and Corrine. Our families were really close for a while. But after the divorce," she shrugged, "they stopped coming to England. They sent me though and I always stayed with the Andrews for a few weeks during the summer."

The neighbor's estate was half the size of the Andrews', but still *huge*. Beyond the main house were outbuildings that contained dozens of horses. Ashley explained, "The Westboroughs buy, sell, and breed thoroughbred horses." The large sign at the entrance to the stables read WESTBOROUGH MEADOWS.

"Are you sad that you stopped competing?" Nora asked as they turned down the long tree-lined lane. White fences went on for as far as the eye could see. Soon the house came into view.

"No, but I really miss riding." Bree spotted Corrine, who waved from the lawn. Corrine ran up as the car pulled to a stop in the curved driveway.

After hugs and introductions, they mentioned to Corrine they'd just been talking about the competitions. "Corrine, of course, won every competition," Bree admitted.

"True," Corrine beamed. "But I've been riding since before I could walk. And we have the best horses." Similar to most riders, she wore tan pants with fancy stitching and shiny black boots. Thick blonde hair hung in a fat braid down to Corrine's shoulder blades.

"I can't wait to see Gray Dove," Bree exclaimed. "It's been almost a year since I've seen her. She's my favorite horse."

"Well, *surprise!* You are going to get to ride her! The horses are saddled and waiting for us!" she sang.

"What! That's awesome! Thanks, Corrine. It's been too long." The girls dropped off their stuff in the front hall and headed out another exit. Corrine chatted the whole way to the stables. Nora just soaked it all in. The large estate offered a homey, lived-in feel. Unlike Ashley's cavernous house, Nora learned this home was occupied year round.

"There's my girl!" Bree cooed as they left the sunshine, crossing into the shadows of the stable. Nora counted four horses with saddles.

"Umm, Bree…" Nora hesitated as she watched her pull on a slim pair of riding boots she borrowed from among several pairs on a shelf. "I hope you won't mind if I sit this one out. I've never ridden a horse before."

"Oh, Nora, I'm so sorry. We don't…"

Nora stopped her. "Oh, no no no. I insist you go. I'll just enjoy everything here." She fanned out her hand to encompass the stables and yards. There was no way she wanted Bree to miss out because of her. With everything Bree dealt with lately, Nora just wanted to see her friend happy.

"I feel awful," Ashley confessed. "I'm sorry, Nora. I should have asked if you rode. I didn't even think."

Corrine chimed in. "I can stay and keep Nora company. We can hang here. It's no problem. I can ride whenever I want."

"No. Please go with them. Bree came all this way. Really, I'm fine here by myself."

Corrine seemed torn, then said, "Well, I could have Ben show her around while we take a quick ride. He's somewhere around here." Corrine glanced from Ashley to Bree. "What do you think?"

Ashley piped up. "That's a great idea."

"You'll like Ben, Nora. He's Corrine's older brother. He knows everything about the horses." Bree nuzzled Gray Dove's neck.

"Perfect." Nora smiled.

They led the horses outside and mounted, and Corrine called to a staff person and asked him to fetch Ben. He pointed toward a field and said Ben was in the pasture. Corrine nodded at the worker and turned to Nora. "I'll send him over."

The girls trotted off toward the low-lying pasture and Nora could hear their excited voices and laughter from a distance. She shielded her eyes as she watched them disappear. Slight jealousy of their longtime friendships tugged at her heart. She never kept in touch with any of her childhood friends, though most of them still lived in her hometown. She had no excuse. Nora shook off her melancholy, focusing on enjoying this amazing place. *I'm fortunate to be here and to have Bree as my friend.*

Nora waited around for a few minutes in the sunshine before walking into the coolness of the barn. It was a bright day, and she had forgotten her sunglasses. One horse poked its head beyond the stall to see who was coming in.

"Hi, there," Nora said to the brown nose that stretched in her direction. She examined the horse's large black eyes and long lashes. Then she heard two male voices outside.

Nora noticed the profile of the taller man, who had an angular jaw and a sandy-colored overgrown crew cut. The other man, who wore a uniform, was closer to her stature in height. The taller man gave some instructions as he relinquished the lead line attached to a large black horse. He pulled off work gloves and tucked them into the back pocket of his tan cargo pants. As the horse was guided away, the tall man turned his attention inside the building. Just then, a Golden Retriever who had been standing a safe distance away from the black horse trotted over to the tall man, who bent to give his companion a quick head pat.

He approached with the dog in tow. The retriever reminded Nora of Polly so much her heart constricted momentarily with longing for her beloved dog. Then she got a better look at the man. *Wow, is this Corrine's brother?* He advanced and smiled. The dimples in his cheeks gave him an endearing quality. *Wow, he's handsome.*

"Hi. I'm Ben, Corrine's brother. You must be Nora?" He reached out to shake her hand. The skin of his palm was rough. They were working hands.

"Yes, nice to meet you, Ben. Sorry to disturb you. I didn't want to hold them up from riding. It's nice of you to stop what you were doing to show me around. I hope it's not inconvenient?" She smiled, batting her lashes more often than necessary. "And who is this?" She squatted to give the dog a proper hello.

"This is Molly."

Nora's eyes crinkled with laughter, and she looked up at Ben. "That's so weird. My parents have a Golden Retriever named Polly." *Molly and Polly*.

Ben chucked. "That is weird." Ben pulled his sunglasses off.

Nora stood and froze, ensnared by his eyes. *Whoa. His eyes. So dreamy.* They were green—not a striking emerald green, but a stormy-day-at-the-ocean green. A lock of sandy hair curved above his forehead where his thick eyebrows perfectly balanced his broad aristocratic forehead. At the slightest tug from his full lips, his dimples appeared.

He chuckled at the nosy horse stretching in his direction, the same horse Nora had been admiring. "This inquisitive girl is Bellefleur. She came from France a long time ago. She is very old but very friendly." He gave her nose a scratch. Molly laid down on the cool cement floor, watching them, pumping her tail and looking up for some attention. After a moment she rested her head; plainly human attentions were elsewhere.

"I don't know anything about horses. Do you still ride her?" Nora tentatively held her hand near the brown nose.

Ben covered her hand. "Rub her neck, here. She loves it." He guided Nora's hand to Bellefleur's neck. She glanced over her shoulder at him; their faces were too close for strangers so he released her hand and leaned against the stall. "No one rides her anymore. She's retired. She was my mum's favorite. My father bought Bellefleur for her as a wedding gift. That was..." He paused to think. "Thirty-one years ago."

"She *was* her favorite?"

"Yeah, my mum passed when I was young. We keep Bellefleur as a reminder of how much she loved this place and these horses."

"Oh, I'm sorry. I shouldn't have asked." *Ugh, could you have brought up anything more awkward?* He waved a hand, dismissing her concern. She narrowed her focus on the horse again. "Bellefleur–what a romantic and beautiful gift." After Nora caressed her she felt at ease with the gentle but large animal. She stroked her soft coat, flashing a bright smile at Ben.

"Would you like a tour of the grounds?" Ben asked.

"I'd love it." She couldn't stop smiling at him like an idiot. She turned to the horse. "Nice to meet you, Bellefleur."

They walked comfortably side by side as he pointed out other horses with funny names. Molly followed along behind them. They passed into four other buildings that held more horses and some equipment. He explained the estate was renowned for its horses and how they not only bred horses but acquired show-quality horses throughout Europe for local competitors. "My sister Corrine has done well competing over the years."

"How about you? Did you ever compete?" Nora asked.

He flashed a devastating smile at her inquiry but shook his head. "No, I'm more of a behind-the-scenes kind of guy." He was soft-spoken but friendly as he called out to others who passed by. They stopped a couple times when employees asked him questions.

"So do you run this place?" People seemed to regard him as an authority, and he had obviously been working hands-on with a horse earlier.

"No, my father and his board keep Westborough Meadows in working order. I *am* on staff, however. I'm the resident veterinarian. I specialize in equine welfare." He sounded humble despite his impressive position.

"You're a veterinarian! Wow, that's so cool." Usually people said to her, "You're a flight attendant... Wow, that's so cool." So it was interesting to be on the other side of those words. Why that just made Ben *more* attractive she did not know.

"I've grown up around horses all my life. Hanging out in the stables with the vets all those years made it a natural transition for me." Ben seemed very comfortable, like he fit this place perfectly. "How about you? What is it you do?" They had passed the buildings and were walking up a grassy hill, away from the estate. Molly paused with a wistful look back but decided to follow her master up the steep hill.

"I'm a flight attendant, like Bree. That's how we met."

"Oh yeah, I remember Corrine mentioning something about that." He didn't display the glassy-eyed stare most men usually exhibited. In fact, he did not even comment. "I've known Bree since we were kids. She rides well. She was pretty good at the competitions, as I remember." He paused. "She stopped competing around the time her parents split up."

"Bree and I are roommates. We've only known each other for five months, but we've become good friends." They continued the climb, both breathing deeply.

At the hilltop the panoramic view of the surrounding countryside spread before her and she shielded her eyes, gazing slowly from right to left, soaking up the scenery. "Beautiful." The stone house nestled in the rolling hills and the outbuildings fanned out below her, connected by a network of white fences. There was activity as men and horses moved about, but not much could be heard on the remote hilltop. It was peaceful.

They stood in silence for several moments and allowed their breathing to slow.

"Too bad the girls didn't ride up here," she said over her shoulder, catching his eye before he darted his gaze in several directions. *Did I just catch him staring at me?*

After a moment, he chuckled. "Then this place wouldn't be peaceful. Corrine and her friends continuously talk over one another."

Nora understood what he meant. In just the short time she'd been around the three friends, she realized their overlapping conversations were hard to follow. They grinned at each other and admired the scenery, waiting for the other to say something.

Nora spoke. "Lately I've been fortunate enough to travel and see so many wonderful sights. And I have to tell you, this English countryside is one of my favorites. The air is so cool and fresh. On the drive here I couldn't get enough of those brilliant green rolling hills dotted with sheep. Sheep are so cute. The architecture of these elegant country estates embedded with history hits me with a sense of nostalgia. You must love it here, Ben."

Ben appeared captivated by her speech, touched by her heartfelt words. He let out the breath he had been holding, nodding in answer to her question. "Westborough Meadows is especially dear to my heart." He pointed to a shady spot under an oak tree, where Molly already sprawled out. "Shall we sit and enjoy it for a while?"

After they settled, Ben asked, "What's it like where you grew up?

"I grew up in rural Pennsylvania. Kind of a small town. Have you been to America?"

"Not to the States. I've traveled some around Europe. Pennsylvania is East Coast, if I remember correctly."

"You are correct." *Cute* and *smart*.

"Do you have brothers or sisters?" Ben inquired.

"I have sisters. Two." She offered him the brief version of her family life: she was the middle daughter, her dad worked in a factory, her mom and sister ran a catering business. She added how she had worked in an office but needed a change of scenery.

He picked up on the catering and asked bluntly if she could cook. She smirked at his question. "Yeah, you could say that."

"More than boil water? I can boil water, but that's as far as it goes!" He joked easily with her.

"I didn't attend culinary school like my sister Victoria, but I'm a pretty good sous chef."

Time seemed to fly by. Soon they saw the girls galloping up the distant pathway toward the stables.

"Looks like they've returned," Ben said, sitting up straighter.

"Ben, I had a nice time this afternoon. Thank you again for taking the time to keep me entertained. I'm sure you had more important things to do. I really appreciate it." They regarded at each other.

"Anytime, Nora." He stood swiftly, holding out his hand to her. He pulled her up with a little more force than necessary and drew her close to him. They paused that way for a moment, steadying each other.

Nora adjusted her footing in the grass, chirping, "Thanks."

They met the girls in the stable. Bree called, "Hey, Ben! Long time no see." She jogged over and gave him a big hug that expressed their longtime friendship.

"Good to see you, Bree."

Nora could not help but wonder if there had been any romance between the two. After all, they were both extremely good-looking. But they conversed and joked with ease. No sign of a failed romance Nora could see.

"You took good care of Nora, I hope." Bree asked Ben, "You didn't bore her with horse talk, did you?"

Nora quickly came to Ben's defense. "Ben was wonderful. He gave me a tour of the grounds, and we went up the hillside to take in that glorious view. And best of all, he introduced me to Bellefleur."

Ben grinned appreciatively at her, the look they exchanged unnoticed by the others.

"Bellefleur! Is she still around?" astonishment filled Bree's voice.

Corrine piped up, "She's down there, stall forty-six."

"Oh, I have to visit her!"

"I've got to get back to work. It was nice meeting you, Nora. Ladies." Ben waved a general good-bye as he turned away. The four girls went toward stall forty-six while Ben strode the other way.

"Oh, Ben!" Ashley yelled. He slowed and turned. "We'll be at the bridge tonight. Come by." He shrugged and sent her a smirk before he walked out of sight.

Chapter Eleven

Nora, Bree, and Ashley ate in a small, private dining room off the kitchen. The room accommodated ten people at most. The larger formal dining room seated up to forty-eight guests. During her house tour, Nora thought her mother would love a banquet facility like this. The cook served shepherd's pie filled with ground lamb and vegetables and topped with mashed potatoes. Nora let the steam from the food fill her nostrils. *Yum, I missed this comfort food.* When she could eat no more, a peach cobbler appeared with fresh whipped cream.

Nora's eyelids drooped. The time change had caught up with her, and her full belly did not help. She glanced across the table at Bree, who did not look tired at all and entertained Ashley.

"Let's get going. I told everyone we'd meet up around nine," Ashley said.

As they drove off in Ashley's car, Nora asked, "Where are we going? You mentioned a bridge?"

"It's literally a bridge." Ashley addressed Nora through the rearview mirror.

Bree swiveled to face the backseat. "There is a bridge not too far from here where we've been hanging out for years. All our friends usually come into town for the big charity event, and it's tradition we meet up, catch up…and drink up."

"And drink up!" Ashley repeated, dancing in her seat so her curls bounced.

They drove for ten minutes, and then pulled alongside dozens of other cars parked on the grass. The waning full moon provided adequate light. Music played through beefed-up audio speakers from someone's open hatchback. Introductions were made, and someone handed Nora a beer. Nora found herself searching the socializing groups for Ben. Cars continued pulling in, and the noise got louder. Corrine arrived, calling out to them. Nora hoped she had brought her brother along.

"Is Ben coming?" Ashley asked.

"Who knows?" Corrine rolled her eyes. "We have a mare about to foal any day now, and he doesn't like to be too far from her. I can't wait to see when he's expecting his own kid." They laughed in unison. "He's too bloody serious. If only he'd show as much interest in girls as he does the horses–"

Bree interrupted. "Wait, what about Pam…or maybe Patty? What was her name? Is he still dating her?" Bree looked to Ashley for help.

"Caroline," Ashley stated flatly.

"Oh, I thought it started with a *P*."

Corrine informed her, "No. The relationship with Caroline is long over and it only lasted a few months."

Nora smiled inwardly. *Ben doesn't have a girlfriend.* She didn't consider Antonio a boyfriend. In fact, she didn't plan on seeing him again. He should be nothing to her, but she waffled. And Sergei? Those were jumbled feelings. Nora definitely felt attracted to Ben, but thought he probably wouldn't be interested in a flight attendant from America. She sighed, figuring she needed to forget about Ben in the romantic sense.

A bonfire blazed down by the river and everyone migrated to it. Stumps and logs, used as makeshift seats, were placed around an existing fire-pit encircled with large rocks. They sat round it, amused by their friends' tales. Nora laughed so hard at one guy's animated story about how his car was surrounded by sheep on the roadway and he'd been stuck for two hours. He tried everything he could to move them until at last the farmer and his dog came by. After one whistle from the farmer, the one dog had moved the entire herd in minutes.

Out of the corner of her eye, Nora noticed someone walking up. Even in the dark she could tell it was Ben. When he came into the circle of firelight he waved at her. He headed in her direction but was stopped by a group of friends. Nora forced herself to look at the girl telling a story about a roommate, a pole, and some panties, but she could not quite give the anecdote her full attention. *Ben is here!*

After a few minutes Bree announced, "Hey, look who showed up." Ben broke away from the group and came over, sitting next to Ashley. "Want a beer?" Bree offered.

"You came after all. How's the mare?" Corrine asked.

He accepted the beer. "She's doing well. She could foal any day now." He took a swig from the bottle. "How did you enjoy your ride this afternoon?"

The three girls talked over each other about how great it was to ride together again, like old times, how far they had ridden, and how the horses behaved. When the conversation died down Ashley slipped away to talk to a friend. Bree announced she needed a potty break.

"Me, too. To the loo we must go!" Corrine chimed in. Bree and Corrine headed toward the woods arm and arm. Others around the bonfire had wandered off too. Nora found herself alone with Ben. Ben stood and moved to sit beside her.

"Are you cold?"

"A little," she confessed. He shrugged out of his jacket and draped it over her shoulders. She basked in the body heat lingering inside his jacket. "Thanks, but won't you be cold?"

"I'm used to the drop in temperature at night. I dress in layers." He still had on a collared shirt and sweater.

"This is pretty chilly–it's June!"

They laughed and talked quietly until Bree and Corrine trudged up to the bonfire. Nora glanced up at the sound of throats clearing and giggles. Corrine elbowed Bree, giving her brother a grin.

"What did we miss?" Corrine asked innocently.

Ben stood and stretched. "You missed nothing, Corrine. I'm heading home. I just came for a beer." He held up the empty bottle. Nora noticed the siblings shared a similar endearing smirk.

"Oh, your jacket." Nora shrugged her shoulders free, preparing to hand it over.

Before she could pull it off Ben said, "Keep it. I'll see you tomorrow." He smiled that crooked, dimple-in-the-cheek, devastatingly handsome smile. "Good night."

"Good night, Ben," the girls sang in chorus.

Bree and Corrine sat close to Nora wearing expectant gazes. "So, you two are really hitting it off," Bree said. "Ben's a really nice guy, and he doesn't have a girlfriend."

"He must really like you. For him to leave a mare about to give birth any day now is..." Corrine held out her hands, "monumental. I had no idea you two got along so well this afternoon." Corrine studied Nora as if to see what her brother found so interesting.

"He's really nice." Nora couldn't help but smile. She crossed her arms, hugging his jacket tightly around her. "I'm sure he didn't leave his mare to come here just for me. He talked with his other friends. And he offered me his jacket because I was cold. He was just being thoughtful." Nora knew she didn't sound convincing. The two girls nodded but said no more. Nora was thankful when they headed home soon after Ben left.

The next day Ashley drove them over to Westborough Meadows to pick up Corrine, and the four girls traveled to a neighboring town for an outing. Nora had surveyed the paddocks hoping she might get a glimpse of Ben, but no luck. The girls got manicures in preparation for the big charity event and stopped at a soup place for lunch. They visited a few boutiques and sat in a coffee house drinking lattes until four o'clock.

Nora got to know Bree's friends pretty well. Ashley worked in London for a non-profit company. On the dating scene, Ash said, "I met this guy, George, one night after work when I went out with some coworkers. We've had one successful date so far, but I'm hoping to reconnect with him next week."

Corrine claimed, "I'm too busy to date. Running my family's London branch of the business spills over into all my spare time. I haven't had a serious boyfriend in two years."

Ashley rolled her eyes and rasped, "I am definitely getting you out more." Even though they didn't live far from each other in the city, they admitted they hardly had the chance to get together.

Bree and Nora nodded in mutual understanding. Bree said, "With our hectic schedules we sometimes don't see each other for a week or two–and we live together!" Bree described what life was like in Philly and tried to convince them to come for a visit.

Corrine's phone rang and she took the call. Hanging up, she said, "That was my mum. She's invited you all for dinner this evening."

Ashley focused her expressive eyes on Nora. "Good, you'll get a chance to meet Mr. and Mrs. Westborough. Wait until you meet Judy. She's great." To the others she announced, "We should get going so we'll have time to change for dinner." Ashley nonchalantly tucked a mass of auburn curls behind her ear. They gathered their bags and headed for the door. A young man coming in held the door open, giving Bree a wide smile and nodded hello only to her. The girls were used to the attention Bree received, but they teased her about it all the same. They dropped Corrine off and went to Ashley's regal residence to change for dinner.

Nora took extra care applying makeup and used her straightening iron. Nora slipped into a girly dress and paired it with a denim shrug and some flats. She was latching a bracelet when Bree knocked and stuck her head around the door.

"Hey, are you ready?"

"Yes, I think so." Nora wiped her sweaty palms on her dress and picked up her purse. She also grabbed the jacket Ben had lent her. *Why do I have butterflies in my stomach?* She closed the door behind her, and they moved down the hallway on the plush carpet.

"So Ben mentioned his mother passed. His dad remarried someone named Judy?" Nora inquired.

"Yes, he remarried. Hmm. Ben mentioned his mother?"

"No, when we were with Bellefleur he just mentioned she'd passed." Nora waited intently for Bree's next words.

"Oh. Yes, their mom died when they were little. Corrine doesn't really remember her. I never had the chance to meet her. Did he tell you it was a car accident?"

"No. That is so sad." Nora's heart constricted, thinking of Ben as a little boy without a mother.

"Yeah." They reached the bottom of the steps where Ashley waited. "Well, his stepmother is wonderful. Her name is Judy," she reiterated. "We all love her."

Corrine welcomed them at the door and led them into a room with comfortable seating. Corrine introduced her parents to Nora. The biggest surprise—Judy was an American who grew up in Maryland. Nora's mother had also grown up in Maryland, so they chatted for a while about that. Judy sent Corrine to fetch the hors d'oeuvres tray. Corrine and Ben's dad, Derek, poured them some wine from the decorative tray set with wine glasses. Nora thought Judy Westborough was abundantly warm and friendly, and Derek Westborough was pleasantly agreeable, although somewhat reserved.

Corrine returned with not only a platter of bite-sized delights but with her brother.

"Hello, ladies," Ben greeted the guests.

Nora fidgeted, attempting not to stare.

He asked Ashley, "Where is Evan? I thought he was coming up today." Nora knew Evan was Ashley's older brother who worked for an investment company in London. Bree had told her as kids the boys were best friends.

Between bites Ashley answered, "Yeah, he got tied up. Mum is furious. He'll either arrive later tonight or in the morning. This will be the first charity event of Mum's he'll attend this year."

Ben sat across from Nora and poured himself a glass of wine. He glanced up at her and gave her a panty-dropping smile.

She nearly choked on her cracker. *Why of all people do I have the hots for Ash's brother!*

"How is your mother, Ashley?" Judy inquired. Nora shot her gaze to Judy pretending to listen. "I don't know how she pulls off these charity events year after year. I invited her to come tonight, but she declined, saying she was dealing with an issue with the florist,"

"She's fine. There are always problems with these events, but she's in her element. I know tomorrow night will be epic." Ashley attended every event her mother put on, forever the socialite.

Judy excused herself to finish making dinner.

"Would you like some help?" Nora offered.

"Oh no, honey. Sit and visit." Judy smiled and seemed touched by her offer.

Nora stood and made her way to Judy's side. "I don't mind. Let me help you. It's the least I can do." She would have liked to talk with Ben, but she felt she was under the watchful eye of Bree and Corrine, who seemed to think Ben was interested in her.

Bree said encouragingly, "Her family has a catering business. Nora likes to cook."

"Oh well, in that case…" Judy beamed and led the way to the kitchen. "I'm glad to get a chance to chat with a fellow American."

As they worked side by side in the gleaming gourmet kitchen, Nora enjoyed talking with Judy, who reminded Nora of her mother. After about ten minutes, Ben wandered into the kitchen, just as Judy and Nora were discussing the best ingredients for a vinaigrette. "Excuse me, ladies, but how much longer until we eat dinner?"

"About twenty minutes. Why, Ben? Where are you off to?" Judy placed a hand on her hip.

He chuckled. "I'm just going out to check on my mare, Judy. I'll be five or ten minutes, tops." He grabbed an apple from a bowl on a distant counter as his smiling eyes lingered on Nora. He did not call Judy Mom or Mum as Corrine had, and she wondered why.

"Don't get dirty," Judy shouted after him, as if he were a boy. After he left, she turned to Nora and resumed their discussion.

Judy and Nora passed the stairwell on their way to announce dinner was ready. Ben was coming down, fastening the sleeves on a new shirt. Judy smirked up at Ben and said accusingly, "You got dirty."

"Yes, but I'm here in time for dinner. And I have on a clean shirt." He reached the bottom of the stairs as the others filed into the hallway.

The group crossed into the dining room and took their places. Ben pulled out a chair for Nora and circled around the table to sit across from her. From this vantage point, they could easily glance at each other all night. She blushed every time their gazes met and lingered.

Nora became better acquainted with Judy and Derek over dinner, and Judy insisted she stop calling them Mr. and Mrs.

Westborough. Her casual American attitude was just one of the things that made everyone love her. Nora noted earlier when Judy slipped her arm around Ben's waist to give him a motherly squeeze, he seemed used to it. Judy rested her fingers in her husband's palm at the dinner table reminding Nora of her own affectionate parents. Derek adored his vivacious wife, and it seemed his children did to.

Ashley and Corrine were great at including Nora over the weekend and making her feel welcome. Because Bree was like family to Nora, this group of her friends felt like extended family. Then there was Ben. She learned he liked British football, better known to Americans as soccer, and he enjoyed playing when he had the time. He had been playing the guitar and the piano since elementary school, and Corrine vouched for his talent. Nora told them she played piano as well and that all three sisters had taken piano lessons since they were little. She and Victoria were good, continuing with lessons until eighth grade, but Lizzy had dropped the lessons by fourth grade; she became more of a jock.

After dessert, they moved to a less formal room in the rear of the house. Corrine and Ben cleared the dishes and were heard laughing from the kitchen. Derek opened another bottle of wine and offered his guests another glass. Bree recounted the tale how she met Nora on the van going to flight attendant training.

As the hour grew late, the chattering died down. Their yawns seemed contagious.

"Well, we have a big day tomorrow," Ashley said as she stood.

Nora and Bree thanked their hosts. Each girl received a warm hug from Judy. "You girls are welcome. Come visit me anytime. Nora…" Judy gripped both her hands. "*Please* come again soon. You are a joy." She leaned toward Bree. "Bree, promise me you'll bring Nora back."

"Of course."

"I'll walk out with you." Ben followed them, as did Corrine.

"Ben, change your shirt if you're going out to the stables," Judy softly called after him.

Ben pressed his lips together and turned slightly to give her a slanted gaze and a curt nod. Derek directed his wife inside and shut the door.

Nora observed as the siblings, Ben and Corrine, shook their heads at each other and rolled their eyes. Judy's mothering seemed to have had become a joke between them.

Nora suddenly remembered the jacket. "Oh, Ben, I have your jacket. It's in the car." Ben trailed behind her as she retrieved it while the others stood off a ways talking. "Thanks again." She handed it to him. His handsome face was all angles in the dark shadows.

"Sure, no problem." He flickered a glance in the girls' direction, and then asked quietly, "So how long are you here for?"

"We leave the day after tomorrow."

Ashley piped up as they walked to the car, giving Ben a stern look. "Ben, you *are* coming to the charity event tomorrow?"

Ben's attention stayed on Nora as he answered. "I'll be there." He turned and strolled toward the stables.

The girls got in the car and Ashley turned over the engine. Bree twisted in her seat. "What were you two whispering about?"

"We weren't whispering. I was just returning his jacket," Nora replied, her eyes wide with innocence.

When they returned to the Andrews estate, the lights were on and the place buzzed with activity. Nora followed the girls past people carrying furniture, hanging banners, and cleaning and polishing. Nora heard distant sounds of pans clanging in the kitchen.

As the girls reached the landing Mrs. Andrews walked past the stairwell. Once she'd caught their attention, she asked, "How was your evening with the Westboroughs?"

"Great," answered Ashley. Nora and Bree nodded in agreement.

"Good. We'll be done here soon, sorry for the noise. Good night, girls, sleep well." Mrs. Andrews strode away, calling after some furniture movers. The girls trudged up the stairs to their rooms, stifling yawns, saying goodnight to one another.

Chapter Twelve

Nora awoke to the beeping of a delivery truck backing up. She rolled out of bed and pulled the window shade aside. Several guys were unloading tables; others were carrying in linens. The florist's truck parked below, and two guys got out. One man carrying a clipboard headed inside while the other rolled open the truck door. She glanced at the time, half passed nine. She dressed quickly and knocked on Bree's door.

Bree laid in bed thumbing through a magazine when Nora entered and exclaimed, "Wow! This is exciting. How many people are coming to this thing?"

Bree grinned. "Around seven hundred–or more?" she guessed. "I told you it is *the* charity event of the season."

"How many times have you been to this event? What's it like?" Nora asked, jittery with anticipation.

"I've been to countless events similar to this, but Mrs. Andrews' annual charity event? I'd say seven or eight times." Bree sat up and folded her feet under her, pretzel-style. "She selects a different organization every year. She's been hosting this for like twenty years."

"I'm getting excited!" The nicest event Nora had ever attended was a wedding at an upscale country club.

Bree paused in thought. "Oh, here it is." She reached for an envelope on her nightstand and slipped out a fancy invitation. "It says…it starts at five o'clock." She read silently. "Guest speaker at seven and dinner at nine, followed by another guest speaker… Here." She handed it to Nora. "You check it out." The invitation was printed on thick paper and embossed with gold lettering.

Ashley's raspy voice called from the other side of the door. "Are you up?"

"Yeah, come on in!"

The door opened, and Ashley shuffled in. She crawled onto Bree's bed and lay face down. She wore a T-shirt that said GIRLS RULE and baggie pajama bottoms with Sponge Bob images splashed all over them. Her kinky hair pointed in every direction. Nora chuckled to herself at the contrast between Ashley, the charity hosts' daughter, who looked like an oversized kid, and the elegant invitation she held in her hand.

Bree retrieved a message on her phone and tossed the phone away in disgust after listening to it.

"What's up?" Nora asked, forgetting about her excitement for a moment. Ashley opened one eye.

Bree shook her head and dragged her hand through her strawberry blonde locks. "It's my parents. They are fighting over who's getting the beach house for the Fourth of July. They decided to split the time at the beach house in the divorce, because neither of them wanted to spend the whole summer there. And so they keep leaving me messages, each insisting they are getting it and want me to come." She cursed, exasperated, "I can't even go. I'm working."

"That is tragic," Ashley said as she rolled over.

"I know! My parents are crazy." Bree sounded dejected.

"Yes, they are crazy, but that's not what I'm talking about. It's tragic that you have to work on your American holiday. Aren't there barbeques and fireworks? I love fireworks," Ashley remarked. Bree rolled her eyes and laughed.

Ashley came up on one elbow. "By the way, we have to leave here in an hour. I booked us hair appointments at the Gloria McPhee salon."

"Ash, that's perfect! I'll get dressed. Then let's get some coffee." Bree climbed over Ashley and grabbed some clothes on her way to the bathroom.

"If you're hungry, my mum always puts out a big spread of food for the service people and the staff on event mornings. Happy people, better service." She shrugged. "The raspberry scones are my favorite."

Nora thought Ashley resembled a little kid with her freckled face and cartoon pajamas. "Ash, I'm glad we are getting to know each other. I hope you know I really appreciate everything. I'm glad I came." Nora placed the invitation on the nightstand.

Ashley sat up and swung her feet to the floor. "Aw, anytime, Nora. I'm glad you are here."

The time came for the girls to make their grand entrance to the gala. Nora and Ashley sat chatting in Bree's bedroom while they waited for Bree to finish with her makeup. "Okay, how do I look?"

"Gorgeous." Nora admired her.

"Wow, Bree. You look fan-*tas*-tic!" Ashley applauded. Bree's golden hair was swept to one side and tied in an intricate knot. Her strapless cocktail dress was snug on her size-two frame. The dress was a radiant blue that complemented her azure eyes.

"Thanks. So do you." Bree admired Ashley's little black dress with its matching shrug. Her kinky hair was smoothed out and braided in a ring around her head, courtesy of the Gloria McPhee salon, which employed a team of girls who could do amazing things with braids.

"Nora, every time I see that dress on you I love it even more. It was made for your body."

Flattered by Bree's blatant praise, Nora smoothed her hand over her flat stomach. She was a couple sizes bigger than Bree, her hips were fuller and she had two cup sizes on Bree's slender boyish figure. Nora reached up to touch her hair. It was parted in the center with an intricate maze of braids that interconnected and hung down her back. The girl at the salon had done a stunning job. Nora's indecisiveness over getting her hair cut last month had paid off. It had grown to her elbows, giving the girl plenty of hair to work with. Everyone in the salon had ooohed and ahhhed.

Nora peeked out the window for the past hour at the steady line of limousines pulling up to the majestic front entrance. Attendants opened doors and ushered in regally dressed guests laden with expensive jewels and watches. A hired photographer discreetly captured photos.

The trio walked carefully down the stairs, each in five-inch heels. Nora noticed a guy standing at the bottom of the grand staircase with his elbow propped on the thick newel post. He was tall, his auburn hair the same shade as Ashley's and he watched them with a smirk on his freckled face.

"Hey, Evan," Bree called to him. "That's Ashley's brother," she said in a rush to Nora as she hurried down the remaining steps to give him a big hug. "I'm glad you made it."

Evan held Bree at arm's length and said, "You look lovely, as always."

"You look pretty good yourself." Bree paused a moment and turned to Nora. "Evan, I want you to meet my good friend and roommate, Nora Clark."

They shook hands and made some small talk. The group worked its way through the crowd in the corridor toward the dining room. The two sets of double doors were swung open; the ornate formal dining room doubled as the ballroom where guests mingled. All the furniture had been removed. Drinks were served in crystal glasses, and staff members wearing white suits and white gloves offered hors d'oeuvres to guests on silver trays.

Nora sipped champagne, her eyes scanning the crowd. She recognized a few faces from the evening at the bridge, although those people were almost unrecognizable in their finery. She was introduced to a variety of polite strangers. Nora was relieved to see the familiar faces of Derek and Judy Westborough and their daughter Corrine. Her chest tightened in disappointment when she did not see Ben with them. *He told Ashley he would come.*

"Where is Ben?" Evan asked. "Don't tell me he was excused from this event," he joked.

"He'll be here soon," Judy reassured everyone.

Corrine explained, "His mare is probably going into labor tonight. We'll be lucky if he stops by. He was still in the stables when we left." Judy shot her stepdaughter a warning look.

After the briefest lull a tall man sauntered over to them with a drink in his hand. "Son." He eyed Evan. "I'm glad to see you made it." The deep voice preceded the man as he approached. Evan shook his head, chuckling.

"Hello, Father. I'm glad to see you made it as well."

Even though the two men didn't look alike, Nora noticed they shared the same mirthful sparkle in their eyes. She heard from Ashley both men arrived late that afternoon, much to her mother's irritation. After all her mother accomplished, the least her son and husband could do was arrive on time.

"Hi, Daddy." Ashley said, competing with her brother for her father's attention.

Ashley was receiving a peck on the cheek from her father when Mrs. Andrews caught up with her husband. She gave him a tight smile, but her eyes clearly said, "You have finally arrived!" She then turned her attention to her guests, greeting them graciously. Nora was charmed by Mr. Andrews' loud and infectious laugh. He spoke to them for the appropriate period of time and then excused himself to continue working the room alongside his wife.

A small stage had been set up at one end of the ballroom to accommodate a podium and microphone. At the other end of the room, a seven-piece band played soft classical numbers. At seven o'clock, Mrs. Andrews announced the first guest speaker. The room quieted, and Nora listened respectfully. As the speaker droned on, all Nora could think about was how much her five-inch heels were hurting her feet. She excused herself and headed for the ladies room.

On her way back, she paused outside the ballroom. Listening from the hallway was much quieter and cooler. She'd been thrilled to meet celebrities, though somewhat anticlimactic since she hadn't heard of those particular British personalities, or musicians or politicians either. *If only Ben were here.* She glanced over her shoulder.

Ben stood in the hall gazing at her. *Better than any celebrity.* He looked amazing in his black tuxedo and bow tie, his hair combed neatly. Nora abandoned the ballroom and snuck off toward him.

"Hi. You made it. How's the mare? Corrine said she could go into labor tonight," Nora said in hushed tones.

"Hi. Yeah, I can't stay long, but I had to see...umm." His grin widened and his gaze lingered on her face.

See you? Is that what you were going to say?

He cleared his throat and glanced away before he said, "I had to make an appearance. I would never want to disappoint Mrs. Andrews."

Right, an appearance.

He added softly, "You look beautiful, and your hair is stunning."

Although noise filled the air, the sudden silence between them was palpable. A strange longing filled her awareness. She thought anyone nearby would sense the crackle of electricity in the air around them.

"Thanks." She smiled self-consciously, her fingers grazing her braids.

Ben glanced away, the din of the party apparently pulling him to the present. He shifted and inhaled, visibly collecting himself. Light reached his eyes, and he smirked, "Maybe you could braid some manes. You've quite a talent." The joke broke the spell and lightened the mood. "For the horses?"

He got the result he wanted. Nora burst out laughing but quickly stifled it with her fist. She glanced over her shoulder, hoping she hadn't drawn attention. "I didn't braid it! I went to the Gloria McPhee salon."

Ben laughed quietly, his shoulders pumping, but she knew he'd meant his compliment. She caught him still admiring her under his lowered lashes. They heard applause, and then guests spilled out into the hall. Nora and Ben worked their way against the crowd toward their friends.

They found the others snatching more champagne from the unending stream of silver trays. Evan and Ben greeted each other like old friends with a robust hug. The group stood together gossiping about who was who until the dinner announcement. Everyone funneled in the direction of the outside tents. The tables were beautifully adorned with white linens and bouquets of flowers, with specialty chocolates at each place setting. Dinner was efficiently served. Later, guests migrated to the island of curved tables laden with desserts and ice sculptures in the adjacent garden.

Nora and her friends were walking away from the dessert island when another guest speaker was announced. Beyond the garden stood an outdoor theater. Ben hung back, looking at his watch. Nora paused to wait for him.

"I've got to go," he said apologetically.

"Oh." Disappointed, Nora crossed her arms.

"You could come with me."

"Oh!"

"Sorry, I'm sure you don't want to leave all this to hang out in the stables." Ben sniffed, as if he made a foolish suggestion.

"Ben, I'd love to go with you."

"Really?" He sounded doubtful.

"One second." She turned and called to Bree, who had started following the crowd, channeling down the lawn to the theater. "Bree, do you mind if I leave with Ben? He wants to get back to the mare and asked me to join him. I might get to see her give birth."

"Okay. Sure. I don't mind. Birth sounds dirty and gross, but since you're excited about it...have fun, I guess." Bree's gaze strayed to Ben, who glanced everywhere but in their direction. Then she cocked her head at Nora, raising her eyebrows.

"Okay, bye." Nora walked as fast as her five-inch heals could take her to Ben, and together they made their way to the house.

They slipped inside, and he directed her down a darkened hallway to the rear staircase. When Nora looked at him, puzzled, he said, "You might want to change into something you don't mind getting dirty."

"Right! Give me five minutes." Her foot paused on the first step at his voice.

"Are you sure you don't want to stay? You can change your mind." When she shook her head he replied, "Nora, you are an interesting girl."

She didn't want him to see her grin at his words, so she turned and clacked up the stairs, feeling his gaze on her behind.

Chapter Thirteen

Nora returned in jeans and a tank top, a sweater tucked under her arm. Ben gestured for her to walk in front of him. When they passed a gilt mirror, Nora paused to make sure her braids were intact. In the reflection she observed his inconspicuous glances were repeatedly returning to her. They proceeded out the back to his Land Rover parked in the service lot. He opened the passenger door for her and then rounded the hood. He drove on the grass, avoiding the limousines parked everywhere.

"So what made you decide to come? Have you ever seen an animal give birth before?" Nora could not quite see his face in the darkness of the vehicle, but she could see the outline of his profile.

"Actually, I have. The annual county fair in Pennsylvania has a birthing tent. I saw a cow give birth when I was nine. Even at that age I thought it was pretty cool. The fair runs for a week. It's a big hit with the local kids. The schools in my hometown close for one day, appropriately named Fair Day, so local families can attend and support the community."

"It sounds pretty rural where you grew up. So you're a country girl?"

"Yeah, lots of farms. My parents still live there. It was a great place to grow up."

The vehicle pulled down the tree-lined lane and stopped in the gravel lot. "Come on in. I'm going to change," he said, already tugging at his bowtie.

He returned to the hallway he left her in dressed in socks, a white T-shirt, and a flannel shirt over it. He wore the same kind of tan cargo pants he had on the other day. She followed him to a mudroom, where he slipped into work boots. "Okay, it's show time." He smiled up at her as he tied his boots.

"Tell me about the mare."

Ben told her the horse's breed and where she came from. "She's a valuable show horse, and her name is Duchess." Inside the stable, Ben stopped at the stall and focused on the mare, apparently in an advanced stage of labor.

Ben entered the stall. "How is she? Stats?" he asked the guy who was bent down, pressing his palms around the horse's belly. The honey-colored mare was lying on the hay, her breathing labored.

The man stood, reached for a clipboard, and discussed the information with Ben. "Okay, good." Ben nodded in satisfaction. "Ah, Keegan, this is Nora. Nora, this is Keegan, the assistant veterinarian."

Keegan's eyes brightened and a big smile filled his whiskered cheeks. "Hello," Keegan said in a heavy Irish brogue, eyeing Nora, who stayed out of the way. "I can see why you attended the gala even with Duchess so near her time," he remarked to Ben. "Did you kidnap this lovely lass from that fancy party?"

"Something like that." Ben grinned. He stepped over the mare's front legs and squatted down beside her. "All right, Duchess," he cooed. "I'm sure you are excited to meet your new foal. Take it easy." He pressed around her distended belly like Keegan had been doing. "Good Duchess. Good girl."

Nora laid her sweater, unnecessary in the warm stable, on a nearby bench and stood watching Ben. "Nora, come here," Ben encouraged. "Come feel." Nora stepped onto the thick straw lining the stall. Ben dropped a knee to the floor, leaning to the side so Nora could fit in the space before him. He circled his arms around her, clasped his hand over hers, and guided it over the soft coat of Duchess's belly.

"It's in position. The head is facing down."

Duchess lifted her head and then laid it down with a loud breath.

"Wow. What do you do next?" Nora's hands were splayed over the horse's swollen belly, feeling something hard under them. *Fascinating.*

Ben stood and helped her up. He raised his thick eyebrows. "We wait."

It turned out they did not have to wait long. Soon Duchess was blowing through her nose, her body struggling to push out her new foal. Out ballooned a milky white sac. Nora could eventually make out two long legs and a head. Duchess's belly contracted for several minutes. The sac tore open, and Ben assisted in uncovering the foal's head when it was halfway out. Ben spoke to Duchess calmly while he pulled gently on the foal's front legs. Nora held her breath, her hands clamped together. Duchess, obviously in pain, did not squeal or whinny. She just continued her labored breathing until, with one final contraction as Ben pulled, the foal slipped out.

Nora let out a sigh of relief. Ben motioned her closer. She had tears in her eyes as she gazed at the foal. "Remarkable."

Ben slipped the rest of the milky sac off of the foal. The slick foal flopped around until it suddenly stood on wobbly legs. Although slick with afterbirth, the foal was honey-colored, like its mother, a mini version of Duchess.

Keegan stood nearby jotting something down on a clipboard. Ben and Nora watched the new mother clean her baby. Once the mare was on her feet Ben examined her. He inspected the foal and smiled with satisfaction. "It's a boy. We'll name him Grand Duke. Everything went well." Ben beamed. Nora followed him out of the stall. "I'm going to go clean up." He glanced down at his stained shirt with a crooked grin. "And change my shirt. There is a wash sink just there, at the end of the stalls." He pointed it out to Nora so she could wash her hands. Other than feeling Duchess's belly, she had stayed clear of the birthing mess.

She waited for Ben outside the stable. The air was cool and refreshing, not so chilly as the night at the bridge. *What an amazing night. First the over-the-top charity event, and then a birth. This is a trip to remember.*

Ben returned and strode toward her; she could feel the slight quickening of her heartbeat.

"Sorry to have kept you waiting. It's getting late, but of course the gala will still be going on. As I remember, usually a midnight buffet is served." Ben wore jeans and a button-down shirt. The edges of his hair were wet from a thorough washing up. He did not plan on returning to the festivities. "Shall I take you back? Or can I interest you in a nightcap?"

"I'd love a nightcap."

In the deserted kitchen, Ben swung the refrigerator door open and offered, "Beer? Wine? Apple cider?"

"Oooh, can I have my cider heated?" It was early in the season for apple cider, but the thought of it reminded Nora of her youth, when she and her sisters would drink warmed cider out by the backyard fire pit.

"Warm cider it is then." Ben moved easily in the kitchen. He gathered two mugs, poured the cider, and placed the mugs in the microwave. He then opened a cabinet and pulled out a mason jar filled with cinnamon sticks. "This cider comes from a nearby orchard. We've known the family since I was a boy. They've grown a new apple variety, one producing an earlier crop, hence the early cider. I never had the chance to work for the orchard when I was younger. During the fall harvest half the county got hired. I always had a full load at school and just couldn't swing the extra hours."

Ben dropped a cinnamon stick in each mug and handed one to Nora. He slipped a tin of cookies off the counter and tucked them under one arm. She followed him to a cozy room down the hall, and together they made themselves comfortable on the sofa. "Hope you like oatmeal-raisin cookies."

"One of my favorites." Nora took a cookie from the tin Ben offered her. "These are delicious. Who made them? Judy?"

"Judy. She made them because they are my favorite." Ben chuckled.

"She loves to mother you. It's really sweet. And you are very obliging." Nora admired Ben for always being gracious to Judy, even when she unwittingly stepped over the line.

"You've noticed." He feigned surprise. "Yes, Judy is a mother hen to a fault. But, honestly, I couldn't have asked for a nicer stepmother." Ben plucked another cookie and offered Nora the tin again.

"No thanks. Ben, can I ask you something?" At his nod she inquired, "Why do you call her Judy and not Mom? Corrine calls her Mom–Mum."

Ben was thoughtful and didn't speak for a moment. Nora regretted her nosy question, but Ben spoke as if remembering a fond memory. "I was seven when my mother died unexpectedly in a car accident. Corrine was almost five. She remembered our mother for a while, but her memories faded." He slowly scratched at his chin. "My father met Judy a couple years later. Corrine was elated to have a mommy, but it took me a long time to get over it. I felt if I called Judy Mom, I'd somehow be betraying my own mother."

She held the mug in one hand and the other was braced over her heart. Nora realized he just revealed something very personal. "That's so sad. Do you still remember her? You were pretty young."

"I have some memories, but pictures really help," he admitted.

"Do you have a picture of her?"

Ben smiled while reaching into his back pocket to pull out his wallet. He slid out a well-worn photo and handed it to Nora. A studio picture of a woman with shoulder-length sandy-colored hair was seated, a young boy standing at her side and a baby in her lap. Their clothes dated, and poses formal, but Nora noted the woman's broad smile. She had passed down the dimples in her cheeks to her son. Nora was concerned her nosy questions might have annoyed him or made him melancholy, but he seemed comfortable about sharing the picture.

"She's beautiful." Nora handed him the photo. "You look like her."

Ben nodded as he tucked the photo away.

Ben said no more on the subject, so Nora sipped the cider, wondering why she had come here tonight. "You were amazing tonight, by the way."

"Naa, Duchess did all the work," Ben said modestly. "I have to admit I was surprised you agreed to leave the party to spend the night in a stable."

"I'm glad I did. I admire you for what you do, Ben." She noted his modest smile and his adverted eyes, as though he was humbled by her comment. Before the silence stretched any longer, she added, "So you only work with horses?"

"No, I work with other animals. I worked with domestic and farm animals during my training." He told her about the school he went to in Scotland, where he delivered a lot of sheep. Their conversation roamed to include sheep, the English countryside, and the Westborough's horses.

Nora hung on his every intelligent and well spoken word. And yet he worked outdoors with his hands. She found the combination very sexy.

"So how do you like being a flight attendant? Do you fly with Bree?"

"I like it. I haven't been doing it that long. And I don't get to fly with Bree, because I fly international and Bree flies domestic." Nora paused in thought. "It's been liberating."

"How so?" He sounded intrigued.

"Well, I was a small-town girl living a small-town life. I was engaged," she admitted. Ben waited politely for her to continue.

"I just had this ominous feeling. Like that couldn't be all there was in life…for me. I just knew there was something out there…and I had to find it. So I changed my life. I broke off my long engagement and…broke away. I left everything that was familiar and comforting."

"And now?" Ben appeared fascinated.

"Now," a humbleness settled in her voice, "now, I'm absorbing everything. I'm embracing new places and experiences. I'm savoring this time of change, this time for myself. I've met so many great new friends. I'm happy…truly happy."

"Wow, that sounds brave. Good for you."

They talked for a while about the places Nora had traveled so far. Ben had traveled in Europe some, and they traded stories.

"Will you come back? I mean here, to visit–with Bree." He brought up the subject again. It seemed he tried to sound casual, but there was a hint of hope in his voice. "Of course you are welcome anytime without Bree, too, since you fly international and all. Bree is like family, and any friend of Bree's… Well, you understand."

"I'd love to come and visit. Maybe next time you can teach me to ride? Ashley suggested I learn."

"That could be arranged." Ben set his empty mug on the table. "Are you interested in learning? Really?"

Is he personally inviting me? "Yes, it's on my bucket list!"

"Well, then, definitely give me a call when you're in London." He pulled out his phone, and they exchanged numbers. "What time do you leave tomorrow?" He glanced at the clock on the mantel. It was two. "Or should I say today?"

"We fly out around four this afternoon." Nora could not believe they had talked so long. She was tired and a little melancholy at the thought of leaving Ben.

"Let's get you back." He collected their mugs and the cookie tin. He dropped them off in the kitchen on their way out.

At the Andrews' estate, Ben drove around and parked in the service lot. It appeared the guests had all gone home, but the clean-up crew was in full swing. Ben turned off the motor and turned to Nora. "I don't think I'll get a chance to see you off tomorrow. I've promised a friend I'd look at a stallion he wants to stud, but he's presenting with... Never mind." He refocused on his next words. "I had a nice time talking with you. I hope you visit us again."

"I enjoyed myself too. Thank you for everything." Nora took a deep breath, and Ben swallowed nervously.

"Let me walk you to the door." Ben jumped out, and Nora scrambled out the other side. Not a word passed as they walked to the door. They stopped and turned toward one another, their gazes locking.

The door swung open, and Ashley called out, "There you are, Nora! You missed all the fun."

Nora gave Ashley a weak smile, not appreciating the untimely interruption, but Nora didn't really think anything would happen with Ben. Truly, at this point she didn't need it to. Just because they shared a mutual attraction it likely wouldn't turn into anything. Turning to Ben, she sighed. She didn't even know if she would see him again. "Good night, Ben."

"Good night, Nora. I hope you find what you are searching for." He spoke softly so only she could hear.

His words touched her.

Reaching the door, she exchanged a wave before Ashley closed the door behind them, talking all about the events of the evening. Nora was lost in her own thoughts as they mounted the stairs to their bedrooms. Suddenly Ashley's words caught Nora's attention.

"What did you say?" Nora stopped on the soft carpet, her feet sinking in where she stood.

"Bree and Evan smooching! And not like brother and sister, I tell you! Yeah, they got cozier as the night went on, and then I accidently spied them kissing again out on a private balcony." Ashley's eyes were wild in her freckled face. The braid that circled her head was starting to unravel, and her shoes were missing altogether. She had obviously been drinking–a lot. Nora thought perhaps Ashley was mistaken. Evan seemed nice enough, but he certainly did not fit Bree's recent type, by a mile. However Nora was thrilled Bree was indeed turning over a new leaf.

"Wow. Well, let's get some rest. We'll ask her about it in the morning. Is she already asleep?" Nora asked as Ashley swayed along beside her down the hallway.

"I tucked her in myself. She's passed out." Ashley released a long sigh. "Everything go all right with you? You got back late. Did you have to wait out in the stables all night?" She made a face.

"No, the birth was a success. Ben and I just got caught up talking. I hope you didn't mind I left with him." Nora paused outside her room.

Ashley gave a sweeping wave. "I don't mind." She staggered down the corridor. "It's about bloody time the man's interested in someone. Sleep tight." Ashley then started singing quietly, "Llllooove is innn the airrr."

"Night, Ash." Nora suppressed a giggle as she slipped into her room.

She washed her face, brushed her teeth, and slipped into her pajamas. Too tired to deconstruct the network of braids in her hair, she just crawled into bed and fell straight to sleep.

She was sorry in the morning when her hair was all tangled and fuzzy. Some of the pins had slipped out overnight, causing one side to droop.

Nora heard a light knock at her door.

"Nora?" Bree's voice called quietly.

"Come in." Nora had been lying there, wondering when she would see Ben again. He was her last thought before falling asleep and the first thing she thought about in the morning.

"Heeey." Bree slipped in, closing the door behind her. Bree had unraveled her braid, and her hair was brushed into a smooth ponytail. "How did it go with Ben last night?" She sat on the end of Nora's bed while Nora scooted to rest against the headboard.

"It was great. I'm really glad I got to see Duchess give birth– what a miracle. And Ben was so calm." Nora sensed Bree wanted to say something. "What about you? How did the rest of the night go?"

"Well, this is probably going to sound crazy, but Evan, Ashley's brother, *who I've known forever*, and I had this really great connection. We kissed." Bree studied the lack of reaction on Nora's face. "Ash told you?" Nora nodded. "What did she say?" Bree nibbled on her thumbnail.

"Basically what you just said. Is there more?" Nora inquired.

"Humph, it's funny. You know, when we were kids I had a mad crush on Evan. Then around high school graduation he became interested in me. By then I had several boyfriends. My interests strayed in a different direction. Each guy I dated was hotter and more badass than the last," she smirked. "But last night, we started talking, and the old flames sparked for both of us."

"That's great to hear. Evan seems nice–from what I've seen of him so far. You deserve someone nice."

"Yeah, Evan is nice. You deserve someone nice too, Nora." Bree's eyes flicked to Nora's hair. "Speaking of being nice– would you like me to help you remove that rat's nest from your head?" Bree said seriously but her eyes twinkled with mirth.

While Bree deconstructed Nora's braid she was silent for a while. "Nora, do you really think I would be accepted if I applied for an international flight attendant position?"

"I don't know–but it would be awesome. You should definitely try and see what happens."

Chapter Fourteen

Nora spent the Fourth of July in Stockholm, Sweden. The whole crew, even the pilots, went to visit the city's Ice Bar, a bar constructed literally of ice blocks. The crew laughed at each other in the thick, puffy ponchos they were given before entering the bar. They drank out of glasses made of ice. It was a hip place Nora would always remember.

Because Bree and Nora had both worked over the Fourth, they organized a get-together for dinner with some friends a few days after the holiday, when everyone had the day off together. Nora had promised Sergei she'd cook for him, and she was glad to get the chance to do so tonight. Nora served a classic barbequed pulled-pork that had been bubbling on the stove all day. Crusty rolls for pulled-pork sandwiches, steamed corn on the cob, a homemade potato salad, and a green salad waited on the table.

When Rebecca walked in, she cried, "Oooo, that smells delicious!" She displayed two six-packs of hard cider. Rebecca admitted she had bought the cobbler in the bag hanging over her arm, plus flying a homemade dessert from North Carolina wasn't feasible.

Bree stuck her nose in the bag. "Mmm, we can nuke it in the microwave and add some vanilla ice cream. I know we still have some in the freezer." Rebecca nodded and smiled at Bree's brilliant idea.

Sergei and Alexei arrived with beer and a female guest. Alexei introduced his American girlfriend, Ann. After they exchanged greetings, they quickly piled food on their plates and sat around the dining room table to enjoy a relaxing evening. Everyone laughed between mouthfuls of food, and the conversations never ceased. When everyone was done and groaning over full bellies, Rebecca and Bree cleared the dishes. Alexei and Anna moved to the comfortable sofa. Nora and Sergei slipped out the kitchen door. The evening air offered no relief from the heat. Nora began to sweat just standing still. Sergei leaned against the railing, looking down at his beer bottle. When Nora remained silent, he spoke. "Dinner was delicious. Thank you."

Nora shrugged. "It was nothing. I owed you after the amazing dinner you made for me." An uncomfortable silence hung between them. Nora's thoughts flashed to that night, when she kissed him. "I'm glad we got a chance to get everyone together tonight." She wanted to keep the conversation nonchalant but knew she needed to address what had happened between them. The awkward tension between them felt wrong.

"Sergei, you are a real gentleman and a good friend. I owe you a thank you for not taking advantage of a certain situation…" Embarrassed, her cheeks heated. "For not having your way with me when I was drunk." She tucked a loose strand of hair behind her ear. "And I also owe you an apology. I'm sorry for putting you in that situation. You see, I'm sort of seeing this guy, and things were…are…not going…" She trailed off, at a loss for what to call Antonio's inappropriate proposal. "Not going as I had expected. Anyway, I know we've kind of had some interest in each other…" Her words died away again. *What am I trying to say?*

"I get it," he mumbled before shifting to the door.

Nora grabbed his hand before he reached the doorknob.

"Sergei, I just need some time. I don't want to complicate things or be unfair to you." His expression was hard to read, but she could tell he was thinking about what she said. "I've hardly ever had one person interested in me, never mind two at the same time." Even Phillip, who had loved her, hadn't shown her the interest she deserved. He focused his gaze on hers. "Believe me. This is new for me. I'm still trying to sort out my feelings. My life has changed so much in such a short period of time. I'm still trying to catch my breath." She shrugged and laughed at how crazy her new life had become. Antonio's face flashed before her eyes, and then there was Ben whose image lingered. *No, there is nothing going on between me and Ben. He had not made a move or shown any true interest–not really. He was just being nice when he invited me to return.*

Sergei nodded at her honesty. "Are you going to keep seeing this guy? Do I know him?"

"You don't know him. I'm not certain there can be a future for us. His ideas of a relationship are very different than mine." She could keep seeing Antonio and just enjoy what they had, but she would eventually want more. Why had she not considered being in a long-term relationship with Sergei. She had to admit she was still a little curious, but was it worth risking their friendship?

"Okay, Nora, then we will be, as they say, to be continued..." They agreed and went inside. She enjoyed the rest of her evening. Sergei was laid back, as always, and made her feel at ease. However that night in bed, Nora's thoughts were filled with the image of a certain green-eyed man she wished she could know better.

As mid-July approached, Nora picked up a trip to Rome. She arrived at her hotel, took a long, cool shower, and slipped into a sundress. Rome's July heat did not stop its citizens from flooding the streets. The Italians were a loud, hot-blooded lot. Nora knew just how hot-blooded *her* Italian man was. She phoned Antonio and asked him if he'd like to see her.

"Are you here? In Rome?"

She smiled at the excitement in his voice.

"I'm on my way to our favorite coffee shop as we speak. What are you up to today?" She felt butterflies begin to flutter in her stomach. She wanted to see him, to be with him physically, but she also knew it was time to end this for good. Meeting Antonio in a public place would increase her chances of ending their relationship. In private she might not be able to resist him.

"I've been staring at market analysis spreadsheets all morning. I'm ready for a break. I can be there in about thirty minutes."

While Nora waited for Antonio, she rehearsed what she wanted to say. Before long his sports car purred to the curb. He stepped out, looking like a model from a men's magazine add.

Oh no, he looks amazing! How am I going to do this? She was worried, and for good reason. Before she knew it he was pulling her into his embrace; his passionate kiss left her weak in the knees. Her planned resistance was nonexistent. She slid her arms around his neck, locking her fingers in his wavy dark hair before she realized what she was doing.

"What a wonderful surprise. I am very glad to see you." His musky fragrance filled her senses. It was as strong as his presence. As usual, he held her hand, stroking her skin with his thumb. When they sat down he did not let go.

"It's good to see you, too, Antonio."

He reached out to caress a stray lock of hair that had escaped her loose bun. "How long are you here? Did you already check into your hotel?" He always preferred her to stay at his place.

"Yes, I checked in this morning. I leave again the day after tomorrow." His quizzical expression told Nora he knew something was up, but she steered the conversation in a safer direction. "How have you been? How's business?"

Antonio ordered an espresso, and then they caught up for a while. After he paid the bill, Nora abruptly stood.

Antonio asked, "Do you want to come back to my place? I can finish up some work and then take you to dinner later?"

"I think I'll do some tourist stuff this afternoon. I'd like to have dinner with you later." Nora couldn't bring herself to break it off yet. Seeing Antonio again had caught her off guard. She needed time to think–but she would tell him tonight. *Tonight! No exceptions!*

"Okay. I will pick you up at seven? Unless you want me to come earlier?" His voice was low and seductive.

"Seven is fine. We'll talk tonight." *Why am I prolonging this?* She had not said one word she had planned to say.

He leaned over and gave her a lingering kiss.

This is harder than I thought.

Nora walked to her hotel. The concierge called her a cab to take her to the Galleria Borghese, where she spent the whole afternoon feasting her eyes on antiquities, art, and sculptures by Bernini. The seventeenth-century villa housing the collections was magnificent. She wished she had a companion to share the experience with. Antonio had never suggested touring or visiting museums with her except for one time when they drove past some iconic structures on their way to his family's vineyard. His interest in her was clearly physical, but it spoke to her ego, making her feel desirable.

What more do I want from Antonio, besides being his mistress? She focused on a painting and wondered what Antonio would think of it. She realized she didn't feel a deep connection with Antonio intellectually. She didn't get the sense she would ever truly know him. Their conversations were superficial, and he rarely asked anything about her personally. *I want someone to share my interests, not just my bed. Still, breaking up with him is unfortunate since he's the first man to ever show me so much passion. I'm only human, after all.*

She took a bus to her hotel after she unsuccessfully tried hailing a cab. She got a lot better at reading maps and was becoming a pretty savvy traveler. The city bus was overcrowded, and she was pressed up against other sweaty people. Old buildings like her hotel did not have air conditioning. Another cool shower felt wonderful.

Nora met Antonio in the lobby later, and he drove them to a small restaurant that specialized in veal. During their delicious dinner, Nora monitored her wine intake. She told Antonio about her visit to the museum and asked if he visited any of the galleries in his beautiful city.

"They say the best museum in Rome is the city itself." He sipped on his wine. "I don't visit these places. I like the vibe of this city–it has good energy."

Hmm. Nora could not relate to the vibe he spoke of. She loved the ancient buildings and carvings but found the city dirty and congested. She did not say that to him though. Instead she said, "It has an amazing sense of history."

After their dinner dishes were carried away and the wine bottle stood empty, Antonio asked, his voice deep with concern, "Nora, what is troubling you?"

"Antonio, the last time we were together you told me you would be marrying someone else someday, but you still wanted to date me now." Nora focused her gaze on a tiny oil stain on the tablecloth to avoid his intense stare. "I've been struggling with that being...okay. I care about you. I really enjoy the time we spend together. You make me feel amazing, but…I don't think we should continue seeing each other." She looked at him. "It's not what I want." She spoke apologetically, but her voice was firm.

"No, Nora, don't say this. You are breaking my heart."

The waiter came toward the table.

"Please. I have more to say." Antonio said to her, and then turned his attention to the waiter. He pulled out his wallet and handed over cash. The waiter gave a pleasant nod and wished them a good evening. Nora mustered a smile in response. They stood and moved toward the exit.

Antonio guided her to his car. Once inside he drove them to her hotel and parked. They had been silent, each considering how they should proceed.

"Nora, please let me try to explain this again. The thing I want you to know–you must know–is how I feel about you."

His voice is so seductive; he can be so convincing! He twisted in his seat to look at her, but she looked straight ahead to avoid being tempted by him. *I was rebounding from a long-term relationship. Rebounds are never a sure thing. Everyone knows that. We have a physical relationship–that's it. This relationship can't really be so important to him. After all, he is gorgeous and successful, and he admitted he has many girlfriends. I am a plaything to him. But to be fair, he had been honest with me.* "Feelings aside, we want different things."

"We want to be together. That is the same thing. I told you, you have my heart. And I'm not getting married for a very long time. Things may even change. But right now, I know we are supposed to be together. Please consider this. We can make it work."

She turned to him. "I don't think so." She rested her hand on his cheek. "I think this is our last night together." He closed his eyes and leaned toward her. Their foreheads touched, and she whispered, "You know I'm right."

He opened his eyes. They were filled with sorrow. *This is hard on him*, she realized.

"I hope you change your mind. Can I see you when you are here on your next layover?" He leaned back, giving her puppy-dog eyes.

"I'm going to take trips to other cities for a while." Her heart felt heavy. "Antonio, this is hard for me, too, but I think it is for the best."

"Can I call you? I want to hear the sound of your voice. And I don't want you to forget me."

"That's not a good idea," she discouraged him. Nora felt tears burn her eyes, but she held them in check. She would miss his glorious body, his dark wavy hair, and his soulful eyes. But she held strong, staying her course. Nora knew she wanted more, like when she'd been with Phillip. Change was hard; decisions were sometimes hard, but she was at a place where she could make them confidently.

But it pained her to see the longing in his eyes.

"Nora, may I kiss you good-bye?"

She didn't say no. He leaned forward, and she slid her hand behind his neck and into his hair. She wanted one last long kiss. She would remember him like a delicacy, something she would savor for as long as she could. She was grateful he had saved her that day in the alley, and she would never forget how desired he had made her feel. She kissed him passionately before pulling away. She slipped from his grasp. "Good-bye, Antonio."

He sighed. "Until we meet again, Nora."

Nora slipped from the car without a backward glance and hastened across the street, the tears she held in check earlier now rolling down her cheeks. She dashed them away, telling herself she could move on to other possibilities.

Nora was already feeling emotional when she rode in the employee bus to the parking lot in Philadelphia. She retrieved an urgent message from her mother to call home right away. Sprinting off the van, she tossed her luggage into the trunk, and slid in behind the wheel of her Ford Escape. She dialed home.

She listened in horror as her mother spoke, "Victoria was rushed to the hospital last night. She's lost the baby."

No! Nora's eyes burned and her throat felt raw. "She'd tried for so long. She was so happy. I can't imagine how distraught she must be. Is she okay physically?"

Heidi sniffled, "She's all right, but devastated. He was six months along. We're planning a small funeral service for him on Friday morning."

After Nora hung up and calmed herself down, she drove to her townhouse to repack her bag. Within thirty minutes she was on the road, heading to her parent's house. Nora called Bree and sniffled her way through the conversation. Bree consoled her as well as a close friend could.

Nora drove down the familiar tree-lined street after spending the ride trying to wrap her mind around this terrible situation. She steered the car into her parent's driveway, where her safe and loving family gathered. She had distanced herself, and she felt the true impact of that now.

Nora's mother met her at the door. "Hello, stranger." Heidi's voice was low, but she smiled at her daughter. The "stranger" part stoked Nora's guilty conscience.

"Hi, Mom." They embraced, synchronized in sadness. "Where's dad?" His car wasn't in the driveway.

"He's at work. He's taking tomorrow off for the funeral. Honey, I've missed you." Heidi patted Nora's cheek before she went to get her daughter some coffee. They sat for a few minutes discussing tomorrow's plans. After a little while, they went to Victoria's house to sit with her for the afternoon.

Perry answered the door. Nora hugged him and offered her condolences. He led them solemnly to the bedroom. Victoria sat propped against some pillows watching the Food Network on the television.

"Eleanor!" Victoria sounded surprised. When Nora rushed to hug her she acted polite. "How are you? Where have you been flying lately?"

"I just flew in from Rome," Nora quickly answered. "How are you feeling? I'm so sorry." She gripped her sister's hand and searched her face. Victoria appeared pale, her lips pinched. Her eyes heavily lidded. Nora glanced at Perry with a question in her eyes, and he nodded. They had medicated her sister.

Nora talked a little with Victoria, awkwardly keeping the conversation light. She wanted her sister to know she was there for her, even when they grew quiet and watched the cooking program. The show ended and Victoria murmured she was tired. They left the room so she could sleep.

Heidi said, "Perry I'm going home to make a casserole. I'll bring it later for dinner along with Russ as soon as he's home from work."

Nora stayed with Perry, wanting to be there when her sister woke up.

Over lemonade, Perry confided in Nora, "There's been a strain on our marriage for years while we were trying to have a baby." Trying to get pregnant naturally had given way to rounds of fertility shots and visits to specialists. "She wanted to have a child so badly—she was obsessed with it. And when she finally was…she's been so happy." Nora watched the play of emotions across his face shift from wonder to devastation. "And then …" His eyes filled with tears. Nora was swallowing her tears, nodding in understanding. *It just isn't fair.*

The next day was awful. The air was static and sticky. The smell of lilies began to make Nora nauseous. No one should witness a tiny coffin in a quiet cemetery. Victoria, sedated for the funeral, had been showing a hefty baby bump. After the miscarriage she couldn't quite fit into her regular clothes, so she had to wear a loose-fitting maternity dress. The funeral was attended by the immediate family and Victoria's best friend and her husband. Nora, who knew Victoria's best friend well, was thankful her sister had a good support system, especially because Nora was so far away. Guilt flooded her; she had hardly been home to see her pregnant sister.

The evening was the hardest to get through. Perry and her mother agreed to stop the medication, and Victoria's dammed-up emotions emptied out. By the time they left her sister's house, Victoria's sobbing had subsided, her emotions spent. She thanked her family for being there for her and held Perry's hand in quiet alliance.

At midnight Nora snuggled in her old bed in her childhood room. It felt nostalgic and comforted her. Despite the tragic circumstance, Nora hadn't realized how much she needed this reprieve. She missed her family.

On Saturday morning, Nora came downstairs to find her mother in the kitchen preparing for the next day's catering job. Lizzy walked in the door carrying grocery bags.

"Good morning, sleepyhead," Lizzy said to Nora as she plunked the bags on the counter.

Nora glanced at the clock, nearly ten. "Wow, you've already gone to the store?"

Lizzy nodded. "Yeah, Mom needs help with the prep for tomorrow's job, a family reunion for seventy-five people. She needed a few things at the store."

"Mom, what can I do to help," Nora immediately offered.

"Nothing, honey. I've got everything under control. Coffee's there." Heidi returned to stirring the pot. "Once this is done we can go see your sister. The doctor wants her off her feet for a couple days, so Lizzy is going to give me a hand."

Nora pondered the idea of irresponsible Lizzy filling her competent sister's shoes. Normally Victoria wouldn't allow it. Nora needed to get to Philly tomorrow morning because she had a trip later that afternoon. As it was, she would be pushing the time limit. She had rushed here and so would need to wash her uniform and repack.

Her old sense of family obligation crept in. *I should help. Maybe I should call in sick. My family needs me.* A sudden sensation of anguish washed over her. *I have let my mom down. I promised to come home often. I selfishly left my family, and they have been so good to me. They love me; they support me.* Her emotions running high, she stood watching Lizzy take her place. *Lizzy!* Nora should be proud her unruly little sister was stepping up, but she felt resentful. *Am I needed here?* Nora silently helped Lizzy unpack the bags.

Nora found Victoria in the decorated nursery. The walls were freshly coated with taupe paint and maple furniture adorned the room. Victoria, a planner, had various ideas gleaned from magazines mapped out for the decor. Her sister sat in the rocker, staring out the window into the backyard where she likely envisioned her child playing. Nora's movement interrupted her hypnotic gaze.

"Hi, how are you feeling today?" Nora spoke softly, as if not to spook her.

Victoria shrugged her shoulders. After a long pause she spoke. "I want a baby, and I'm not going to give up." She sounded resolute. "I need some time to morn my little boy. Eventually we'll try again. Or maybe we'll adopt."

Nora ran her hand along the crib rail. "Of course," she agreed, believing her determined sister would achieve whatever she wanted. "You will be a great mom." Nora focused on the crib sheet with tiny airplanes on it. "If you want, I can call in sick for a few days." The tiny planes had clouds stitched around them. "Mom said Lizzy was around, but I can help, either here with you or with Mom."

Victoria scanned the room until her eyes rested on her sister. "No, don't do that." Nora's head snapped up and Victoria continued, "You need to stick with what you're doing. It's your life, Eleanor. Do what is going to make you happy. I realize I may never give birth to a child, but I will be a mother someday. Find what it is you want and go for it. I know things weren't working for you here. I know I've asked a lot from you in the past." Victoria regarded her a moment, "You were right to break things off with Phillip, even though I thought you were crazy at first."

Nora and Victoria had never been particularly close, but when Victoria divulged her most personal feelings to Nora, for the first time she felt an unusual sisterly bond with her. It was as if she had somehow grown up in Victoria's eyes. Indeed, Nora felt worldly. But most importantly, she felt justified in her choices.

Bree met Nora at the door, and they hugged. Nora related the miserable story but ended on a positive note, explaining she felt touched when Victoria showed her support for the choices she'd made. Nora slipped away then to get her laundry and packing done.

Heidi had sent her daughter home with a cooler filled with homemade comfort food. Nora shared it with Bree. "I told my mom I'm leaving tonight, but she insisted I bring all this food for you." They assembled chicken salad sandwiches on huge croissants and sat savoring the flavors.

"Guess what! I just heard I've been accepted for the international flight attendant program! I report for training in August. I can't wait to fly together! And I can't wait to tell Ash and Evan I'll be flying international soon and can visit all the time!"

"I can't wait to pick up trips together too." They promised each other once Bree transferred, they would take every city by storm *together*. Having a buddy in a strange city would be wonderful and safer. Nora's encounter with a thief taught her that. Then, Nora thought of Antonio. Over the chocolate chip cookies her mom had sent, Nora told Bree about the breakup with Antonio.

On the subject of men, Bree reported things were progressing with Evan. "We've talked on the phone every day. I'm trying to time out so I can go see him. Do you want to come too? We can stay with Ash in London, no problem."

"Yeah, sure, I'd love to come. I have one last trip to Helsinki."

It was Nora's second layover in Helsinki, Finland. She joined a scenic countryside tour. On the comfortable tour bus, she enjoyed the rustic landscape on the way to a quaint historic town. During lunch in an old mill, she sat with a couple from Canada. The establishment offered bear on the menu; she wasn't brave enough to try it. Nora decided these northern countries were *the* places to visit in July and August, when their warmest temperature reached around seventy-five degrees. It beat the oppressive heat of Philly or the baking city of Rome.

Antonio had called her several times, but she hadn't answered. He left messages claiming he was thinking of her and he missed her. She admitted to herself she missed him too. After a week she finally answered his call.

"Nora, I'm going on holiday for three weeks. I'm staying at a place along the Amalfi coast. Come with me."

"You know my answer, Antonio. You shouldn't call me anymore. Have a nice trip." Antonio still believed she would change her mind. Typical.

Chapter Fifteen

Four weeks had passed since Nora and Bree were last in England. As the girls steered their rolling luggage through the crowded London airport, they smiled at each other, anticipating a great weekend. Ashley picked them up and took them to a coffee house in the city. They sipped and chatted the afternoon away. Of course, the first topic that came up was Bree's transfer to international flight training. Though Ashley insisted on calling everyone to tell them, Bree convinced her to wait.

"I hope you don't mind," Bree said to Ashley. "I talked to Evan and he wants to take us out on the town tonight." Ashley's eyes widened above her freckled cheeks. "And I want to tell him my news in person." Bree gave Ashley a coy look, suggesting things were getting more involved with her brother.

The girls stopped at Ashley's to freshen up and drop off their things. The two-bedroom walk-up flat was modest and her building overlooked a busy small-business district. It suited Ashley perfectly. They met Evan at a quaint pub for dinner. Thrilled with Bree's news, he ordered a round of drinks to celebrate.

Nora woke to the sounds of Ashley making coffee in her modernized kitchen. She sat up from the sofa, inhaling. "Mmm, that smells good."

"Good morning. Coffee will be ready in a few minutes," Ashley said as she spooned level scoops of dark crystals into the coffee filter.

"I could definitely use some." Nora rubbed her eyes, still groggy from the time change.

Ashley was handing Nora a container of cream at the table when Bree emerged from the bedroom. "Do I smell coffee?" She gratefully accepted a mug from Ashley. After a few quiet moments sipping caffeine, Ashley fixed her eyes on Bree.

"So–what is going on between you and my brother? Is it finally happening?" Ashley pursed her lips.

"Is *what* finally happening?" Nora's gaze shifted from Bree to Ashley. Bree peered over the rim of her coffee mug, in a stare-off with Ashley. "What are you talking about?" Nora prodded.

"Well," Ashley began, "when we were kids, we played the game of chase with the boys, but Bree always went after Evan."

Bree groaned.

"One day, she chased him into the stables. At her scream we all came running in. She'd slipped and fell. Evan stood over her, laughing and teasing. Bree's clothes were covered in mud and horse manure. Bree stood up, stomped her foot, and yelled, 'This is the last time I'll chase you, Evan Andrews. Someday you will be chasing after me!'" Ashley nodded slowly. "It was quite a declaration."

"Really, so he's finally chasing after you? Why has it taken so long?" Nora inquired.

"Timing," Bree answered, and Ashley nodded.

"Bree was a dorky American kid." Bree made a face at Ashley's description.

"Yeah…when I was nine," Bree said defensively. "I think I told you some of this, Nora. The summer of my junior year in high school I came for a visit. Evan would have asked me out, but he had a steady girlfriend. When I returned a year later, I was dating this musician, so Evan knew I was into someone else. Now…" Bree fiddled with a strand of red-gold hair, "we are both unattached, and he's finally been calling me. Chasing me. So here we are." She opened a palm. "Ta da!"

"I guess becoming an international flight attendant will make seeing him easier? Right? Don't you come to London often, Nora?" Ashley poured herself a second cup of coffee.

"Yes, London flights are easy to pick up," Nora confirmed. Bree seemed to have a good relationship going with Evan, but Nora could not help but feel a pang of jealousy. Her own relationships were stretching in too many directions.

"I'm so excited you'll be an *international* jetsetter now." Ashley's raspy voice squeaked as it went higher. "Too bad you couldn't transfer here to London."

Bree glanced heavenward and shrugged her shoulders.

That "who knows what could happen in the future" shrug alarmed Nora. If Bree left Philadelphia, Nora could not afford to stay in the townhouse on her salary, even with a roommate. Bree's father paid for the expensive residence. She pushed the thought out of her mind. It would be crazy. They just got settled. They'd only been flying for about five months. Besides, Bree wasn't even flying internationally yet. Still, the thought was disturbing.

The girls spent the morning shopping at Harrods, London's well-known department store. Bree tried on several outfits before deciding on a shirtdress. Then they tried on shoes. With a mountain of open shoeboxes stuffed with tissue paper surrounding her, Bree chose a pair of strappy sandals to complete her outfit.

It was a beautiful summer day and they went for ice cream. Bree hung up her cell phone and smiled at Nora. "Evan got us reservations at Bernard's tonight, and Corrine and Ben will be driving down to join us." Bree ate the ice cream off the top of the cone and then tossed the cone into a nearby trashcan. Nora paused for a moment, thinking she should toss her cone too. *I don't need the extra calories*. But she didn't.

Nora cautioned herself not to overreact because she would be seeing Ben. "Cool. Sounds great." She thought she sounded nonchalant.

"Good! Are they staying the weekend? It's been ages since they stayed." Ashley finished her last bite and dusted off her hands.

"Yes. Evan said he invited them to stay with him." Bree said, applying lip gloss and checking her hair in her compact mirror. Watching Bree, Nora reached into her purse, bypassing her everyday lip balm for the new lip gloss Bree had insisted looked gorgeous on her in Harrods. They'd stood at the makeup counter for forty-five minutes, playing with the many samples. Nora thought Harrods was like Macy's on steroids. It was huge and had so many fun things to look at. The prices were well out of her spending range, but she could swing for the thirty-dollar lip gloss.

Bree gathered her shopping bags and stood. "We better get going."

Ashley grabbed the smaller Harrods bag containing the cosmetics she'd bought.

Outside Bernard's restaurant, Corrine and Ben gave hugs all around. When it came time for Nora to hug Ben, she closed her eyes and inhaled his masculine scent. "It's really nice to see you again, Nora." He smiled as he appraised her.

"You, too, Ben. So you're staying for the weekend?" She was staying until Monday and hoped to see more of him.

"Yes, I'm taking a little break from work for a few days. It's been a long time coming–or so everyone tells me." Ben took the seat next to Nora; they chatted easily. Just after the waiter delivered their drinks, Ashley dug around in her bag for her buzzing cell phone.

"Oh, bloody hell!" After listening to a phone message Ashley hung up. Ben and Nora paused to hear what was wrong. "I have to go into work tomorrow. Those idiots have messed up everything, and now I have to go in on my day off." The smattering of freckles across Ashley's face made her look like a pouting child.

"Welcome to the real world," Evan taunted his little sister.

"Bugger off," she whispered venomously to her brother in an unladylike manner. Evan just chuckled.

"Oh, Ash, we were just talking about shopping on Mayfair tomorrow." Corrine looked disappointed.

"Just go without me. Maybe I can meet up with you," Ashley offered. Then she focused on her glass of beer like her life depended on it.

Nora spoke up. "I was thinking about visiting Westminster Abbey tomorrow. I've been dying to go each time I come to London, but I can never fit in all the sights I want to see." She apologized. "I'm afraid I'm a little shopped out."

"That's a London classic," Ben replied, "one of my favorites, in fact. I'll take you if you want. Evan told me after I got here that he'll be working tomorrow as well. So I'm free." He took a sip of the amber liquid in his glass.

"Really, I'd love that. I love history, and I've read a lot about English history. My favorite story is King Edward and Elizabeth Woodville."

"A horse, a horse, my kingdom for a horse." Ben's odd comment made Nora lift her brows, and he chuckled. "In Shakespeare's play, King Richard III, King Edward's brother, uttered those words before he died. Of course, because it's horse related it stuck in my mind."

"Ah, King Richard, King Edward's younger brother, the last of the York kings," Nora said to impress Ben. "I have never seen Shakespeare's *King Richard III*." Nora confessed; she made a mental note to see the play. The waiter returned to take their orders. Nora chose a dish Ben recommended. They continued talking to each other for some time.

"What are you two talking about?" Bree asked as the waiter approached with their dinners. "It sounds like a soap opera."

"It is like one. We are talking about the English court. The war between the Yorks and Lancasters." Nora received admiring looks from her British friends until they were distracted by the meals set before them.

"Nora and I are going to Westminster Abbey tomorrow. Would anyone like to join us?" Ben sliced into his roast beef.

"Ugh, no!" Corrine rolled her eyes. "Dad used to take us all the time when we were kids. We'd come to the city to visit our aunt, and she would always mention the Abbey. I never understood why you liked it so much."

"It never gets old." Ben grinned at his sister and then took another mouthful.

"Ben, I'm so glad you're here, for her sake." Bree pointed her salad fork at Nora. "She is a big history buff, like you." She swung her fork between herself and Corrine. "We're going shopping. So Nora is all yours. You can be Tour Guide Ben." Bree understood she had a threshold for shopping, plus now her friend wouldn't have to feel guilty about dragging Nora into overpriced shops she was unable to resist.

Everyone laughed, and Ben shrugged. "Fine by me."

After they'd finished eating, they continued drinking and socializing. Nora glanced around the table and realized just a few weeks ago these people had been strangers to her. Now they were becoming her dear friends. Nora discovered Corrine was a Madonna fan; they both loved the same 1980's hits. They sang song lines together across the table, the rest of the group were practically in tears from laughing. Evan apparently had a pool table at his house; he beamed at Nora. "You play!"

They split the bill six ways and headed out into the balmy summer night. Ben slowed to walk alongside Nora. "I'll pick you up after breakfast, around nine. The Abbey doesn't open until ten, but I thought I'd drive you around and show you some points of interest if you'd like."

Nora nodded, delighted.

Corrine said to Bree, "I'll catch a ride over with Ben in the morning."

Ashley offered her car to the girls. "It's no bother to take the tube to the office." Then the group dispersed.

The next morning the sky appeared cloudy and ominous. Nora stood on the sidewalk waiting for Ben and wearing a sweater to keep warm. England's weather was unpredictable at best. Businesses hadn't opened yet, and the street was quiet for a Friday morning. Ben pulled to the curb in a compact car, not the same vehicle he drove in the country. She was already feeling nervous about being in a tiny car, driving on the *wrong* side of the road, in London traffic. That was probably why she could feel butterflies in her stomach.

Ben jumped out first. Corrine got out the passenger side and waved hello as she hoisted her bag over her shoulder. "Have a good time, you two." Ben waited for Corrine to disappear behind the entry door that led to Ashley's apartment.

Ben turned to her, his hands buried in his pockets as he squinted at the sky, "Looks like we'll get rain today. Not to worry. I always have an umbrella in my car."

The bright, cloud-covered sky reflected in his green eyes, casting them in a cool, minty shade. *His eyes are so beautiful...* Nora thought she could stare into them all day.

Nora made herself comfortable in the small vehicle. Ben, a tall man, looked cramped. "So what happened to your Land Rover?"

He said with a grin, "This is my city car." He came to an intersection and edged into and around traffic. They motored around the city for half an hour or so before they found parking near Westminster Abbey.

She pulled out her wallet. "How much are the tickets?"

He waved her money away. "I got it."

"No, Ben, I don't expect you to pay. I should be paying for you." She didn't want this to be like a date. He was just a friend.

He laughed. "Our tour is starting." He tipped his head in the direction of the Abbey and paid for the tickets.

Nora was delighted with the short, round, eccentric tour guide. The matching plaid pants and jacket he wore did not say much for his fashion sense but fit his personality perfectly. As he began the tour, his pronounced British accent flowed from beneath his drooping mustache, and his blue eyes widened with every point he made.

Nora swiveled her head, feasting her eyes on the stunning architecture. She could sense the history within the abbey walls. She flashed Ben a brilliant smile and mouthed, "Thank you."

Throughout the tour, Ben added a few points the tour guide failed to mention. When the tour was over he showed Nora where he liked to sit inside the ancient church. He said it was the best view. They sat together, quietly taking in the grandeur and noticing the tourists passing by with cameras around their necks or cell phones in the air.

They exited Westminster Abbey and crossed the road so Nora could take some snapshots. "Ben, let me get a picture with the both of us." She held the camera at arm's length, faced it toward her, with Westminster Abbey behind her, and motioned him in closer. They pressed their cheeks together, and she snapped the picture. Their heads remained close while they viewed the shot. "What's next?" She peeked up at him and blinked as a fat rain drop landed on her cheek. Ben's thumb traced the wet trail down her cheek. Then *splat ...splat... splat...* Nora held her breath. *Is he going to kiss me?* Ben pulled an umbrella out of his back pocket, and they huddled together under it. *No, he wasn't going to kiss me,* she chided herself.

"Not far from here is the Cavalry Museum, if you don't mind walking in the rain."

Horses–of course. Nora found his interest in animals boyishly sweet. "Or we can walk over and see the House of Parliament and Big Ben."

"How could I say no to the Cavalry Museum?" Her heart skipped a beat at his winsome smile.

"Good. If we hurry we can catch the Changing of the Queen's Life Guard parade. The horses are remarkably fine. That was always fun for me as a child. I think you'll like it," he said enthusiastically while he propelled her in the right direction. The rain was bothersome, but not torrential. Nora liked that they huddled together. Ben put his arm around her when he saw her shiver in the cooler air the rain had brought. The parade was just starting as they walked up. When it had finished, they went into the Household Cavalry Museum and watched the troopers working with their horses. Then they strolled around, looking at exhibits. She found it surprisingly interesting and was glad Ben had suggested it.

The rain ceased, but the clouds still looked threatening. They stopped at the House of Parliament, where Nora snapped more photographs. By then it was well past noon. Ben asked, "Have you gone to a chippy or a chip shop?"

"I don't think so. What is that?" British slang always made her laugh.

"It's where you get a plate of greasy batter-fried fish and golden potatoes. You should try it at least once," he urged.

"Oh, fish and chips, of course. Okay, I'm up for that. Do you know a good place?"

He raised his eyebrows. "Indeed I do."

"Lead the way." Nora was surprised when they stopped at a roadside meal truck with a pretty long line. "A food truck?" She said, skeptical.

"Trust me. These trucks park all over London, and they have the freshest fish. Their batter is delicious too." They waited for about ten minutes to get their bags of steaming food and cold drinks. "Follow me." Ben led Nora down an alleyway and up a flight of stairs to a gate that opened to a park. Circling the park was a thick stone wall, which happened to be a perfect place to sit and have a picnic. They followed the wall until it ran under a large old tree. The rest of the wall was wet from the rain, but there, under the canopy of leaves, the wall was dry. They sat down and dug in.

Nora's stomach grumbled when she opened her paper bag and smelled the fried food, sending the pleasure center in her brain into overdrive. "Oh man, this is good!" she said after the first bite. Ben nodded, his mouth full. After lunch they wandered through the park in the direction of Ben's car. As they reached the car, Nora got a call from Bree, who wanted to know if they were done touring and ready to meet up. She said Ashley had gotten off work and was on her way to meet them for coffee. Ben nodded when Nora relayed the address.

It started to pour down rain as Ben turned over the motor. "We got lucky!" she exhaled. They stayed dry during the half hour it took to walk to the car from the park. The rain had lightened up some by the time they reached the coffee shop. They gathered with their friends indoors, ignoring the drenched tables outside. Nora cradled a hot cup of coffee in her cold hands. *So much for a warm summer day*.

Ben ordered tea to go and hung around for a few minutes. "I need to pick up a couple things while I'm here in the city. Are you sure you don't mind if I run off?" He hesitated before leaving.

Nora replied, "Of course not. Ben, thank you. I had a wonderful day."

Bree, Ashley, and Corrine watched Ben and Nora closely.

"Me too." He smiled at her and then looked at the girls. "I'll see you ladies later."

"Wow, I haven't seen Ben like that in a long time," Corrine said as she watched him dash away in the rain.

"Like what?" Nora asked.

"Well...like interested in someone besides his horses," Corrine stated matter-of-factly.

"We are just friends. I don't think he's interested... He hasn't... And anyway, I live in America." Nora stammered through her statement, darting her gaze at each of their doubtful faces.

"Nora, my brother takes his time deciding what he wants. He's very cautious–especially with relationships. He's had a few girlfriends, and a couple who broke his heart. He claims he's waiting to find Mrs. Right. Don't discount him yet." Corrine sipped her tea.

"Yeah, you might have to make the first move," Ashley inserted as she fiddled with the tag on her teabag. Bree only offered her a sympathetic smile, because she knew Nora had just broken off a relationship with Antonio.

Nora shrugged and changed the subject.

Their weekend was rounded out with a ride on the London Eye, another great dinner at a Thai restaurant, and a late night of pool shooting at Evan's apartment. On Sunday, Bree and Evan announced to everyone they were seeing each other exclusively.

When Ben said good-bye to Nora, he suggested she return soon and invited her to stay at Westborough Meadows. Nora promised she would call him when she finished up her work commitment for the next month.

Chapter Sixteen

Nora worked a trip to Denmark. It was her first time visiting Copenhagen, and she loved it. Her fellow flight attendants regularly picked up the trip and guided Nora to their favorite eateries and sites. The colorful buildings along the Nyhavn Canal offered a delightful lunch spot for watching the boats' flags waving in the breeze. The city was small enough to walk around, and they navigated the on/off tour bus with ease. Nora marked this city as a favorite to return to.

In Philadelphia, the air conditioner ran constantly in their brownstone during the sweltering month of August. Nora arrived home before Bree, sprinting to turn down the air first thing. With them both traveling for three or four days at a time, they tried to be conscientious about the heating and air bills. Before Bree headed off to Pittsburgh for two weeks of international flight attendant training, Nora spent the day with her. Bree had some errands to run, so they went together and stopped for lunch.

Sergei joined Nora and Bree for dinner that evening. They ordered take-out Chinese food because it was too hot to cook. Bree turned in early, grumbling she had to get up at the crack of dawn to catch her flight to Pittsburgh for training. Nora promised her it was worth it. Sergei congratulated Bree again on her new position as Bree left the room.

When they were alone, Sergei surprised Nora. "Nora, I was wondering if you would like to go to Russia with me...to St. Petersburg?"

"When are you going?" Russia wasn't a destination for her airline.

"I was thinking in perhaps a couple of weeks. I'm going to visit my family for a few days, and I thought you would like to come along. I'll show you around." He shrugged his shoulders, as if it was no bother.

This visit would give her a chance to get to know him better and see if there might be more to their friendship. She wasn't dating anyone, particularly not Ben, who she wished she was dating, but she couldn't dwell on that. "Sergei, I'd love to see St. Petersburg, but don't I need a visa?"

"Yes. I will help you apply."

"Wow, that would be amazing. Okay. I can use a few personal days." Nora trusted she'd be in good hands with Sergei.

It turned out the visa was no problem to get. It was waiting for her when she arrived home after working a trip to Germany. It had rained heavily the entire three days she was there. She used that time, hunkered down in her hotel room, to read up on St. Petersburg, Russia.

Nora got Sergei a buddy pass on her airline, so he could fly with her free of charge as far as Helsinki, Finland. From there they purchased tickets to St. Petersburg's airport. Then they took a cab to an affordable hotel Sergei selected. They got rooms across the hall from each other. Sergei explained to Nora his family's apartment, while nicer than most, was small and had only two bedrooms. He preferred staying in a hotel. He didn't want Nora going anywhere without him. St. Petersburg was a large city and not very safe for a single American woman to walk around alone.

The hotel was old, with outdated décor. She hung up four days' worth of clothes in the tiny closet and was just finishing freshening up when there was a tap at her door. The layover in Helsinki had been a long one, and it was now well into the evening. They agreed to get some dinner and turn in relatively early.

"Is your room okay?" Sergei inquired, after Nora opened the door.

"It's fine." She wasn't going to complain. She'd stayed in many places overseas, and this one was the worst, but she didn't care. She was just happy to be in St. Petersburg to experience something new. "Where are we going to eat?"

"There is a place not far. We can walk from here. It has good Russian food. Not a tourist place–a place for local Russians." He used his hands for emphasis. "I chose this hotel because we can walk to a lot of places. You will see the traffic in St. Petersburg is very bad."

The sounds of the city were loud, and the streets, as in any other bustling city, were littered with papers and trash. They stopped in front of a generic building with a front window advertising food on a sun-bleached poster. Sergei opened the door for her. Inside the dark paneled dining room they sat at a linen covered table for two, and Sergei described the food options to Nora before he ordered in Russian. Before the meal, a plate of pickled items was served. "It's custom," he said. Nora also tried some berry-flavored water she found slightly tart but tasty. Their dinner was a sort of stew: meat and root vegetables in a thick gravy. She scarfed down every bite.

In the hotel, they went to their separate rooms, and she fell right to sleep. The next morning she met Sergei downstairs in the hotel restaurant for breakfast. Sergei sat in a corner with a cup of coffee, reading a paper. Nora waved when he looked up; she gestured with her thumb to say she was headed to the coffee station.

She returned with a mug and a plate with a hard-boiled egg, a slice of bread, and slices of cheese. The cheese looked like it had been out too long; the edges were dried and curling upward. "Good morning." She settled in the chair next to his. Besides the wafting aroma of coffee, she could smell Sergei's fresh shower scent. She briefly wondered what was up with her new superhuman, hormone-infused power to sniff out the aromas of men she was attracted to. She had enjoyed Antonio's musky smell. Ben had a distinct and attractive scent too. She shook her head to clear her thoughts.

"Good morning. Did you sleep well?" Sergei asked, looking over his newspaper.

"Like the dead." Nora felt fully recharged. "You mentioned meeting up with your sister today. Is she free?" She buttered the slice of bread and sank her teeth into it.

"Yes, Lydia is free this morning. She wants to take you to the Hermitage Museum. It is one of the world's most famous art museums."

"I read about the Hermitage. I picked up a book on St. Petersburg at that used bookstore on Haven Street in Philly. The museum is housed in that pretty blue palace…" She stopped, trying to recall the name.

"The Winter Palace." He grinned at her memory lapse, flashing his teeth. "Lydia has a car and will pick us up in about ten minutes."

"Okay!" Nora sliced her egg, laid it on one of the hard cheese slices, and chewed.

"Do you remember that Lydia is an English-speaking tour guide?"

Nora nodded as she savored the egg and cheese flavors.

"I've arranged for her to take us around for the next couple of days."

Nora choked down some bitter coffee and told herself to stick with tea for the rest of this trip.

As they left the hotel Sergei's sister called his name and walked toward them. They hugged, and he introduced the women to each other. Nora observed that Lydia's blue eyes, like her brother's, sparkled with tears; clearly she was happy to see Sergei after so long.

Lydia led them to her compact car, parked across the street. Nora sat in the backseat and Sergei sat next to his sister; he was apparently complaining to her in Russian about the traffic. Lydia always spoke in English, to be polite.

The traffic was horrendous. The short distant to the Hermitage took almost forty-five minutes. Lydia dropped them off and went to park the car. Sergei walked Nora to the river's edge to enjoy the water views. They watched the boats motor by under overcast skies. Several minutes later Lydia approached and called out, "I've got the tickets," waving them in the air. They followed Lydia inside the massive building. She directed them around the crowds of tourists to a quieter section of the enormous museum. Lydia was very knowledgeable, and she maneuvered them effortlessly through the long halls. Nora was fascinated.

"There is so much more to see, but I have to leave you two now. I have a private tour here in a few minutes. Please finish exploring on your own." She looked at her watch. "I'll see you soon." Lydia disappeared into the crowd.

"Your sister is so sweet. Her English is very good."

Sergei nodded and pulled a map out of his jacket pocket. "Do you want to go down to the café and eat something and then wander around some more?"

"Good idea. I'm thirsty. It's a little warm in here."

Afterwards they waited out front for Lydia to finish her afternoon tour and then inched their way through the traffic to Sergei's parents' apartment. Lydia parked the car in an alleyway, and they walked to the front of the building, which ran the length of the block.

They walked down a corridor to an elevator and took it up six floors. Lydia used a key to open the door. "Hello, we are here," she called.

A woman rushed from the kitchen and met them with open arms. "Sergei!" She hugged her son around his waist.

"Mama." He hugged her and kissed her on the cheek. "You look well." He held her at arm's length and then turned to grab Nora's hand. "Mama, this is Nora."

"Hello, Nora." She shook Nora's outstretched hand. "I am Svetlana."

"She is the friend I spoke to you about who lives across the street from me in Philadelphia. She is a flight attendant."

"Of course." The mother only had eyes for her son. "Look at you; it's been too long, Sergei." Nora could see the love in her eyes and was touched by the tender moment.

"Come. Let me get you something to drink."

The apartment was bigger than Nora expected. Although the furniture looked a little worn, the place was nicely decorated. Lydia told her mother she would fix the tea and disappeared into the galley kitchen. Sergei spoke about living in America. He said, "Things are better since I met Nora and Bree, her roommate."

"We've been living there for five months, since March," Nora added. "Sergei has been great. One night he even made me beef stroganoff. I was very impressed."

Sergei laughed, shaking his head, his eyes twinkling at his mother.

"Sergei, I have not seen you in two years, and now you bring home a girl you've cooked dinner for," his mother replied in a teasing voice.

Lydia entered with a tray and set it on the coffee table. She and her mother exchanged looks.

"What is new with you, Mama?" Sergei glanced briefly at Nora before opening the next subject.

They chatted for a while before Svetlana excused herself. "I am going to prepare dinner, before your father gets home."

"Do you need help?" Nora offered.

"No. You are a guest. Lydia will help me." Lydia followed her mother into the kitchen.

"Is this where you grew up?" Nora asked.

"Yes, my parents got this apartment when they got married. Lydia and I shared a bedroom until I left for my job in America." He chuckled. "Now she has it all to herself."

When his father arrived, introductions were made. Once the men had a chance to catch up, the group ate a dinner of pork chops, potatoes, carrots, and parsnips and shared a pot of tea. Lydia poured, using a strainer to hold back the loose tea leaves. For dessert, Lydia served custard. "We made your favorite." She beamed at her brother.

Nora loved being emerged in new customs. She thanked his parents before she and Sergei left. He had arranged to borrow Lydia's car for the night. They would pick Lydia up in the morning and drive out of the city to visit Peter the Great's palace, Peterhof.

Since the hour wasn't late and the traffic had lightened up, Sergei drove Nora past a few touristy sites. He pulled over just down the river from a cathedral and they got out. "This is the Church of the Savior on the Blood. And it is the best time to see the church, at night when it is lit up," Sergei said.

"Wow, this is beautiful," Nora replied, in awe.

It was everything she had seen in magazines about what a Russian church would look like. It featured beautiful gold-draped onion domes and incredible stonework. The lights reflected in the water of the canal. *This is a truly magical sight.* She took out her camera. "I never want to forget this place." She snapped away.

After another hour of touring the city, Sergei parked Lydia's car near the hotel. When they stopped in front of her room to say goodnight, Nora remarked, "This city has some beautiful treasures. Thank you for bringing me." She stopped and looked up into his eyes. "Why did you?"

"I wanted some time with you, a few days, just us. I want you to get to know me better. I don't want you to hesitate when I try to kiss you again."

"You want to kiss me!" She laughed, waving him off. "Goodnight."

He smiled at her, but the look in his pale blue eyes told her a very clear story. She understood Sergei wanted their friendship to move to the next level. But she smiled at him and opened her door, waving to him as she closed it behind her.

Nora sprawled on the bed, looking up but not seeing a crack in the ceiling. Sergei was thoughtful and protective, tough when he needed to be and gentle when he wanted to be. *He brought me all this way to spend time with him. He wants me to get to know him better. If that isn't commitment, what is?* Why was it so hard for her to figure out if there could be something more than friendship? Nora knew she needed to move on after her torrid relationship with Antonio. And as much as she would love to get involved with Ben, it would be a complicated long-distance relationship she didn't think either of them considered viable.

Chapter Seventeen

She woke to a gorgeous sunny morning. Nora ate the same breakfast as yesterday but switched from coffee to tea. They donned their sunglasses and drove to pick up Lydia. She was pacing outside. "I'm glad to see my car is in one piece."

"Get in the back, I'll drive," Sergei said out the driver's window. Lydia hesitated. Nora figured she must have decided against arguing with her big brother, because she opened the sedan's door and climbed in. They inched their way out of the city and drove into the country. It took about an hour to arrive at Peterhof. As soon as they walked through the elaborate gates Lydia started spewing facts about the famous royal residence. They maneuvered through room after room. Sergei seemed impressed by his little sister's extensive knowledge of the palace's history, including its recent renovations.

"We saved the best for last, in my opinion. The fountains and gardens are spectacular. Have a look at the Grand Cascade. This parkland represents nearly two centuries of aristocratic European fashion in park design." Lydia pointed down toward the magnificent fountains and waterways that led to the sea. The weather was perfect for walking around. Both Sergei and Lydia commented it was rare.

Nora asked Lydia to take a picture of her and Sergei with the fountains and Peterhof in the background. He put his arm around her, and they said "Cheese." They wandered around the grounds for over an hour. A pavilion by the sea housed a café, and they got a little something to eat.

"It's so lovely here with these sweeping vistas, ornate statues, and spectacular flowers. I hate to leave." Nora feasted her eyes one last time on the Grand Cascade as they headed toward the car. Svetlana had invited them for dinner; Nora didn't want to go empty-handed, so she asked Sergei to stop at a gift shop, where she purchased two pretty scarfs. After dinner she gave one to Svetlana in appreciation for the delicious dinner and one to Lydia for being an amazing tour guide. They both gave her hugs and thanked her over and over.

While they sat sipping tea after dinner, Sergei leaned over and asked Nora, "Did you happen to pack anything to wear to go out to a club?"

"Yes, as a matter of fact I did. I'm always prepared." They hadn't talked about nightlife in St. Petersburg, but on their last night there she thought it might prove interesting to sample what the city offered. "Why? Do you have a place in mind?"

"Lydia called a bunch of my old friends about hanging out tonight. Do you want to join us?" At her nod they finished up their tea and said their good-byes to Sergei's family. Sergei drove them to the hotel to get ready.

Nora thought she would try something different from wearing her hair up. She'd brought along her jumbo Velcro hair rollers. She rolled them into her hair before she showered, hoping the steam would help set them. Once dressed, she let her hair down. The waves cascaded to her elbows. She spritzed it and moved on to her jewelry. She latched long silver drops in each ear and slid on a set of bangle bracelets.

Sergei rapped on her door. Nora called, "Come on in."

"Wow!" he said his gaze landed on her.

Nora wore a lavender halter dress and strappy wedge sandals.

"Wow yourself. Good color on you." Sergei looked handsome in a light blue button-down shirt, almost the shade of his pale eyes. His face was freshly shaven, and he smelled great. Nora grabbed her small clutch on the way out the door.

"Mmm, my friends are going to go crazy when they see you," Sergei warned with a flash of teeth as he followed her down the corridor.

"Oh, stop!" She laughed.

They swung by to pick up Lydia, who wore an emerald green blouse with a short black skirt and heels. She added a barrette studded with dark green stones to her hair.

The club was large, and Nora was surprised to hear American and British music playing. A group of guys yelled out to Sergei.

While the guys made their noisy hellos, Nora followed Lydia to the bar. Nora usually managed to turn a few heads when she went clubbing with Bree, Bree being the main attraction. But here she felt like everyone was looking at her. It was like "American" was stamped across her forehead. When guys moved in on her, Sergei slid his arm around her and whispered in her ear, "If you get tired of getting hit on I can be your boyfriend."

"Okay. You are my boyfriend tonight." She didn't want to fend for herself with this group of foreign men.

His eyebrows rose at her declaration. "Well, let me introduce you to my friends. They all speak English, but some not very well."

She turned toward the stunned faces of Sergei's friends.

"This is my girlfriend, Nora." He called off their names as they waved or shouted hello. There were seven of them; two were with girlfriends. Sergei got Nora and Lydia drinks from the bar, and not long after, shots appeared for the comrades. Sergei's loudest friend convinced her to do two shots. His friends were funny and jovial, and one tugged Lydia out on the dance floor. Another asked Sergei if he minded if he danced with his girlfriend. Sergei defaulted to Nora, lifting his eyebrows at her.

"Sure." Nora felt buzzed and safe under Sergei's watchful eye. After she danced for two songs, the DJ played an old favorite of hers, and she shook her stuff more vigorously than she planned on. She noticed Sergei stood at the edge of the dance floor, talking to a friend who was pointing to Nora, shaking his head in amazement. He put his palms up as if to say, "You are with her? Go figure." Sergei good-naturedly shoved him aside.

The night was coming to a close, and they walked outside to say good-bye to his friends. Lydia told Sergei she had a ride home, and she left with the guy she danced with.

"It was good to meet you, Nora. Take care of this guy, eh?" said the loudest of Sergei's friends. "I'm glad to see you happy, comrade." He tipped his head toward Nora. "Eh?"

"Thanks, my friend. You take care of yourself." The men hugged, slapping each other's backs.

Sergei and Nora walked the couple of blocks to Lydia's car. Nora slid inside, saying, "My feet hurt." She untied her strappy shoes, kicked them off, and curled her feet under her on the seat. She faced Sergei as he pulled away from the curb. Resting her temple on the headrest, she studied his profile. *He's ruggedly handsome and oh how his thick shoulders fill this small space.* With a long day of touring and a long night of partying behind them, Nora drifted off to sleep and woke when the motor turned off.

"Stay there," Sergei said. Nora held her shoes by the straps, her purse strap looped around her elbow. Sergei came around, opened her door, and effortlessly lifted her out of the car. He kicked the door closed with his foot and carried her to the hotel.

"Sergei! I can walk!" she protested.

"You have no shoes on."

Nora tried to wiggle free, but he held her in his vice-like grip. No one was in the lobby, not even at the front desk, which was a relief to Nora because she was embarrassed at being carried. He pressed the button and the elevator doors opened.

"We are inside. You can put me down now."

His response was to jostle her so she tightened her grip around his neck.

The doors opened on their floor, and he asked for Nora's key. She peered over his shoulder while she opened her clutch and fished around for the key, the old-fashioned kind, not a keycard. She slid the key into the slot and twisted it. After hearing the click, Sergei turned the knob, using the hand tucked under her knees, to open the door. The door closed behind them.

He slowly let her feet slide to the floor, bodies pressed together. When he slid his hands up her back under the soft curtain of her hair, her arms came to rest at her sides. She dropped her shoes and let the clutch slip from her fingers. The bangle bracelets sliding down her arm clanked in the silence of the room. She searched his face, knowing what he wanted, but she hesitated this time, not making the first move. He told her before he wanted to kiss her. So she waited. It was his move. He held her to him.

She tilted her face, opening her mouth slightly, ready to receive his kiss.

"Nora, I want to kiss you."

I know and I want to kiss you!

The room was in semidarkness, the city lights filtering through the window. She could see his face filled with desire. His eyes fluttered closed as he dipped down, and his lips brushed hers only once before they captured hers. His gentle kiss deepened, and she slid her palms up his arms and around his neck. She didn't want to think; she just wanted to feel. She was very buzzed, and his kisses aroused her.

They shuffled toward the bed, pausing at the foot of it as she clumsily unbuttoned his shirt. He tugged her dress up so he could access the supple skin of her behind, kissing all the while. When she touched his bare chest her fingertips tingled at the sensation of his hard muscles. She pressed her palms flat against his pecs and then slowly slid them down his abs, savoring every ripple. The belt stopped her progress. The buckle locked her out. This caused her to pause and to think. She stepped aside, holding her hands up, halting him. She drew in a deep, shaky breath as doubt twisted in her gut—a feeling that she should not continue. She had been caught up in the moment. Sergei tried to pull her to him, and Nora felt the tiniest flicker of panic.

"I'm… It's… I'm not ready. Sergei, I'm sorry." She pushed her dress down and gave him a sheepish look.

"It's okay. We can stop." His rough voice was barely above a whisper, but it was like a loud warning in her ears. She looked into his pale blue eyes in the dim light. *Damn, he is patient.*

"Get some rest. Tomorrow is our last day together."

Nora felt the tension ease from her shoulders. Sergei leaned in and kissed her forehead, lingering for a brief moment. *He is so sweet. And I'm torturing him.*

After retrieving his shirt, Sergei left her room. Nora covered her eyes with her hands. She had almost done something she would have regretted. She felt slightly dizzy. *I'm practically hyperventilating.* Needing to lie down, she unzipped her dress where she stood and dropped it to the floor. She flung her bra away. Her bangle bracelets dropped, clunking to the floor. She climbed into bed and drifted off into a restless night's sleep.

The next morning her head throbbed. When she tried to swallow, her mouth was cotton dry. She screwed her eyes shut against the pillow, wondering what had occurred the night before with Sergei. She cracked one eye open to survey the situation.

Her clothes were strewn around. Focusing on the alarm clock, she remembered Sergei had gone to his own room hours before. She gingerly crawled out of bed, pulling the sheet around her naked body. She went straight to her toiletry bag to find something for her pounding head, and she drank every drop of water that was left in her water bottle from the day before. After all the alcohol she'd consumed, Nora felt dehydrated. She eyed the tap, not sure if she should drink out of it, but she hoped one glassful would not upset her stomach.

She didn't want to think about last night, but after the pain medicine kicked in and the sweaty stickiness from dancing was washed away under a hot shower, she replayed everything in her head.

It was their last day in St. Petersburg and already late morning. She dressed, wondering where Sergei was. She was pinning her hair up when she heard a knock. When he entered he bent and kissed her. It was a gentle brush of lips like the kisses old lovers shared. "Good morning," he said. "I brought you some coffee and something to eat."

"Mmm, you are so sweet." She took the cup with a thank you. After a few sips of strong coffee Nora felt the hangover clearing. Sergei pulled from a paper bag what looked like a glazed croissant, and he handed it over to her with a flash of a smile. She nibbled on it, all the while contemplating what to say about last night. All she could come up with was how delicious her breakfast was.

Sergei ate his in three bites and told Nora Lydia would be by in twenty minutes to take them to see Pushkin. "We'll have time to see the palace and stop by to say good-bye to my mother before Lydia drops us off at the airport."

"Okay. It'll only take me a few minutes to pack everything up." She learned to live out of her suitcase and had never left anything behind so far, but she glanced around the room to make sure she hadn't carelessly left something in an "out of normal" place. She spotted her bangle bracelets on the floor where she had discarded them last night.

Sergei broke her train of thought. "I'm going to get my things together."

Nora nodded and watched him close the distance between them. He bent and brushed a soft kiss across her lips again, but ended it there. She allowed him to do so.

"I'll be right back." His Russian accent seemed thicker in his native country. Nora nodded, giving him a sweet smile, and then he was gone.

She bent to pick her bracelets up off the floor and prayed she could shake this feeling of regret.

Nora stood outside her townhouse in Philadelphia with Sergei, thanking him again for the lovely time in Russia. "I truly wouldn't want to have visited with anyone but you. You and your sister were amazing guides, and I couldn't have asked for a more authentic visit. It is a trip I won't soon forget," she concluded sincerely.

Sergei wrapped his arms around Nora in a big hug, lifting her toes off the ground. Captured in his arms, he gave her a lingering kiss. When her feet returned to the ground, Nora retreated a little too quickly, which she thought probably wasn't lost on Sergei. "I have to fly out soon," she said vaguely, hoping to discourage the question "When am I going to see you again?"

"Yes, I have to leave as well. Tomorrow. I will call you in a couple days after I return."

Nora nodded and made her way up the steps. She paused with her key in the door to look at him. As he crossed the street to his townhouse, Sergei carried his duffle bag slung over his broad shoulder. *He really is so sweet.* Based on appearance, someone else might not necessarily label him sweet, but that's what she liked about him. She knew the real Sergei. She was lucky he cared for her.

Stepping inside, her heart skipped a beat when she saw Bree standing at the window. Nora could tell by her friend's raised eyebrows she had been watching them.

"Hello. It looks like you two had a nice trip," she said slyly.

"Hey, Bree." Nora stashed her luggage by the stairs and headed for the kitchen. "Yeah, Saint Petersburg was amazing." As she moved around the kitchen and poured a glass of water she gave a monologue about the places she'd visited and how great meeting Sergei's family was.

"And?" Bree prompted. As Nora innocently stared at her, Bree pulled a face. "Sergei and the kissing I just saw! Is there something I should know?"

"Ugh." Nora glanced heavenward. "There've been a few times when we've had this...tension... This attraction. On the last night things got steamy, and we almost hooked up," she admitted.

"I knew it! I thought it was weird he asked you to go to Russia with him." Bree pulled out a chair and sat down, waiting to hear more. With a roll of her eyes Nora sat across from her.

"We had separate hotel rooms. It's not like we were planning this or anything. We went to a club, and I drank too much. We ended up in my room. But I stopped it. It just didn't feel right." Nora shrugged, not knowing how else to explain how she felt. She didn't mention the earlier kisses.

"It's obvious he is interested in you, but I didn't know you were interested in him." Bree said. "So? Why did you stop it? Was he a bad kisser or something?" she joked.

"Noooo!" Nora laughed, relieved to feel the mood lighten a little. "To tell the truth, after my love affair with Antonio... Well, he might have ruined it for other guys. And besides, I think a need a little break. Antonio was intense."

"I'm jealous!" Bree sighed dramatically.

"Shut up!" Nora chuckled.

Nora stood, placed her glass in the sink, and leaned against the counter. "Sergei is such a nice guy, you know. I just hope I don't mess up our friendship when I tell him I'm not interested." Nora's eyes focused on the floor, but she was far away in thought. "Anyway..." Nora feigned a cheery voice. "How are things with you? How was training?"

"Great." Bree beamed. "I'm officially an international flight attendant. Training went well. We had to become qualified on all the big international planes." Nora had done the same when she'd gone to training. Being qualified meant they needed to be able to operate emergency windows and doors and know where the emergency equipment was stored and how to use it on each type of aircraft.

"How did the exams go?" Nora remembered memorizing the European airport codes. At the time she was glad their flights were limited to one other continent, which made codes easier to learn, but now she wished their airline would expand to include Asia or South America.

"I did fine." Bree collected her thoughts. "I know this is going to sound crazy, but while I was in Pittsburgh the trainer was telling me about other hubs, international hubs, that we could work out of." Nora knew about this, but she didn't say anything. "There is a hub in London. We could transfer. Do you think you'd ever consider moving? You already have great friends in England." She added, "We could still be roomies."

"Wow!" Nora was stunned. She could lose Bree *or* she could move to England. Ben's face came to mind, and longing stirred within her. Would Ben want her there? Nora didn't know. Ben had kept their friendship casual. What about her family? But more importantly, she couldn't imagine losing her friendship with Bree. Now they were both flying international, they were supposed to take every city by storm…together.

"Bree, I'm glad things are going well with Evan, but it's only been a month or so."

Bree held up her hand. "No, no, you are right about Evan. I'm not just considering moving there for him. I miss my old friends. I know we've only had this job about six months, but I feel like I'm ready to keep moving forward. I think I want to move to England. I always wanted to live there when I was younger, and I feel like now is the right time. Really, the only thing holding me here is you. So, Nora, come with me!" she pleaded. "At least think about it. I can't even put in the request for thirty days."

"Well, I'll think about it, but right now I need a shower and some food."

"Thanks for not saying no. I'll call for a pizza?"

"Veggie?" Nora suggested.

"Yeah, then we can skip the salad." Both girls grinned at each other.

Nora grabbed her bag on the way up the stairs and made a mental checklist. She needed to do laundry, refill some items in her toiletry bag, sew a loose button on her uniform, find the needle and thread kit she'd stashed somewhere in her room, and iron her uniform shirts. Keeping herself prepared for each trip was tedious. Living out of a suitcase left her feeling as if she didn't belong anywhere, because she was never in one place long enough. At the same time, it allowed her freedom to seek out where she wanted to eventually plant herself.

She pulled out her cell phone to look at the time. She noticed a missed call from Antonio. The thought crossed her mind it was getting late in Italy. She compared spending time with Sergei to spending time with Antonio. For a few moments, Nora reminisced about Antonio's touch. *Oh, what is wrong with me!* She needed to forget about Antonio and figure out how to deal with Sergei.

Chapter Eighteen

The warm days of August were over, and so was Nora's trip quota for that month. She took the first week in September off. In her room in Philadelphia, she unpacked her bag. Spontaneously picking up her cell phone, she called Ben.

At the sound of his voice Nora smiled. "Hey, Ben, how's the weather?"

"Nora! I was thinking of you today. I spent the morning with Duchess."

She clamped her teeth onto her bottom lip. *He was thinking about me!*

"Aw, how is she doing? And her foal–Grand Duke, right?" They talked for twenty minutes before Nora got around to why she was calling.

"I have this week off and was thinking of coming over for my riding lesson if you are still up for it. Only if you have any free time, of course."

"Yeah, you're welcome anytime. When can you come? I'll adjust my schedule." His accent was evident in the way he pronounced *shed-ju-l.*

"I know its short notice, but I can come the day after tomorrow. Bree's coming in tonight from a trip, and she wants to see Evan. We'll fly together, but she's going to stay in the city. I'm not sure what day she's returning to Philly." Nora hoped he remembered offering her a place to stay with him and his family in the country.

"I can pick you up, and you can stay with us. We have plenty of room. What time do you get in?" Nora was relieved he remembered and excited she would get some alone time with Ben.

When she hung up she hugged herself. She almost hadn't called. Nora had done a lot of soul searching over the last couple weeks; she wanted to see Ben again, and this time she was going to make a move. She didn't want to look back and regret missing an opportunity with Ben. If things went well after this trip, she would seriously consider transferring to England with Bree.

In the meantime, Nora kept things casual with Sergei. She had avoided seeing him for a couple weeks, which was easy since they had opposite work schedules. They spoke briefly on the phone before Nora caught her flight to London. She told him she was visiting friends and she wanted to talk to him when she returned.

Several times Antonio had called from Italy, and when she answered their conversations were always same. He said he missed her terribly and begged her to come visit him. She continued to keep him at bay but was secretly flattered he still pursued her.

Nora's mother and Victoria relentlessly called to see what she was up to and when she was coming home for a visit. "We never see you, Eleanor!" her mother said, tears choking her words.

Nora was going through a life change and needed space, but it was hard to disconnect from the family. They were a close family, and they'd been through a lot with the loss of Victoria's baby. She knew her parents were concerned when Nora told them about her trip to St. Petersburg with a Russian neighbor. They wanted to know who this man was. Nora sent photos and assured them Sergei was a good friend who was just showing her around. Nora felt guilty and promised to come home soon, but all Nora could think about was Ben. She missed *him*.

Nora flew into Heathrow, butterflies in her stomach. A million times she rehearsed in her mind how she would make a subtle but pointed move on Ben. But how would he react? Did he have feelings for her? Would she make a fool of herself? *I have to know.*

Evan met Bree and Nora in the baggage claim, holding a dozen red roses. The two lovers kissed and snuggled close, murmuring intimately to each other. Nora waited, giving them some privacy, until Bree broke their embrace.

"Hi, Evan. Beautiful flowers!" Nora exclaimed.

"Isn't he so sweet?" Bree and Evan exchanged an intimate glance.

"It's nice to see you, Nora. Do you have a ride?"

"Yes, Ben is picking me up. He offered to teach me to ride, so I'm finally taking him up on it. He'll be here soon."

Bree tucked her hand into Evan's arm. "Okay, I'll see you soon, and I'll call you." As Bree and Evan disappeared from view, Nora scanned the crowd for any sign of Ben. She spotted someone waving, smiling, and moving quickly toward her. She propelled herself and her bag forward until they clasped each other in a snug hug.

"You made it! How was your flight?" he asked. He took her bag, as any true gentleman would.

"The flight was fine. You just missed Bree and Evan."

In Ben's Land Rover, they drove into the green countryside. The rolling hills were dotted with sheep. Worn old stonewalls encircled cottages from another era. Ben tuned in a station on the radio and smiled when they both simultaneously commented, "I love this song!"

"Nora, I have to admit I was completely, but pleasantly, surprised when you called a few days ago. It's a long way to come for a riding lesson. Or maybe to an international flight attendant flying across an ocean to hang out for a few days is nothing?"

He seemed thrilled to see her, which was what she hoped for.

"I'm happy I had some free time to come visit." She beamed, "I am used to traveling a long ways in short bursts, like my recent trip to Denmark." They then chatted about her adventures in Demark.

When they reached the house, Molly the dog greeted them exuberantly at the door before Ben carried Nora's bag up to the guest room. "Wow, this is lovely!" Nora looked at the papered walls, the dark antique furniture, the lushly adorned bed linens, and the artwork depicting the English countryside. The windows were framed by satin material with a subtle pattern and edged in a heavy bullion fringe. The room was rich, yet cozy. "This whole house is amazing." She crossed to the window and grinned, seeing it looked over the stable yard.

Ben stepped next to her, glancing at the view. "I'm glad you think so. It's an amazing place to grow up." He stood so close Nora could smell his scent of fresh air and aftershave. "This room was my grandmother's when she visited." His eyes flickered through the room, as though he could picture his grandmother there. "She'd sit by this window, doing needlework. Said it had good light. I'd sit by her feet playing with my toys." He rested his gaze on Nora's face. "So I think you will be comfortable in here."

"I will." *This seems like a special room to him, and he purposely put me here. Should I kiss him now? His sexy lips are so close, and we are alone.* She swallowed the lump in her throat. *I just got here. Don't need to rush it.* She said quietly, "Thank you, Ben, for letting me stay here. I'm looking forward to my riding lessons. Although, I have to admit, I'm a little terrified. What if I fall? Or the horse doesn't like me or something?"

Ben laughed at her admission. "Well, falling off a horse does hurt. But we won't be doing any crazy galloping this week. And the horse I have in mind will adore you. I think you'll do okay."

Nora squeezed her eyes closed and said, "I hope you are right!"

"Let's get some lunch. Then we can start our first lesson," Ben suggested. "No sense wasting a perfectly good day."

Nora's hand flattened over her stomach. "I don't think I can eat. I'm too nervous."

"All right, then, we'll pack a lunch. Once you've successfully maneuvered your horse down to the river we'll picnic there. That's the best way to eat anyway, in my opinion." She nodded, pleased by his comment.

Ben asked about her footwear. She unzipped her bag and showed him the boots with heels she had packed on Bree's advice.

Nora freshened up and changed her clothes while Ben went to the kitchen to pack their picnic lunch. The kiss could wait. She needed to feel him out more and find the right time. What if he rejected her? How would she face him again—or Corrine, or Bree? She realized she was second-guessing herself.

She joined Ben in the kitchen. "Okay, I'm as ready as I'll ever be."

"Let's go." He grabbed the small cloth cooler bag from the counter. "After you." He pointed to the door and looked over at Molly. "Stay."

The day was warm for early September, but the shade cooled the air inside the stable. The smell of horses filled her nostrils. She could also discern the smell of leather and sweet hay.

Ben introduced Nora to her horse for their afternoon ride. "This is Stargazer."

Stargazer was on the smaller side, compared to the other horses she had seen in their stalls. "Hello there," she cooed.

Ben named each piece of equipment as he saddled the mare. Nora was a little surprised to see Ben lifting a western saddle onto Stargazer's back. *Oh, good, it's not one of those postage-stamp saddles!*

"I'll go saddle my horse while you two get acquainted." Ben left the stall.

Nora moved closer to Stargazer and stroked her soft coat. When he returned they led their horses out into the stable yard. His horse was outfitted in a brown leather English saddle, which looked insubstantial and slippery to her eyes, and she breathed a sigh of relief.

"Some people use a mounting block, but you look athletic enough to mount from the ground. And Stargazer's not too tall." Ben instructed her to put her left foot in the stirrup. Nora gave five noble attempts before she finally stepped up and swung her right leg over Stargazer and landed soundly in the saddle.

Nora beamed. She wasn't sure if mounting the horse had made her giddy or if it was Ben thinking she looked athletic that set her heart pattering. It was a plus he noticed her physique. He held the reins from the ground and led the horse in a wide circle so Nora could get a feel for the mare's movement. He gave her tips after he observed her rigid body struggling to find the right rhythm. With Ben's astute tutelage, it did not take Nora long to get the hang of it. Before long they were walking the horses east toward the river.

It took them just over an hour to reach the grassy knoll, a secluded spot between the forest and the river. In the narrow river large boulders protruded just above the water from its bed. Ben helped Nora down and then let the horses drink from the river before he tied them to a nearby tree. He fished around in the saddlebags behind Stargazer's saddle for a blanket and their lunch.

"Let me help you with that." Nora took a corner of the blanket, and they stretched it over the soft grass. They knelt and spread out the contents of the bag. Ben had packed two sandwiches, chips–Nora thought, *I have to remember to call them crisps*–two bottles of water, and a few oatmeal raisin cookies. They settled in and ate their sandwiches.

"Thanks, this is great." Nora took another bite.

"Sure. I didn't think I could mess up ham and cheese." Ben took a swig of water as she chuckled. "What did you think of your first riding lesson? Do you like being on horseback?"

"I love it. It's so freeing, and it makes me feel connected to nature." Nora stared off in the distance, feeling peaceful. "Riding through the countryside on the back of a large animal seems daunting right now, but I can see how it would be very relaxing." Nora focused her gaze on Ben. "I'm really happy I tried this. Thanks for teaching me."

"You are a natural. I'm glad you don't hate it." He grinned for a moment but his voice changed as he added, "I really enjoy riding and regret I'm too busy to take long outings. This is one of my favorite spots. And it's great for swimming during the warm summer days."

After their lunch they strolled along the river. Ben collected some flat stones while they chatted about various things. He stopped and skimmed the stones over the water. "It's my boyhood pastime–I can't resist!"

Nora thought his adorable grin was as boyish as his skipping game. She bent to retrieve two choice rocks near her feet and positioned one in her hand. "Mind if I try?" Nora threw the best skim of her life. One stone kissed the surface of the water five times before sinking into its depths.

"Wow, good one! I didn't know you were an expert," Ben joked.

"Two words: Summer. Camp."

They spent the next ten minutes hunting for more stones and watching each other try to beat the other's skims. Nora was proud that her five hops held the record.

"Okay, I can't beat you. I give up." Ben's green eyes twinkled with delight. "We'd best get back."

"Are we having dinner with your dad and Judy?" Nora asked as they folded the blanket.

"No, they are out of town for the week attending a wedding event. The son of a friend of my father's is getting married at the end of the week in London. Apparently there are going to be several days of golfing beforehand." He cast a glance at her. "So it's just us. Don't worry. Judy left us something for dinner, and I picked up some beer." He buckled the saddlebag. "I thought we could hang in tonight. I figured you might be tired after flying through the night. If you are up for it tomorrow night, there is a pretty cool pub in town where I hang out sometimes."

"I'm sorry to have missed your parents," Nora said as Ben helped her mount. He handed her the reins. After Ben was in the saddle, he clucked at the horses to move forward and they swayed along together. "It's thoughtful of you, Ben. The first night overseas is the hardest for me. Like everyone else, I don't sleep well on a plane. Relaxing and watching a movie sounds great."

When they returned, Keegan, the other veterinarian she met, welcomed Nora back to Westborough Meadows.

"Good to see you again, Keegan. Ben is teaching me to ride."

Ben tended to their mares as Keegan went on about Ben's special knack with horses, and added, "Corrine is the best horsewoman I've seen. Can ride any horse. Too bad Corrine didn't come by. She's really something to see."

Nora detected admiration in Keegan's voice.

Keegan needed Ben's attention about a stallion, so Nora took the opportunity to head inside and take a shower before dinner. After a soothing shower to wash away the dust, she checked her phone and saw Bree tried to call her.

The sun shone low on the horizon when Nora wearily entered the kitchen. The thought of spending the night alone with Ben in the empty house sent the butterflies in her stomach fluttering, but she felt so tired she didn't think anything could possibly happen that night.

Ben came in and began to wash his hands. Nora hung up her cell phone after leaving a quick message for Bree. Ben dried his hands while Nora filled Molly's bowl with fresh water at the sink next to him. He leaned his hip against the counter watching her with interest. "I noticed the bowl was empty." She realized she made herself at home; she shrugged and placed the dish down. Molly lapped the water noisily.

Nora wore yoga pants and a tank top, her long, wet hair dampening her shirt. "Everything go okay?"

Ben gave her a brief version of the stallion's medical condition as he dragged a large Dutch oven out of the refrigerator and lifted the lid.

Nora peeked over his shoulder. "Beef stew?"

"Yeah, it slow-cooked all day yesterday before they left, and it smelled delightful. I can't wait to try it." Ben reached in the cabinet for some ceramic crocks and loaded them with stew. He positioned them in the microwave, clicked the door closed, and then pressed buttons until Nora heard it *whirl* to life.

"I'll feed Molly. Where's her food?" Ben directed Nora to a cabinet stocked with canned dog food and various dog treats. Molly gave Ben a glance before following Nora around the room. When Nora noticed the dog's confusion she smiled at its owner. Continuing with her task she felt Ben's eyes following her as she fed his dog.

The hot beef stew, accompanied by some crusty bread, was on the table within a few minutes. Ben grabbed two pale ales from the refrigerator.

After their meal, they washed and dried the dishes side by side, Nora commenting on Bree and Evan's plans for their weekend in London.

"Another beer?" Ben asked as he opened the refrigerator.

"I'll just have some water." Nora already had a full belly and she knew another beer would put her right to sleep. She helped herself to a glass of water from the tap before they went into the den. "Should we watch a movie?"

"Yeah, I have a thriller in mind." He told her the name of the new release.

"Haven't heard of it." She dreaded watching anything chilling, truly hated scary movies. But she didn't want to be rude, so she replied, "Sounds cool."

Ben grabbed the remote control, switched on the movie, and lounged on the sofa. Nora sat in the armchair and curled her feet under her. Molly settled in on the floor under Ben's outstretched legs. After fifteen minutes, Nora transferred to the sofa next to Ben. At his questioning look, she explained, "This is creeping me out." Several times she covered her eyes. Ben offered to shut it off, but she toughed it out. Nora said a silent prayer when it ended. Ben switched over to a music station, and they chatted for a little while.

Nora's yawns and drooping eyelids forced Ben to declare, "It's bedtime."

They climbed the stairs, stopping at Nora's door. "There are extra blankets in that chest." Ben pointed to an ornately carved chest at the foot of the bed. "Sometimes summer nights can get cool."

"Thanks, Ben. Goodnight." Nora watched as he strode down the hall and went to the next room across the hall where Molly sat waiting in the doorway for him. He gave Nora a silent wave, and Molly followed him into the room. The door closed.

Nora brushed her air dried hair and changed into her summer pajamas. As tired as she was, she couldn't turn off the small lamp on the bedside table. Scary images from the movie were haunting her. *I am such a scaredy cat.* She got out of bed and grabbed a book from her suitcase. Chilled in her tank top and shorts, she dashed under the covers. Every time her eyes drifted closed, the twisted face of the killer in the movie entered her mind. *Why didn't I confess I can't watch that stuff?* Just then she heard a noise. She sat up, frozen, listening as the noise drew closer. Gooseflesh rose on her neck and she squeaked at the quiet knock on her door. The door remained open a crack, but she couldn't see anything in the dark hallway.

"Nora? Are you still awake?"

Relief washed over her when she recognized Ben's voice.

"*Ben!*" she whispered. "Come in."

The door swung slowly inward, and Ben emerged from the darkness wearing a plaid robe. He was barefoot, his hair damp.

He rested his shoulder against the doorframe. "Why are you still up? I saw your light on."

"Um… Well...I'm freaked out. I confess I can't watch scary movies. I'll never be able to fall asleep. I know I'm ridiculous." She offered him a pretty pout of her bottom lip.

"Nora, why didn't you tell me? I'm sorry." He raked his fingers through his hair, the wet points askew. "I should have asked what you preferred." He sat at the end of her bed.

"It's okay. I'm just silly. I slept with my parents for a week after I saw *Jaws*," she admitted.

A thought played across Ben's face. "Move over. I'll keep you company until you fall asleep."

"You don't have to do that!" Nora felt foolish. She shouldn't have said anything. *Ben is so thoughtful.* But she worried about how she would handle him lying in bed next to her.

"It's my fault. Move over."

Nora closed her book and placed it on the nightstand. She scooted to the other side of the double bed. Ben kept his robe on and rested on top of the bedding. Before he reached over to shut off the lamp, he turned to look at her face, washed clean of makeup. She watched his eyes move to her hair, which cascaded around her bare shoulders over the covers she held snug to her chest.

Ben whispered, "Goodnight."

He turned off the lamp, and she heard him swallow and sigh. He lay very still. Nora tried not to think about his warm, hard body next to her. Comforted, she stifled a yawn. "Thank you, Ben. Goodnight."

Chapter Nineteen

Without opening her eyes, Nora listened, but only heard the birdsong outside the window. She slid her hand into the space beside her, empty, the sheets cool. *Ben must have left after I fell asleep. How did I fall asleep with him next to me? Why didn't I have the energy to kiss him then?*

Nora found a note on the kitchen counter. MEET ME OUT IN THE STABLES. HELP YOURSELF TO BREAKFAST. After drinking a cup of coffee and eating a vanilla-bean scone, Nora made her way outside to look for Ben.

Keegan lead Nora to Ben "This is his hideaway," Keegan announced. "See you later."

Ben sat in his makeshift office, a horse stall at the end of a barn that looked like it belonged to the Nutty Professor. A large chalkboard rested on a stand with various drawings of horses and stats scrawled across its chalky surface. Several bookcases were stuffed with books, manuals, and papers. The counter space was cluttered with an assortment of medicinal jars. Ben's desk was home to thick bound books, and a laptop computer barely fit on the cramped workspace. *He looks nerdy in the* hottest *way!*

Ben looked up with a bright smile. "Hey there! I was just finishing up."

"Good morning. Take your time. If you need to get other things done, I can–"

"Nah," he cut her off. "I'm done." He shut the laptop lid and slipped it into a worn leather shoulder bag that hung on the back of his wooden swivel chair. When he stood up, Molly appeared from under his desk.

"This is quite an office." Her remark begged the question why he worked in this cramped space.

Ben grinned at his surroundings. Over time he had borrowed unwanted furniture from the main house. "There's a proper office up at the house–" he shrugged–"but it's too far from the horses. Besides, this place helps me think."

"It must be freezing in the winter."

He dismissed her concern. "I dress in layers, remember," he said as he passed her. He continued into the hall, and the dog followed.

They walked to the barn housing Stargazer, where Ben quizzed her on the equipment. Nora was sure she impressed him by remembering each item.

"Do you think you can saddle her?"

They worked together to tack up Stargazer, and a sense of confidence filled her as she walked the horse into the paddock. This time it only took two tries to mount the mare. Ben praised her success, and Nora blushed under his astute attention.

In the paddock, Ben taught her horses have distinct ways of walking and running: the walk, the trot, the canter, and the gallop. "The gait we'll work on today is the trot." He used a long lead to circle Stargazer around the yard at a trot, instructing her to rise and fall in what he called "posting" until he felt Nora could handle the movement. He removed the lead and allowed Nora to trot Stargazer. After a while, they led the horse to water before removing her tack and putting her in her stall. They took this time to go into the house to pack a lunch and use the loo.

"Where are we off to today?" Nora inquired as she helped him gather sandwich makings.

"We're off to the high ground. A trail will take us up into some higher hills–not too steep. The elevation will challenge your balance some and give you a different feel while riding." He wrapped the sandwiches in parchment paper. He pointed to the cookie jar on the counter. Nora knew he wanted her to get the oatmeal raisin cookies stored inside. She bagged two for each of them and broke the last cookie in the jar in half; they shared it. She rinsed the cookie jar in the sink, and he filled the cooler bag with drinks and a bag of baby carrots.

They saddled up, mounted and trotted off easily. Nora enjoyed the quicker pace. By the time they reached their destination Nora started to feel her inner thigh muscles, butt, and knees ache. Even her back began to hurt. Dismounting seemed like a great idea, and her legs nearly buckled when she hit the ground. She laughed and remarked, "Gosh, I thought riders just sat there!"

Ben took halters and leads from the saddlebags; he haltered and tied the horses loosely so they could graze on the bright green grass. He hung their bridles on a dead branch and returned with the blanket and lunch bag. "Are you holding up all right?"

"I'm fine. I'm just using muscles I haven't used–probably ever…" She pursed her lips. *I definitely need to exercise more. Riding is a great workout. I bet Ben is in amazing shape. He looks like it, even with his clothes on.* Then she wondered what he would look like with his shirt off. She cast her eyes downward to avoid his gaze, feeling guilty, as if he caught her with that naughty thought.

Ben chuckled at her comment. "We can picnic at the top of the ridge." He pointed to the hilltop, shaded by an old oak tree. "Do you think you can make it?" he teased.

"I think I can manage," she said and followed him up the hill. "Wow, look at that!" Just over the rise was a view of the whole valley. A village nestled there, three church spires pointing toward the blue sky. She swiveled to look down the hill they just ascended and then at the valley. She breathed in the cool, fresh air and sighed. "Ben, this is a great spot. How did you find this place?"

He laughed. "It's England. There are lots of great spots, especially by horseback." Nora turned. Ben had already spread the blanket under the shade. He stretched out across the woolen fabric, and she quickly joined him. He folded his arms behind his head and gazed up at the passing white clouds. She sat with her legs curled to one side and admired Ben's handsome face. The bright day had turned his eyes a lighter shade of gray-green. A relaxed grin rested on his full lips, and the breeze ruffled his hair.

"What a nice day. There is always a great breeze up here," he murmured.

Nora observed the outline of his flat stomach, his ribcage, and his smooth chest through his T-shirt. "It's lovely. You said you're too busy to ride, so how often do you come up here?" When he fixed his gaze on her, she fidgeted. She reached up and unfastened her hair clip to adjust her hair, loosened during the jostling ride. It cascaded down her back, and she raked her fingers through it until it poofed out like a cloud around her shoulders and streamed to her elbows. She made a mental note to visit the salon when she returned home. It was getting too long and was harder to keep coiled in a bun for her job.

"Aahhh." Ben seemed distracted by Nora's hair. "It's been awhile. To tell the truth, I'm always working. I only take time off to be with my family and friends when something is going on. I'd like to spend more time riding though." He gestured toward her. "Now, thanks to you, I have someone to enjoy this day with. Otherwise, I'd have my nose buried in a medical journal."

Nora scooted down on the blanket and lay back, mimicking Ben. She swung her hair over one shoulder and dropped her hair clip on the blanket as she got comfortable. Her hair fanned out to tickle his underarm, forcing him to roll to his side with his head propped on one elbow. "Yeah, I could get used to this," she sighed.

Ben stared at her intently.

This is it—the perfect moment to kiss Ben! She had dreamed of this moment so many nights. Her heart started to drum a little faster as she rose up on her elbows. Her tongue poked out and wet her lips… Ben leaned in. The world slowed around her—and then her cell phone buzzed in her pocket, making her jump. So startled, she shot up into a sitting position and yanked it from her pocket. *No! Antonio! Ugh. Figures he'd pick the perfect time to ruin my first kiss with Ben!*

"Sorry." She shot Ben a frazzled look.

Ben had sat up and suggested they eat lunch.

The moment was gone.

Nora cautiously broached the subject of last night. "So, umm, thanks again for coming to my rescue last night. I feel like such an idiot."

"I thought it quite endearing." His broad smile revealed his white teeth. *What a smile!* It made her heart pulse. "Actually, I'm not a big horror/thriller fan, but a friend of mine recommended that movie." After discussing movies awhile, they discovered they pretty much liked the same genres: dramas, historic epics, and comedies–the exception turned out to be romantic comedies. Nora rattled off several of her favorite British romantic comedies. Shaking his head, Ben said they were as silly as horror movies. Nora feigned disgust, but she couldn't help laughing at his typical male response.

After lunch, they mounted the horses and traveled along roadways and across fields before finally stopping at the river's edge to offer the horses some water. Achy, she dismounted and found a shady spot to sit and rest while Ben held the horses. She pulled out her cell phone and snapped a few pictures of Ben with the horses, a few more of Stargazer. She wanted a memento of this time spent with Ben even if it didn't go anywhere romantically; she knew they were becoming good friends. She made a mental note to ask Ben to take a snapshot of her on horseback so she could send it to her family. As she thought about her family it reminded her of her old life, and Nora was enjoying her new life. She missed her family, but she needed this space, this time, to reinvent herself.

Ben secured the horses. He sat next to her and stretched his long legs out across the grass. He pulled his cell phone out of his pocket and checked for messages. "I told Keegan to call me if there were any problems. I guess he has everything under control."

Nora tucked her cell phone into her pocket ignoring another missed call from Antonio, hoping he would get the hint. She wanted him to stop calling.

Nothing from Sergei. *Thank goodness.*

"Are you still up for going out tonight?" Ben inquired. "Want to see if Bree and Evan want to drive up?"

"Sure, I'm up for it. But Bree and Evan have dinner reservations tonight at some swank wine bar." Nora had mentioned it last night.

"Oh, right, you said. How does Bree like her transition to flying internationally?"

"She loves it, but she's only had one international trip so far. She seems really happy, and things are finally going well for her. In fact, when she came back from training last month she learned she could be based out of a European city." Nora's eyes swept across the scenery and settled on some far-off steeple. "She wants to transfer to London."

"Really! Aren't you two roommates?" His curious eyes searched her face.

"Yes. In fact, Bree's dad pays for us to live in a townhouse in a great neighborhood in Philly. He won't take my money. It is so nice of him. So I buy the food and pitch in in other ways when I can." Nora gazed over the pasture, seeing an uncertain future.

"What are you going to do?" Ben seemed to calculate what Bree's relocation meant for Nora.

"I'm not sure. Bree wants me to transfer with her to London."

"Really! You considered that? You would leave America?" He paused, intent on her answer.

"I'm thinking about it." Under his intense gaze she dropped her lashes and picked at the grass by her feet. "I'd miss my family, but I really like it here. London is a great city. Bree is my best friend. All of you guys have become my friends. I wanted a change. I just didn't imagine it could be so drastic. But I'm open to anything." His ear-to-ear grin made her blush.

"That would be great." He reached for her hand, giving it a squeeze. "That would be really great. I hope you do consider it."

Ben's phone buzzed, and he released Nora's hand. "Ah, I spoke too soon. Keegan's calling." Ben spoke briefly before hanging up. "Sorry, Keegan needs me to look at something. Do you mind if we head back."

"Of course not." They got to their feet, and Ben gave her an apologetic look. Nora wished she could read his mind. *How do you really feel about me, Ben? He is so handsome.* She adored the gray-green color of his eyes and his straight, aristocratic nose. The angles of his jaw were covered in soft stubble. Around his mouth the skin was clean-shaven and smooth, but she could see where the darkening shadow would grow out. She sometimes felt overwhelmed by him, like she was the luckiest girl in the world to have his attention. He moved toward the horses and she followed, his words ringing in her mind. *I hope you do consider it.*

In late afternoon they arrived at Westborough Meadows. Keegan met them at the stable entrance. A young lad followed Keegan, ready to take care of the tack and brush down their

174

horses. Molly came trotting over at the sound of her master's voice. Nora headed for the house, Keegan, Ben, and Molly heading in the opposite direction.

Nora took advantage of the free time to shower and blow-dry her long hair. She took extra care applying makeup and slipped into a navy and white sundress. She was on the phone with her mother when she spied Ben approaching the house from the stables. She stood at the window watching his purposeful stride, and her heart quickened at the sight of him. She assumed he would come in and shower, and then they would head into the small town. Nora pulled away from her thoughts of Ben and directed her attention to her phone call.

"Yes, Mom, I promise I will visit when I can." After Nora hung up she reflected on the call. Lizzy had a new job as a basketball coach for a girl's league and she loved it. Through a mutual friend, Victoria landed a client who wanted a dinner catered on his fifty-foot yacht. That would be a first, catering on a boat. Heidi remarked Victoria seemed happier now that she and Perry were taking a break from the fertility treatments. Dad was the same, of course. They had to take Polly to the vet, though; her arthritis flared up, poor old dog.

The sun was a burning orange disc as it dropped lower in the sky. The Land Rover motored into the center of town, where the buildings were casting long shadows. Past the church and several stone houses, they finally reached an area with several restaurants and shops.

The pub, Atlas, was a typical English-style pub with dark wooden booths, tables, and a long bar. As the name suggested, there were maps of England everywhere inside. Some were medieval, and some were seafarer friendly, with named ports. Others were topography or road maps. The friendly locals gave the place a great vibe. There was a wide selection of beers on tap, and the menu posted at the entrance looked promising. They got a table and ordered dinner.

The tables quickly filled up. Many hands waved in Ben's direction. He explained he had helped out at the veterinary clinic in the next town over for a while, and he had gotten to know everyone from their pets. Ben mentioned he wanted to open his own small animal clinic. "As great as it is working with the horses at Westborough Meadows, I'd like to take the next step and do something on my own. Establish my own practice and, you know, get a house of my own."

"I could definitely see you with your own practice. And it looks like you'd have a lot of customers." Nora opened her hands toward the crowded room. "And yeah, I definitely know what you mean about doing something of your own. I could have easily stayed employed with my family's catering business, but it never really felt like it was my thing. I always felt like I needed to accomplish something." She laughed at herself. "I think I'm still figuring out what it is I *am* trying to accomplish."

Ben nodded in agreement, but before he could say more, their attention was directed to the nearby door.

Someone was propping open the pub's side door. A musician carrying a guitar case and amplifier walked in, setting down his heavy load by the makeshift stage directly across from their table. A woman followed, carrying a solid black box, a coiled cable wrapped around her other arm. The woman, in her late thirties, had thin blonde hair parted to the side, sweeping dramatically across her forehead. The back was clipped short behind her ears. The blonde's large, expressive blue eyes surveyed the crowd until landing at their table, she exclaimed, "*Ben!*" This caught the musician's attention, and he also turned to greet Ben.

"Hey, man," Ben said just loud enough for them to hear above the din of busy restaurant noise.

The musician stood closest to Ben, and he reached his hand out to rest on Ben's shoulder. "You made it. I haven't seen you in a few weeks." The man was tall and extremely slim, giving him a lanky appearance. He appeared older than the woman, though he wore his black hair pulled back into a trendy short ponytail at the nape of his neck, and his goatee was neatly trimmed. The woman scooted over and bent to give Ben a little hug.

Ben introduced Nora as his friend from America, here this week to take riding lessons. "This is Will and his wife Liza." After the introductions, Will went back out to his car for a couple things. Equipment accounted for; Will closed the pub door behind him before sitting down to join them. Liza waved to the waitress, who held up two fingers. At Liza's nod, two beers were soon delivered.

"We'll take another round," Ben said to the waitress after he asked Nora if she was up for another.

"Wow, so you'll be playing tonight?" Nora gestured to the pile of equipment. She was impressed Ben knew a musician famous enough to play in a pub.

"Yeah, in a bit. I play here a couple times a week," Will said, soft-spoken.

Nora noticed his long fingers as he reached for his beer. "How do you know each other?" Nora expected Ben to say he had performed some lifesaving procedure on their pet but was utterly surprised to hear she was meeting Ben's music instructor.

"Oh, that's right. I knew you played–both piano and guitar, right?" Ben's musical talent impressed her.

Ben finished the last swallow from his bottle and nodded. "Yes, I play both, but Will taught me guitar. Mrs. Heinz taught me the piano. She was my German music teacher all through my early-education years." Ben chuckled. "In my preteen years I begged my father to learn guitar. Judy helped convince him learning another instrument would be valuable. Mrs. Heinz had pursed her lips and harrumphed at the idea. And then William Prescott was hired for private lessons." The men both chuckled at the memory. "Will is not only our local celebrity, but he is director of the music program here in town. Liza is a teacher at the same school."

"I teach fifth grade math," Liza said. She and Nora then chatted for a while about the school. Before long, Will rose to set up for his gig. Keegan strode in and took Will's seat. Keegan ate with them, and soon the little table was full of empty beer bottles.

Will sang sensitively and soulfully into the microphone. Nora was mesmerized by his voice. She and Ben stayed for two sets and then made the twenty-minute drive to Westborough Meadows. They said goodnight at the top of the landing.

The house was quiet when Nora stepped from the bathroom into the hallway in her pajama tank top and shorts. Molly padded up to her, seeking a familiar pat between the ears. Ben step out of his room, looking for Molly. Nora heard his breath catch and knew he saw her curves outlined in the softened light. He exhaled a long breath and then cleared his throat. Nora flushed knowing she caused his reaction.

"I have a visitor." She squatted to pat the golden head, using the dog as a shield to hide her semi-dressed state. Molly turned to look at her master, but she didn't budge.

"Molly, go lay down." Ben advanced toward them, and the dog obediently headed to the room from where she'd come. Nora stood and waited for him.

"I can still hear the music in my mind. Will was amazing. Can you play your guitar for me sometime?" The sweet smile she gave him was meant to beckon him closer.

"Nora." Ben's voice was a whisper. He placed his hand on the doorjamb just above her head, so close she had to tilt her head up to look at him. Her lips parted, and her breath quickened in anticipation. *This is it.* She rose onto her toes as he lowered his mouth to hers. A soft, delicious kiss. He shuffled closer, cupping her face in his hands. Ben slightly pulled back, searching her rich, brown eyes. He must have found what he was looking for because he drew her in for a deeper, fuller kiss, tasting her mouth. Nora slipping her hands inside his robe, stretching her fingers and palms against the skin of his abdomen. He inhaled a sharp breath at her scorching touch. "Nora..." His voice was tortured. "I've wanted to kiss you for a long time."

"I've wanted that too." They moved deeper into her room, staggering together until they stood at the edge of the bed. They kissed and stroked each other until breaking away for a breath. They pressed their foreheads together and held each other.

"I've had an amazing time with you. I want to see more of you."

She captured her bottom lip between her teeth, basking in happiness. "Oh Ben, you're amazing and I want to see more of you, too. I'll pick up more trips to London for now. And I have a big decision to make about moving here."

"If this could work..." He stared longingly into her eyes before he kissed her again.

Nora knew he wished to tell her to move to London. It would give him more confidence about forming a real relationship with her. Ben was a cautious guy. Who could blame him when it came to fickle females? Nora felt she fit into his life in a compatible way. Bree mentioned plenty of girls liked Ben, even chased him, and explained his family name came with social status and always seemed to draw eligible females.

"I know from experience I need to do some soul searching for every decision I make. Moving here would make seeing you a lot easier." She traced her finger down his downy jaw before she stood on her toes to kiss him again. She was burning for him to touch her, but soon he pulled away and sighed.

"Umm, I think I should return to my room." Regret filled his husky voice, and his eyes expressed his true feelings—he wanted to stay.

Nora understood he could pull her down on top of him, the bed being so nearby, and make sweet passionate love to her, but he wouldn't. They would wait. Taking this slowly would be best; it would guard both their hearts in the long run.

"Goodnight, Ben." He slipped from the room with a modest smile, trying to keep himself reserved, but Nora heard him blow out a long, ragged breath as he strode to his room. She touched her lips in wonder. She had taken a risk; she came here wanting to kiss him. And she had.

Now what am I going to do?

Chapter Twenty

Nora organized her suitcase for tomorrow morning's flight, sadly this being her last full day in England. She confirmed her next scheduled trip before tucking her phone into her pocket. She would return to Rome. *I won't call Antonio this time. It will be strange going to Rome without being with him, but it's for the best.* With her new love interest, Nora felt assured breaking off their relationship had been the right thing to do. She also needed to talk with Sergei when she got home. Their passionate moment in St. Petersburg was clearly a mistake.

Nora followed the same routine as the morning before and found Ben in his office. On her way across the hard-packed dirt she repeatedly cast her gaze upward. Judging by the look of the dark gray sky, they might not be riding today. She entered and was greeted by Ben's broad smile.

"Good morning," Ben said softly, gaze openly sweeping over her.

"Good morning," she replied. "Did you sleep well?" She waggled her eyebrows at him.

He laughed, getting her meaning. "Yeah. It took me a while to fall asleep though."

"Mmm, me too." She reddened, reminded of her wild midnight thoughts of him.

"Hey, come look at this." He pointed to the laptop computer on his desk. When he clicked on a tab, a web page came up, displaying a beautiful castle.

"Oooh, that's cool. What is it?" she asked, leaning over to get a good look.

"This is Warwick Castle. I was planning to take the horses out on an easy ride with a few scenic stops, but it's going to be rainy today, so I was wondering if you wanted to be a tourist.

Actually, I have an ulterior motive for visiting Warwick. A friend of mine wants me to take a look at a horse out that way. I'd only need about thirty minutes, and then we could go straight to the castle from there. What do you think?"

"Right. Warwick, home of the Kingmaker." Nora inwardly grinned, loving the stories she'd read about historical kings and queens of Europe. "I'd love to see it!"

"You know who the Kingmaker is?" He laughed. "Why do you know that?" He raised a quizzical eyebrow at her.

"I'll have you know I've read quite a bit about the Earl of Warwick." She placed her hands on her hips, pausing for dramatic effect. "In fact, I could probably name more English kings and queens than American presidents. Strange, I know," she stated matter-of-factly.

"Wow. Okay, Warwick it is." Ben feigned surrender.

They climbed into the Land Rover and motored down the highway to a farm, where Nora was introduced to a jovial man with an old horse. A true farmer, the man grew fields of waving barley. They looked like wheat fields to Nora.

"Yes, yes, Mr. Westborough, good to see you, lad," said the stout Mr. Topper with a gravelly voice. He pumped Ben's hand. After the introductions, they went to the modest barn, where a few horses raised their heads at the new arrivals. Ben tended to the horse in question, and Nora listened in on his conversation with Mr. Topper, who explained the old horse was very dear to him, and he wasn't ready to bury her under the pasture. Ben was sincere and sympathetic. He advised the owner how to care for the horse during the last of its days.

The men stepped out from the stall and chatted a few minutes with Nora. She learned the barley Mr. Topper grew was primarily for animal feed. Ben had met Mr. Topper through a local grain supplier he used for Westborough Meadows. They soon said their good-byes and were on their way within Ben's estimated thirty minutes.

It had sprinkled on and off during their drive, but there was a break in the weather when they arrived at Warwick Castle. Nora slipped an umbrella in her purse, and Ben tucked his in his pocket. With tickets in hand, on the other side of the admittance building they stood before a sweeping view of the castle's medieval exterior wall. The bulky stone structure topped with crenellations was an impressive sight. Ben reached for her hand, and she breathed out excitedly. "Oh, this place is awesome. Let's go check it out."

They passed through the Barbican and Gatehouse area, where once a drawbridge would have been raised against an invading enemy. Nora opened the pamphlet and read aloud. "It says here the curtain wall is the main wall that connects all the towers and main castle structure. Along the wall, walkways were built, which meant that crossbowmen and archers could move swiftly from one end of the castle to the other during attacks at any points on the perimeter. Once in position, they could pick off the enemy from the battlements." Nora paused, sneaking a peek at Ben to make sure he was listening before she continued reading. "The tops of the towers were encircled by crenellated parapets that added a further layer to the castle's defenses. Cut into the floor of the parapet at regular intervals are openings, or machicolations, through which the defense troops could drop stones or pour boiling pitch and quicklime onto the unfortunate attackers below." She pulled a face. "Sounds gruesome!"

Ben led her farther into the building, his gaze on her more than the sites. They toured each room, all filled with elaborate furniture, paintings, and wax figures. Nora read the placards and took photos. They climbed the curved stairs in the Defensive Tower, where they were rewarded with a 360-degree view from inside the castle courtyard. Caesar's Tower, the tallest of the castle towers, rose before them, three stories, including the Gaol, which was the original dungeon. Nora admired it. "The cloverleaf shape is impressive!"

A single flight of steps provided access to the lowest chamber in Caesar's Tower, the Gaol. It would have been miserably dark down there in times past with only a tiny shaft high on the wall to allow daylight in. Thankfully there were now discreet, modern lights so tourists would not trip.

"Look, Nora." Ben pointed to the ancient graffiti left by prisoners from hundreds of years ago. "Can you make out the names?" Nora and Ben spent a few minutes running their fingers over the etching in the stones, marveling they had lasted all these years.

They toured Guys Tower, which would have offered an amazing view on a clear day. This structure included the garderobe, or privy. "Did you know?" Nora asked Ben. "It says here a garderobe usually consisted of a single hole, which simply lead to the outside cesspit or moat. It usually smelled terrible and was a haven for disease and vermin!"

"I'm thankful for indoor plumbing," Ben murmured. She shook her head, laughing. He followed her to the next spot.

She continued to play tour guide and read on from the pamphlet. "The Clarence and Bear Towers were never finished. They were started by…?" Nora quizzed Ben as they strolled toward the twin towers. "I'll give you a hint. He was briefly the king of England, and he was married to Richard Neville's daughter Ann."

"Richard of Gloucester," Ben offered. "Have we discussed him before?"

"Wow, lucky guess." She narrowed her eyes at him.

In Clarence Tower, Nora checked out the well and ovens constructed inside the building for times of siege or attack. "This tower was named after Richard of Gloucester's eldest brother, the Duke of Clarence," Ben read. "Let's check out the Bear Tower. They apparently kept live bears there for baiting," Ben shared.

After milling around inside and reading as many plaques as they could, they stepped outside and were blasted with fresh air. Nora realized there had been a stuffy, damp smell within the thick stonewalls.

As the drizzle tapered off, they reached The Mound, one of the oldest parts of the castle grounds, first built in 1068 for defensive reasons. "On a clear day you can actually see as far as Stratford-upon-Avon." Ben looked up at the gray sky. "Next time I'll bring you on a sunny day."

"Next time?" Nora stood close to Ben. "I would like that very much."

Ben dipped his head to steal a kiss, but not before looking around to be sure no one was watching.

On the drive, Nora asked Ben about his childhood and what it was like when Bree used to stay with them as a young girl. What Ben described as "a typical childhood" Nora considered a privileged childhood. He had gone to private schools. When his sister wasn't involved in competitions, the family had traveled some around Europe. They skied in Switzerland and swam in the Mediterranean. Ben confided as great as all those places were, he enjoyed their quiet home with the horses around him. "I especially love it around the holidays," he emphasized. "Around Christmas, we gather and have horse-drawn sleigh rides and bonfires."

Nora pictured it in her mind. "Sounds lovely."

He conjured a few stories and then suggested a late afternoon lunch/early dinner; it was almost four o'clock, and all they had that day was some coffee and cookies at the castle's concession stand. The road they took wound up a hill, and Nora remarked at all the beauty the landscape offered. Now the rain had stopped and the sun was breaking through the clouds.

"I know a great spot. It looks down over the valley. It reminds me of the place I took you yesterday on horseback, up on the hill. It should be picturesque now with the sun low in the sky." He seemed excited to show it to her.

Nora recalled the view yesterday. "Yes, I loved seeing the church spires." She smiled at the memory. *There is something about Ben.* The way he spoke of things allowed her to read his sensitive nature. He was impressively intelligent but not conceited in any way. He was thoughtful and romantic. Nora glanced at his profile, wondering what it would be like to be his girlfriend, to be around him often… *Don't put the cart before the horse*, she remembered taking this slow would be a better course.

She concentrated on the passing trees and asked, "Are we nearby?"

"We are." He seemed almost reluctant. "It's just up ahead. Not far from the tavern." He then smiled broadly, rewarding her with his dimples.

They pulled off onto a gravel drive marked by two stone posts. They drove past a small structure, appearing to be under construction. The gravel road divided, and they bore to the right and stopped by a small cottage. "This is it." Ben turned off the motor. They stepped out and walked in the squishy grass to the edge of the property, where the hill sloped down to the valley.

"You're right. This is a lovely spot." Nora slowly spun around, puzzled. "This is off the road a bit. How did you know it was here? Do you know who lives here?"

Ben had a gleeful look in his eye. "Actually, I do know the owner, quite well." He paused for dramatic effect. "You're looking at the *new* owner."

"What? Wow, Ben, you bought this place? Congratulations." Nora was surprised and happy for him.

"Come on, I'll show you around." Ben tried to contain his excitement as she followed him to the cottage.

It had that English charm from the outside, but the inside lacked style and décor. The wallpaper in the first room had a deer-and-stag motif. The pine green shag carpet matched the wallpaper. *Of course, how quaint.* She grimaced. "Wow, hello 1970s." Nora pointed to the light fixture overhead and held up her hands. What could she say?

Ben just laughed, "Yes, this place needs some updating, but I'm planning on gutting and redesigning it in time."

After touring the cottage Ben confessed, "Actually, it wasn't the cottage that sold me; it was the building we passed, just up the drive."

Nora nodded. "The one under construction?"

"Yes. That is going to be my new clinic."

"Really, you've already picked a place? You just told me you wanted to open a clinic. Oh my gosh! Congratulations." Ben looked pleased at her enthusiasm. "Wow, a new house *and* a new business. What does your family think about all this? What did your parents say?"

"Well, I have actually been saying *for years* I want to start my own practice. I guess I just haven't been quite ready, until recently. It was convenient to work and stay at my family home. But as I told you, I need my own place. I've been training Keegan to take over for me at Westborough Meadows." He moved on to the next room, inspecting the doorway as he passed through. "My parents are supportive. Only they know. It's not like I'm leaving right away. And I'm only about fifteen minutes away if they need a consult."

"Ben, I am so happy for you." *Wow, this is a good step for the two of us–if this relationship works out.* It was somewhat awkward staying at the Westboroughs' house, even when they were not at home. "How long have you owned this place?"

"I became owner about two months ago. I've had a couple contractors out here already, and I've narrowed it down to this one company that specializes in medical installations for the clinic. They gave me a quote and an eight-week time frame. I should be able to open by the end of October or early November."

"What about the house? Will you move in soon?" She knew she hadn't offended him by joking about the dated décor. He had a good sense of humor.

Ben shrugged. "Yeah, at some point. My main focus is the clinic. Come on. I'll show you around."

Ben gave Nora the rest of the tour: kitchen, dining room, bath, three bedrooms, and, of course, the front room with the shag green carpet. They left the house and walked through Ben's future clinic. Nora was fascinated at how much had already been done. The front room would be a reception area with a counter and computer station. There were two exam rooms and one operating room.

Impressed by Ben's detailed descriptions, she said, "It sounds well thought out."

"Yeah thanks, and out back there's a small barn with a couple stalls for my larger patients."

"I can't wait to see it finished."

Ben locked up, and they got in the car as a second wave of clouds rolled in. He told her about a web page he was having done. Also, he would have some local ads printed, as well as mailings.

The pub they stopped in offered shepherd's pie served with rosemary sourdough rolls. It paired perfectly with their frothy beers. "That meal was the perfect comfort food on this drizzly day," Nora murmured, slipping her hand into his as they walked out of the pub. After he opened the car door for her, she slid in. They were at the estate within fifteen minutes.

They chatted easily late into the night, and Nora even persuaded Ben to play his guitar. Professing himself not ready to sing in front of her yet, he just strummed some songs. Nora dreaded leaving in the morning. She snuggled into him on the sofa, and they kissed and laughed until she bid him goodnight.

Chapter Twenty-One

On Monday morning Ben dropped Nora off at the airline terminal. He took her in his arms and kissed her in a long good-bye. This time he didn't seem to care who was watching.

"I'll call you soon," she promised. Nora found a quiet spot in the airport where she could wait for her flight. She often used airport downtime to catch up on her calls. She started with Bree. "Good morning, Bree. When are you flying home to Philly?"

"Morning. I'm in London until tomorrow. I'm at Evan's now, but I'm meeting Corrine for lunch today while he's working. Are you still with Ben? How is everything going? I want details!" Bree sang the last sentence.

"I'm at the airport, heading home. I wish I was still with Ben. We had a great visit." Nora tried to camouflage her delight but knew Bree could hear it.

"How was the riding? Did you ride anything besides horses?" Bree joked. She told Nora before Ben wouldn't rush even if he was truly interested in her.

"No, it wasn't like that, but we did kiss." Nora described their days together in a dreamy voice.

"Are you an expert horsewoman since you've been tutored by Ben? Although," Bree said as an afterthought, "Corrine is the *real* horsewoman of that family."

Nora assured her Ben had been very helpful, and she admitted she liked riding but joked about how sore she was after.

Bree said, happiness filling her voice, "Evan took me to an opera and then to a very romantic restaurant."

"Sounds lovely." However, Nora would never trade trendy city hotspots for her lazy afternoon picnic lunches with Ben. Nora hung up after talking to Bree and called Sergei. With her stomach knotted, she exhaled through the ringing. She hadn't spoken to him since she left for England. In hindsight she wished she just told him before she left that their relationship would not go any farther romantically. On their return from St. Petersburg she allowed him to hold her hand on the plane and kiss her good-bye. They had talked on the phone a few times, just generic conversations. If she had only known Ben had feelings for her, she would not have allowed things to evolve with Sergei. Nora had taken the friendship with Sergei to a level she now regretted. The dynamic in her life was shifting. She had traveled, literally and figuratively, very far in a short period of time.

"Hi, Nora!" She heard the pleasure in Sergei's voice.

"Hey, Sergei. I'm at the London airport, on my way back. I was wondering if you were around tonight or tomorrow."

The loudspeaker announced flight information, so he spoke up. "Yeah, Alexi and I are just leaving the gym. I'm here tonight. What time do you want to meet?"

"Umm, let me text you when I get in town, and we can figure out a time," she suggested.

"Yes, very good. We can figure it out then."

Nora figured Sergei had sensed the apprehension in her voice. He was no fool and probably already recognized their relationship had not advanced since their time together in Russia. She exhaled in relief when Sergei didn't end their phone conversation with "I miss you" or "I can't wait to see you."

Nora napped on the flight home. But her waking hours buzzed with thoughts and questions concerning her future. *Can I really move to London? I don't know anything about where to live, but Bree will know. I'm sure she will want to live near Ashley or Evan. They could certainly help us in the transition. Would Ashley be mad if Bree moved in with me instead of her? Or what if Evan wants Bree to stay with him after I move all that way? As much as I want it to work out with Ben, what if it doesn't? I definitely don't want to move across an ocean for a guy!* Nora shuddered at the thought. She had just won her independence, true rely-on-herself independence. She had to be certain this move would be good for her no matter what.

The alterative to moving to London? Stay in Philadelphia and find another place. She would probably need another roommate. She might have considered asking Rebecca, but she'd already moved to North Carolina.

Nora liked Philadelphia well enough, but she would have no trouble leaving it behind. Besides, if she lived in Europe, she could easily travel on her days off and see more European cities.

She ticked off the pros and cons in her mind. Leaving her family was the biggest con, but she was an international flight attendant who could fly home whenever she wanted. Even though, she hardly saw them now.

Pros included living in England with her best friend and hanging with Ashley and Corrine; that would be great. Traveling the world with Bree was what they had talked about. It was an opportunity to immerse herself in European culture. And dare she include Ben in this equation?

The pros for going to England outweighed the cons.

Nora plotted out a timeline. If they put in their application for transfer as soon as the end of September, a few weeks away, then they might be moving by early November. *Huh, I could be spending Thanksgiving in another country–weird.*

The streetlights were on when Sergei knocked. When Nora opened the door she was welcomed by a balmy September evening. Sergei held up a six-pack of beer and asked if they should sit outside. Nora stepped out and gave him a friendly hug. They hadn't sat out on the stoop in a while, not since the summer heat had pressed in on Philadelphia. During that time they preferred indoor air conditioning to the muggy nights. They settled on the steps, and he handed her a frosty bottle.

"How's your family? Have you talked to them? They were so happy to see you." Nora took a long swallow.

"They are good. My mother and sister asked about you. They like you. Of course, who would not?"

Her lashes lowered at his comment, hiding her thoughts, and she knocked her knee against his. "Your family is great. So nice of your sister Lydia to be my personal guide. It was wonderful to experience Russia with you. I can't thank you enough for inviting me along. Sergei, you are such a great guy–"

"But…" he interrupted.

"What happened between us… Well, I think we should just be friends," she said sympathetically.

"Is there someone else?"

She nodded meekly. Nora had wondered if their time together in Russia would blossom their relationship. She'd been willing to give it a try after she broke it off with Antonio. And besides, at that time she did not know Ben was truly interested in her. Now she just felt…bad.

Sergei cupped her knee with his large hand. "I knew there was someone else before we left. You even spoke of a complicated relationship. It does not matter. I am glad we went to Russia together. I am glad for any time we have spent together, and I do not want you to think this will ruin our friendship."

"Really?" She held her breath.

"Yes! But if you want to have sex I am available any time," he joked.

She laughed out loud. The complicated relationship Sergei mentioned had been with Antonio. And the "someone else" was Ben. She laughed to herself about the tangled web she had woven.

All her tension eased away while they talked for the next two hours. They drank all the beer. Nora insisted on a big hug before she went up to her room alone. She no longer felt regret about what had *almost* happened between her and Sergei. She chalked it up to a lesson learned.

In September, although the temperature in Rome was pleasant, the smog was a bit stifling. The flight crew's taxi was just dropping them off at the hotel when Nora's cell phone rang. *What a coincidence, it's Antonio.* Nora regretted answering the call as soon as she hit the button. "Hey, Antonio."

"Nora, it is good to hear your voice."

Just then, a very loud doorman called to a porter in rapid Italian. The crew's captain waved away the porter and assured the doorman they could handle their luggage. The crew entered the quiet lobby of the hotel.

"You are in Rome!"

Damn! Antonio had heard the exuberant doorman.

"Ugh…yep." She didn't fancy herself as a liar, so she couldn't say she was just *leaving* Rome. *Why did I answer the phone!* "How are you?" She tried not to sound caught off guard. She rolled her bag up to the desk and collected her room key.

"I am well. And I am so pleased to hear you are in Rome."

Her heart compressed. She felt melancholy; as much as she enjoyed their brief relationship, Antonio wasn't for her. He had other plans in life, including marrying and having children with a nice Italian lesbian. She was not going to settle, even if it meant losing a remarkable lover. He was a broad-minded thinker, a little too broad-minded for her taste.

"Nora, can I see you?"

She could picture his perfect full lips on the other end of the phone.

"I'm stepping into the elevator, so I might lose you." The crew squeezed in and the doors closed. The elevator went up four floors and the doors opened. *Figures, the call didn't drop.*

Antonio continued. "I know what you said, but I have been thinking about us. We should talk some more. Let me take you to dinner."

Nora entered her room, now safely away from listening ears. "No, I'm sorry. I think it's best we don't see each other. Please, Antonio. Please stop calling me."

"You are playing hard to get. That is very sexy." His voice purred.

What! "No, I'm not. I mean it." Her tone reflected the seriousness of this conversation. He was the one who didn't want a serious relationship, so why this reaching out? Then it dawned on her it was all about the pursuit. *"Hard to get!" He has probably never been rejected in his life. I mean, the man was romance novel cover worthy. He just can't stand the idea I don't return his calls with baited breath.*

"I have to go. Good-bye." Nora disconnected with a heavy sigh. True: she had been flattered he found her attractive. True: she had been flattered he had pursued her. True: she was his plaything, just as he was hers. This Italian Stallion was too wild for her.

Nora had met a new crew member named Debra on the flight to Rome. They got on well, so while in Rome they hung out, visiting sites and restaurants. They had just walked to the hotel from dinner when Debra said out of the side of her mouth, "Oh Lord, look at that hunk."

Nora followed her gaze to a darkly handsome Italian guy leaning against one of the hotel columns, looking like a Roman statue for all to admire. Antonio.

Debra inhaled a sharp breath and whispered franticly. "He's coming this way!"

"Good evening, Nora," Antonio purred, sauntering up to them.

Debra's eyes grew wide. "You know him?" She sounded astonished. Nora gave a weak laugh and tight smile.

"Hi, Antonio, this is Debra. Debra, Antonio." He shifted his smoldering eyes to Debra, and Nora thought her companion might faint. Debra barely squeaked out a hello.

"It is very nice to meet you, Debra, but would you mind if I spoke with Nora?" He smiled, alluringly.

"Oh no, nooo, not at all." Debra couldn't walk away fast enough. "I'll see you tomorrow," she said to Nora. Past Antonio, Debra almost tripped, thanks to her gawking and lingering look backwards.

"Please don't be mad." He put his hands up in surrender. "I have to tell you something, eh?"

Nora couldn't see a way around it, so she just nodded. They walked away from the bright lights of the hotel entrance to a quiet nearby garden, where they found a secluded bench. Antonio grasped her hand as he always did, bringing it to his lips. After a moment he began. "Nora, I have to tell you, you have captured my heart. I cannot stop thinking of you." At her closed expression, he plowed on. "I told you how much you mean to me, but I realized what I needed to do. I have spoken to my mother and told her the engagement is off. I told her I would be the one to choose who I spend my life with, whether she is Italian or not."

"Wait! What?" Nora couldn't quite grasp what he was saying. "You are going to break up with her for me?"

"It is done."

Truly shocked, she scanned his handsome face. This was a *huge* move for him. Nora shook her head. Before she could deny him, he spoke. "I think you are worth getting to know better. And I think I am finally ready to settle down and...see what happens."

"Antonio, I am overwhelmed by your grand gesture. I have to admit, I wanted that at one point in time, but now... I don't really think it was only because of that, that I allowed our relationship to end. We are very different."

He waved away her excuses. "We have passion." He leaned in closer. "You cannot deny this." He defiantly played his irresistible card. He tucked a lock of hair behind her ear and slid his arm around her shoulder. He dropped his head next to her exposed ear, whispering, "Nora, I want to love you." His breath hot on her neck, and she shuddered at the sudden chill up her spine. He brushed his lips in her neck, and then his hot tongue licked her salty skin.

Nora jumped to her feet. "I'm sorry, Antonio. Please don't call me again. I'm sorry." Striding away, she left him on the bench in a beautiful garden drenched in moonlight. She couldn't look back. And she didn't know why tears were blurring her vision.

Nora curled up in her bed, listening to the evening sounds of Rome's traffic, distant sirens, and loud pedestrians, reflecting on all that had happened in the past year. Last September she was planning her wedding with Phillip. In October she broke off her engagement and moved home with her parents. She managed to survive the holidays, biding her time, until she left for her new job training. The New Year took her to Pittsburgh, where she spent six weeks of her life learning everything there was to know about becoming a flight attendant. She met a new best friend. In March they became roommates in Philly. Then she was off, visiting amazing countries and meeting new people, making some good friends. She had been flying for six months now. In just six months she had met and become involved with three very different men.

My life has changed so completely. A year ago, I was a wallflower. Engaged for years, no other guy paid her any attention. She lived like a ghost in her own life. But something changed. She made a choice. She left a man who loved her and wanted to marry her. She broke up with a hunky Italian lover who still wanted her. She made up her mind a relationship with Sergei would not work out. And within six short months, was she now ready to fall completely for Ben? It seemed too soon. She was glad she *dated*–she used this word loosely in her mind– both Antonio and Sergei. A part of her thrived on the new sense of freedom, but the other part of her, the part that grounded her, was her sense of normalcy. She relished this fun freedom, but she didn't want this to always be her life. She just wanted to meet the right guy, who would complement her, respect her, and keep her interested, both mentally and physically. Ben could be that guy. She held her phone in her hand and swiped to the picture she had of Ben.

She decided to transfer to London. She was going to take a chance on having a great life. After all, that was what she wanted all along–a chance to change her life and be happy, no matter what. She couldn't wait to tell Bree. She knew her best friend would be elated.

Days passed before Nora and Bree finally had a day off together. Nora sat in front of a basket of clean laundry, drinking her second cup of coffee, when Bree came in from an early-morning run.

"Hi, Bree! I was wondering where you were. I didn't hear you leave. Actually, I didn't even hear you come in last night. Was it late?" Nora was not alarmed at the thought of Bree not coming home, because often enough a flight schedule was altered. When that happened, the airline would put the crew up for another night at a hotel. Sometimes mechanical or weather-related problems delayed or canceled a flight.

"Hey." Bree kicked off her sneakers. "I got in around ten. You were out like a light when I peeked in to say hi."

They sat on the living room sofa, sorting and folding clean laundry while they watched the Travel Channel on television. Nora studied her friend as Bree prattled on about some designer handbag shop she found in London. After describing a bag she had to have, she said, "I didn't get it because I'm going to stick to a budget." Bree talked about wanting financial independence from her parents, but confessed her extravagant taste was way more expensive than she could ever afford on her salary. Still, she was going to give the concept of a budget a try. "So I resisted the urge to buy it," Bree concluded with a sigh. She matched a pair of socks. "So have you considered moving across the pond?" Her voice sounded nonchalant, but she pinned Nora with an anxious gaze.

"I think this is your sock. I've picked it up three times." Nora tossed the cotton gym sock in Bree's direction. Bree did not even blink. "Yes," Nora replied, hunting for the mate to her sock.

"Yes, you're considering it? Or yes, you want to move?" The excitement built in Bree's voice.

Nora smiled at her friend. "Let's do it!"

"Yippee!" Bree tossed her folded laundry aside and hugged Nora. They settled in their seats, grinning. "Have you mentioned it to your family?"

Nora frowned. "No, not yet. I'll call and see if they're around tomorrow. I plan on driving over for the day. I should have been visiting them more often. My mom is going to be upset."

"I told both my parents I was considering moving to London. My dad thought it was a great idea, London being his old stomping grounds. And he mentioned the Andrews family. I told him I'd been visiting Ash and Evan." Bree got up and headed for the kitchen. After a dramatic pause in front of the refrigerator, she continued. "My mother wasn't receptive at first, but after I told her I've been dating Evan she warmed up to the idea pretty quickly."

"What about this place? Your dad leased it, and your mom decorated it." Nora glanced around at their posh quarters.

Bree retrieved a cup of yogurt from the refrigerator and waved her hand before she opened the drawer to root around for a spoon. "He'll just sublet it furnished. And Mom will ship over anything we want to keep." Bree dropped onto the sofa, squealing with glee. "I can't believe you said yes! I really wasn't sure what you were going to decide."

"I know, it's crazy, but I think it will all work out." Philly was never going to be Nora's final destination.

Nora had a funny smirk on her face. Bree had to ask, "Does this decision have anything to do with Ben?" Bree got her answer when Nora's smile broadened. "Well, is there more to the story? You said you guys had fun but kept things friendly. Just kissed, huh?"

"Just kissed," Nora confirmed. She didn't want to jinx their relationship somehow by making it more than it was.

"Nora, that's great! He must really like you if he's willing to take your friendship to the next level. Like I've said, he had his heart broken a couple times. When he falls, he falls hard. Do you really like him?" Bree sounded protective of Ben, her longtime friend. "I mean, what about Sergei?"

Nora nodded. "Sergei and I had a talk. I broke it off. He was kind and understanding. He really is a great guy too, just not for me." Nora let out a long sigh. "Ben is remarkable. I want to take things slow. His heart isn't the only one needing protecting."

Bree seemed satisfied with that answer. The girls decided to call Ashley and share the good news about them moving to London. Ashley mentioned the couple in the flat upstairs was moving out next month; it wasn't yet rented. She gave them the landlord's number, and they started to make plans.

After they hung up with Ashley, Nora decided to drive to her parent's house that afternoon. She wanted to talk to them first before she filled out the final transfer paperwork. How would she break the news gently? She had to tell them she would be moving to London, thirty-five hundred miles away.

Chapter Twenty-Two

When Nora walked into the kitchen of her childhood home, the welcoming smell of beef stew filled her nose.

"Hi, Eleanor, how was the ride?" Heidi hugged Nora and then untied her apron and hung it on a peg in the kitchen pantry.

"Fine, no traffic. Dinner smells great. Is there anything I can do to help?" Nora swept her gaze across the kitchen counter. Bowls were stacked up next to the crock of stew. A pitcher was filled with iced tea. The bread rolls were already snuggled in the bread basket, wrapped in a towel to keep them warm.

"No, you go ahead and put your bag up in your room. Dinner is already." Heidi moved around the kitchen. "I just finished working on some pastries for a baby shower. I'll just get them in the fridge, and then we can eat. I'm sure you're hungry."

Nora nodded emphatically and rolled her suitcase into the family room, where her dad sat watching the news. "Hi, Dad. Mom says dinner is ready."

Nora lugged her suitcase up the stairs with some effort. The long drive and the weight of what she wanted to say to her parents left her feeling exhausted. She rolled her suitcase into the center of the room and abandoned it. She plopped down on her bed, riding out the bounce of the old springs. She melted onto the quilt and looked blankly at the white ceiling. *Home. Home?* This was her *old* home, where she grew up. It would always be a comforting place. Philly was where she lived, but not her *home*. *Will I find what I'm searching for in England?*

"Mom, Dad, I'm moving to England," she murmured to the ceiling. She inhaled a long, steady breath and drew herself off the bed. Time to make this change a reality.

When Nora entered the kitchen, the table was set and her dad was grabbing a can of Coke from the refrigerator. "What can I get you?" Russ asked his daughter, holding up his can.

"I'll take some milk." Nora headed for the cupboard to retrieve a glass while her dad placed the gallon of milk on the counter.

They ate and chatted for a while before Nora steered toward the subject of her move. "So–Bree and I have had a great time in England. I've made so many new friends through Bree. She spent a lot of time there growing up. In fact, now that she's flying international, she wants to transfer over there, to England. Meade Airlines has a hub in London." Nora pinched off a piece of her roll and stuffed it into her mouth, watching for any reaction.

Her parents exchanged looks. Heidi took a sip of iced tea. "That's nice. Bree seems like a charming girl. Are her parents concerned she'll be so far away? And what about you? You'll need a new roommate."

"It's not that far, just across the pond, as they say." Nora said, dismissively. "Bree's parents are really supportive, and they know the families of the friends I was telling you about. And this may sound crazy, but…I've decided to go with her."

All eating movements stopped.

Nora's dad finally spoke up. "Eleanor, you want to move to England?"

Nora nodded. It was all she could manage with the lump in her throat. The last bite of bread seemed to be lodged in her throat. She reached for her glass of milk.

"But you just moved to Philadelphia," her mother protested, "and we hardly ever see you now."

"When would you be leaving?" Russ's voice was low and calm.

"In a month, maybe six weeks. We actually might get a place in London in the building where our friend lives." Nora rested her gaze on her mother's face. Heidi's brown eyes were wide with shock, shifting to her husband and back again. "I'm an international flight attendant, and I want to get out there and see the world. This move puts me at a better advantage and makes travel to other countries more accessible. And now with Bree flying international, too, I can have a companion. It's what I want. I want to give this a try."

"Sounds like you've thought this through. We support you, kiddo." Russ nodded across the table at his wife, who followed suit.

Heidi added, "We love you, Eleanor. We only want what is best for you."

Relief swept over her at how well the conversation had gone. When had she learned to assert herself, especially with her parents?

The next day in Philadelphia, the girls applied for transfers. Nora had stepped out of her life "in a nut shell" and found freedom with her career in a new state, and soon, a new country. Seeing the world is what she set out to do and she felt more confident and comfortable with her jetsetter life. She was excited to continue her pursuit of happiness. Nora talked to Ben frequently. He responded cheerfully when she told him she decided to move to London. Everything was falling into place.

In the meantime, with Bree's new international status, the girls worked a trip to Paris. It was everything Nora imagined for a girl's getaway. They were shopped out, exhausted from sightseeing, and aching from laughter–and they couldn't wait to do it all over again in another city.

As they waited eagerly for the transfer to go through Bree had an idea. She arranged for their British friends to come across the pond and celebrate Nora's thirtieth birthday. This was the gang's last-ditch effort to visit Philadelphia before the girls made their overseas move. Before their friends arrived in early October, the girls received permission to transfer and were lining up a place to stay with Ashley's help. So by the end of October, Nora and Bree would be living in England, but in the interim they made big plans with the gang.

Ben and Corrine came with Evan and Ashley for a long weekend and checked into hotel rooms a few blocks from the girl's townhouse. The first night in Philly, during their slow pub crawl, the gang ran into Alexei at one of the bars. Nora asked him privately, "Where's Sergei? He around this weekend?"

Alexei replied, "Sergei's working, but will return tomorrow."

Nora felt some relief her former love interest wasn't going to be around to make things awkward for her while Ben visited. A part of her was sad she might not see him again after she moved. Despite their short-lived romance, she did care for him.

The next morning, the gang met at eleven for a historic city bus tour. After the tour they walked over to sample the famous warring cheesesteak shops of Philadelphia. Half the group ordered from one shop, and the other half went directly across the street to the competition. They shared the Philly cheesesteaks and voted. Laughing and joking, they attempted to figure out what type the gelatinous yellow cheese actually was. They agreed it would remain a mystery and headed to the townhouse to relax before they could even think about dinner.

The friends walked side by side on the sidewalk under the tree shade. Nora and Corrine were followed by Ashley and Bree. The guys lagged behind, immersed in conversation. As the girls approached the front steps, Nora heard Ashley's breathy voice: "*Who is that?*" Ashley referred to a man sitting on the stoop, watching them approach, a dozen long-stemmed red roses in his lap. He stood as they neared.

"Oh my God." Bree exclaimed under her breath. She had seen his picture several times on Nora's phone.

Antonio.

Nora stood in shock for a moment, staring at Antonio. *How can he be here, in America...in Philadelphia? Why is he here?*

"Ahhh..." Nora nervously turned to her friends. "Will you excuse me for a minute?" Ben and Evan caught up to the three girls, who stopped in their tracks. Their curious eyes observed something was amiss.

Nora forced herself to move forward toward the man she thought she would never see again. She made things clear to him. *What is he doing here?* Nora's heart hammered against her chest.

Antonio smiled as Nora approached. He waved to her group of friends, who lingered with wide-eyed stares. The girls couldn't help eye him up and down; the guys stood a little taller and exchanged glances.

He met her at the bottom of the steps. "Nora." Antonio, devastatingly handsome, caressed her face with his dark, dreamy eyes.

All Nora could think about was getting rid of him. *Ben is watching! What the hell is happening?*

"Antonio, what are you doing here?" Nora could feel five sets of eyes burning into her skin.

"I have come for you, Nora." He reached out to caress her cheek, but Nora snatched his hand away and pulled him down the street in the opposite direction from her friends. She didn't want them to hear what Antonio was saying. She prayed they hadn't heard him say he'd *come for her*. Maybe they would go inside since she moved him away from the door. He stopped only a few steps away, turning her to face him.

"I have come all this way to tell you in person how much you mean to me, Nora. I needed to see you. You have not left my thoughts for weeks." He glanced sideways at her friends, who were talking quietly and sending glances their way.

Nora looked at Ben under her lashes and watched his fidgety posture. *What must he be thinking?*

"Antonio, before you go any further…" She intended to tell him she was with someone else. And *someone else* was standing right there! But he interrupted.

"These are for you, a symbol of my love and passion for you." He thrust the roses into her hands and got down on one knee.

Oh God. This can't be happening. A wave of heat washed over her, though her hands were ice cold. Her stomach twisting, she felt like she would vomit.

"I told you I am not going to marry an Italian girl to make my family happy." He shook his head; his dark, glossy waves tussled over his forehead. "That doesn't matter. What I realize is I want to be with you. I love you, and I know my family will be happy with my decision. They will love you too." His smile accentuated his sensuous lips. "Nora, will you marry me?"

Nora tried to swallow, but there was a huge dry lump in her throat; she couldn't even speak. After an extended moment of silence, Antonio stood up and continued. "You don't have to answer right now. I can see I have chosen the wrong time." He glanced at her friends.

Nora sent a pleading look in Ben's direction. But when their eyes met, Ben looked away, hurt and disgusted. It prompted her voice, raw with emotion. She tore her eyes away from Ben. "I think it would be best if you left *right now*. I'm sorry, but my answer is *no*. I just want you to go. I can't talk to you right now." She shoved the roses at him and turned to leave.

The roses fell to the ground. Antonio grabbed Nora's arm.

"Hey, let her go!" yelled a heavy Russian accent from across the street.

"Oh shit!" Bree's voice caught everyone's attention. And the group once more watched with open mouths as a large man crossed the street and faced Antonio with fury.

"Is there a problem here?" Sergei said in his thick accent to the Italian man, who swept Nora behind him, out of the way.

"There is no problem here, friend. Why don't you mind your own business and go over there?" Antonio gestured in the direction from which his opponent came. The two large men were puffed up like peacocks, staring each other down. Nora, now released, held up her hands and stepped between them.

"Stop!" she shouted, anger at the ridiculous situation mounted. Nora flicked her gaze down the sidewalk for Ben, but he walked away. Corrine sent Nora an accusing look before following her brother. Evan left too. Bree and Ashley waited to see how this would play out.

There were tears in Nora's eyes when she glared at Antonio.

"Nora, I am sorry." Antonio's voice was tender, and he reached for her.

"No. *No!*" she repeated louder. "My answer is no. Antonio, please, just go home. I'm sorry you came all this way."

Sergei stepped back, dropping his eyes to the red roses strewn across the ground. Nora moved to stand next to him, once again her protector. She hadn't seen him step out of his house across the street or heard his car door close after he placed his gym bag inside. She guessed he'd watched the scene unfold and figured there was trouble.

Antonio looked like a wounded boy, his dark eyes questioning her choice, and he said a quiet "Oh." His gusto deflated.

Nora clamped her teeth on her upper lip, trying not to cry, but hot tears spilled when she blinked. Antonio gave her a curt nod and strode up the block. He crossed the street, got into a rental car, and sped away. Ben was out of view. Sergei was the last man standing.

Nora turned to Sergei and allowed him to fold her into his arms. She cried for a few minutes before Bree and Ashley approached. Nora felt safe and cared for in Sergei's arms, her protector and friend. The thought flickered briefly across her mind: *Why didn't it work out with us?* But Ben's hurt expression resurfaced in her mind.

"We've got it from here," Bree said to Sergei. Sergei let Nora go reluctantly. He crossed to his car as Bree ushered Nora inside. Ashley curiously eyed Sergei before disappearing inside.

Ashley closed the door and stood in front of the sofa, regarding Bree and Nora. Nora sat with her face buried in her hands, Bree with her arm around her shoulder.

"What the bloody hell was that all about?" Anguish filled Ashley's voice.

Nora knew all too well how deeply her friends cared about Ben and they would protect him at all cost. They'd been so happy when he took a liking to her. Nora felt terrible. This farce was not her fault. But it didn't matter. *Ben must hate me now. They must all hate me!*

Bree knew the whole story and defended Nora. She cautioned Ashley to calm down, holding up her hand. "Ash, that guy with the roses was an ex-boyfriend. *Ex.* Nora broke up with him a while ago."

Nora peeked over the top of her fingers at Ashley feeling nauseated, but grateful to Bree for explaining things.

"*She* broke up with *him*?" Ashley accused doubtfully.

"It's complicated," Bree stated flatly. "He's been pursuing Nora since she broke up with him. Ash, that guy was engaged and basically asked Nora to be his mistress." Bree let out a frustrated breath. "I'm telling you, he's messed up!"

"What?" Ashley plopped down next to Nora and nudged her for more information.

Nora stopped crying, dropped her hands from her face, and sat against the cushions, folding her arms over her chest and hugging her broken heart. She gave a sarcastic chuckle before explaining the saga of Antonio to Ashley.

Ashley whistled. "Sweet Fanny Adams." Nora never heard that phrase but got the gist. Ashley cocked her head to the side so her auburn curls bounced on her shoulder. "And the other guy? The Russian?"

"That's Sergei, our neighbor and good friend," Bree answered. "Do you remember meeting Alexei the other night? He and Sergei are roomies. They've been our friends since we moved to Philly. They're both great guys," Bree added emphatically.

Nora exchanged glances with Bree; they would not soon forget how Sergei stood up for Bree with Tyron. They left the subject of the Russian at that.

"I need to talk to Ben." Nora pulled her phone out of her pocket and dialed his number. It went to voice mail. She hung up and headed for the door. "I need to find him. We need to talk."

"Hold on," Ashley said, digging in her purse for her phone. "I'll call Corrine and see where they are."

According to Corrine they were at the hotel. Ben was upset and didn't want to talk to Nora. Nora decided she would go over to the hotel anyway and the three of them walked the few blocks in silence. Evan and Corrine were in the lobby, having a heated conversation.

Corrine saw them enter and marched over to Nora. "My brother doesn't want to see you." A mixture of anger and hurt occupied her voice. Nora and Corrine had become good friends, but Ben was Corrine's brother. Nora did not blame her for her raw, mixed emotions.

"Corrine, I'm sorry that happened. That guy is my ex. We've been broken up, so I don't know why he came all this way. I told him it was over before your brother and I ever got involved. I swear. I would never deceive him—or any of you," Nora pleaded. Bree nodded emphatically, backing up Nora in her dilemma.

Corrine's shoulders visibly dropped as she exhaled, clearly relieved to hear her friend say so, but Nora understood she still hurt on her brother's behalf. "I'm sorry, but he doesn't want to see you," she said with more sympathy.

Nora glanced at Bree, Evan's arm around her shoulder.

Evan confessed, "He left."

"What do you mean? Where did he go?" *Surely if he is out walking, clearing his head, I can catch up to him.*

"He grabbed his things, checked out, and took a cab to the airport. He said he got the last seat on the five o'clock flight." He glanced at his watch.

Nora didn't hear Evan telling them that he and Corrine had just been arguing about whether to leave on a later flight tonight or wait for their original flight tomorrow afternoon. The pounding in her chest had elevated to her ears. She trembled with panic. *He's so upset he just left! He left without any explanation!*

Nora's head snapped up. "Right!" she declared, interrupting Corrine, who was talking about leaving on the eight o'clock flight. "I'll come with you, Corrine. I can make the eight o'clock flight."

"No. I don't think that would be a good idea. If Ben chose to leave, then he's choosing to be alone, probably for a while." The rest of them nodded and murmured in agreement.

"I have to explain this to him. He's going to end our relationship without even knowing what happened. He won't even hear me out? You are saying he will refuse to talk to me? To see me?"

Evan and Corrine looked at her sheepishly.

"He's like one of his animals. He'll need time to lick his wounds," Corrine reasoned. "Knowing Ben, he'll brood and throw himself into his work. If and when he is ready, he'll contact you," Corrine said softly. "He will reach out to you in time."

"Ben really likes you, Nora. Probably this was a wakeup call as to how much," Ashley added. The girls nodded in unison.

"Yeah. He watched another man profess his love and propose to you. That was a blow to him," Evan added matter-of-factly.

Tears of frustration welled up, but Nora blinked them away. "Fine. *Please* tell Ben I am *truly* sorry my *ex*-boyfriend showed up out of the blue and proposed to me *in front of him*—and I obviously said *no*." She paused, taking in a shaky breath before she went on. "And I would very much like for him to call me so we can fix this."

"Of course." Ashley rushed over and hugged Nora. "I'll explain everything you told me to Ben when I see him."

Nora nodded mutely into the fall of auburn hair tickling her face.

Ashley's hug was replaced by Bree's. "Come on, I'll walk you home." Bree squeezed her roommate around the shoulders. Nora apologized to Ashley, Corrine, and Evan for ruining their visit and said her good-byes.

At home, Nora went to her room and traded her jeans for pajama pants. She dropped her cropped knit sweater on the bedroom floor and pulled a hoodie sweatshirt over her tank top. She tossed the bracelets that tangled in the sleeve of her sweater on her small nightstand.

When Bree knocked briefly before pushing the door open, Nora was lying in bed. "Hey, I made you some chamomile tea." She held a steaming mug with a geometric pattern on it, the tell-tail string and tea bag label hanging over its side.

"Thanks," Nora murmured, but she didn't move to sit up. Bree set the mug on the windowsill and sat on the bed. "Bree, what am I going to do?" Nora rehearsed in her mind what she would say to Ben. Surely he would realize none of this was her fault! "He's being childish," Nora accused. Defensively she added, "Maybe it's for the best. If he's acting like this now, then maybe our relationship wasn't going to go any further anyway."

"Nora, remember how long it took Ben to get to know you and show interest? He is a deep thinker. He has to mull everything over before he decides on anything. He's always been like that." Bree mused, "He probably left so he could give you space to make your choice."

"What choice? I wanted him to stay."

"I mean about Antonio. Maybe Ben thought you might still have feelings for the guy and might want to say yes to his marriage proposal. Ben's like that! If Ben thought you'd be happier with someone else, then he'd back off. I've seen it happen before," Bree warned.

Oh Ben, so sweet and sensitive. Nora hated the woman before her who broke his heart. But now she'd done the same thing. Anger slipping away, she curled into a ball on the bed, deflated.

Bree's phone rang. She pulled it free from her pocket, glancing at it. "It's Evan," she said without answering it.

"Oh, it's their last night here." Nora cried, lifting her head slightly off the pillow.

"Yeah, they were looking to go to dinner, but I'm staying with you. I'll call him in a few." Bree rested her hand on Nora's arm. Nora felt the prick of tears again, grateful to have a friend like Bree.

"No, Bree. I *insist* you go with them tonight. They came all this way. And besides, I already feel terrible for ruining their visit. I'll feel even worse if I keep you from them." She dropped her head onto the pillow. "Honestly, I just want to wallow alone."

Bree considered her words, before finally nodding in agreement. "Okay, if you're sure." Nora smiled with relief. "Promise you'll call me if you need me for anything." Nora agreed, and Bree slipped off the bed, calling Evan as she left the room.

Chapter Twenty-Three

Nora cried herself to sleep. She dreamed of the drumming of horse hooves on a dirt road—Ben on horseback, galloping down a dusty road toward her. She stood against a white fence, shouting and waving her arms to catch his attention, but he acted as if he didn't see her and galloped right past. The loud drumming of hooves had drowned out her shouts.

Nora woke, her gaze searching the near darkness. She listened intently. Someone knocked on the front door. The persistent knocks sounded much like the horse hooves in her dream. Nora raced down the stairs. *Can Ben have changed his mind? Or maybe Antonio is back. No, not Antonio—I can't repeat that again.*

Surprise was evident in her voice when she swung open the door. "Sergei!"

He displayed a bottle of vodka in one hand and a six-pack of beer in the other. "I saw Bree leave earlier and figured you needed some company."

Why not? At this point I'm all cried out, and Sergei has always proven to be a good friend, always manages to cheer me up. She waved him in and went to collect two glasses.

The next morning, Nora squinted at the bright sunshine pouring through her window. Her bare arm was chilly, and she yanked the sheet, to no avail. She wiggled, trying to dislodge the sheet, but it wouldn't budge. She heard a male grunt behind her. She bounced away as Sergei rolled onto his back. The sheet suddenly gave way, and she yanked it, covering her body to her chin.

"Oh my God, Sergei, what are you doing here?" she whispered fiercely.

He briefly opened his eyes and then they fluttered closed. "We fell asleep."

"I can see that!" Nora glanced nervously at the closed door with a massive head ached, and a bad taste in her mouth. White knuckled, she peeked under the sheet and breathed a sigh of relief to see her pajama pants and tank top. She sprang from the bed, bumping the nightstand and sending her bracelets clanking to the floor giving her a flash back to the hotel room in St. Petersburg where she had disregarded that same set of bangle bracelets.

Thank goodness I'm still wearing my clothes and nothing happened. But why are we in bed together? And what if Bree saw us? "Sergei, get up! You have to go. Sergei." Her whisper was more of a hiss.

He mumbled something in Russian.

"Shh!" Nora warned. She climbed into the bed and got close to his face. "Sergei. Please! You have to go before Bree sees you and thinks..." She didn't finish her sentence. Sergei opened his eyes; the hungry look he gave her filled with desire. She sensed he was ready for her under the sheet. She stood. A glance down the length of the sheet confirmed her suspicion.

She felt empathy for him, because although her tears were caused by Antonio, and had been for Ben, Sergei was the one with her now.

"All right," he answered and moved to sit up.

Nora crept to the door to listen. He stood, a large man in a small room, stretching his brawny body. His T-shirt was rumpled, and he adjusted the front of his jeans. Nora averted her eyes. He swiveled his blond head around until he found his shoes resting at the end of her bed. He sat down to slip them on. Nora waited, impatiently tapping her bare foot. When he rose, she listened at the door again. All was quiet; she gave him a silent thumbs-up. He made no sound on the stairs, and the click of front door closing was barely audible.

Nora surveyed the room to be sure there was no sign left of him. She began to remember now how Sergei had practically carried her to bed after she had started to cry on the sofa while they watched television. She mumbled as he laid her carefully on the bed, "Thanks for being here when I needed you. Don't go yet." She remembered the weight of him sitting on the bed and his protective hand resting warm against her back. She must have drifted off to sleep after that.

Bree was just coming in when Nora was walking out the door, her duffle bag over her shoulder. Nora dropped her bag to the floor. "Hey, I was about to call you. I'm heading to my folks' house for a couple days. I don't have to fly until Thursday."

"Sorry I didn't come home last night. I stayed with Evan." Bree sounded guilty.

"Seriously, don't even worry about it. I can take care of myself." But she hadn't been alone, and Nora couldn't imagine explaining that to Bree at this moment. Nora was suddenly startled by Bree's sharp intake of breath.

"Oh, Nora, after everything that has happened... It's October eighth! Today is your birthday! Happy birthday! I have a card for you." Bree opened her purse and produced an envelope. Nora opened it and thanked her friend for the gift card. She hugged her with an extra squeeze.

Bree commented on the red-rimmed eyes of her dear friend. "I'm so sorry all this happened, and on your birthday too!" They had been through a lot together in the past year. "Everything will work out, Nora. Just give it time. This has certainly been a year of change for you."

This has certainly been a year of change for you... The thought haunted Nora on the long drive to her parent's house. Today she turned thirty. Three decades old. Nora had made a different life for herself, since a year ago in that bar with her fiancé and family celebrating her twenty-ninth birthday. She vowed then, "I'm going to live a better life." *Is this a better life?* She answered her own question. *Yes. Even if Ben breaks my heart, I know this is where I should be. I accomplished what I had set out to do.*

Nora considered the old Eleanor had been trapped in a life without fulfillment. She compromised too much. Through her experiences, she learned it was okay to say no and still be a kind person. She was proud of herself for becoming successful, worldly, and independent. She struggled with guilt and felt selfish at times, but had come to understand *settling wasn't good enough*! Despite her family and Ben, she was still determined to move to England. She would take every city by storm with Bree. But at this vulnerable moment, when she felt uncertain about what would happen with Ben, the one thing she was certain of was the love and comfort of her family. She needed to be with them now. After all, today was her birthday.

When she phoned her mom to say she was coming home, she felt the love wash over her with the sound of her mother's elated voice. Heidi declared she'd gather the family for dinner.

Nora turned onto her family's street and breathed a sigh of relief. She needed a pause in her hectic life.

The girls said good-bye to their American friends. Sergei told Nora to call him anytime and to stay in touch. It was hard saying farewell to him, but it was even harder when Nora endured the tearful good-bye with her family. They encouraged her, and she appreciated it.

Nora and Bree officially settled into their British life. Meade Airline allowed them to take an unlimited quantity of luggage on their transfer flight, which held the majority of Nora's belongings. Although Bree talked of wanting independence from her parents, she was glad her mother had swooped in and taken care of every detail for their move. Mrs. Royce hired a company to pack what the girls wanted for England. She'd flown to London, where she oversaw the unloading of furniture and goods. She checked out the area with Ashley, since Ashley lived on the fourth floor of their building.

Nora listened to the mother and daughter arguments about Bree working on Thanksgiving, only two weeks away. Bree tried to explain to her unyielding mother she just transferred to international status and she had low seniority, which meant she had to work no matter the day.

Mrs. Royce was relentless. "It's not even a holiday here!" Mrs. Royce usually got what she wanted, but not this time. It was resolved when Bree promised she would spend all of the time over Christmas she had available with her mother. Nora was sure this would spark a huge fight between Bree's parents. Eventually, when Mrs. Royce deemed the apartment was safe, clean, and tidy, she kissed the girls good-bye.

A couple weeks later Nora entered her new London apartment building after a long morning run. As she started up the stairs, a door opened on the second floor, and a silver-haired lady called hello to her.

"Good morning, Helen." Nora smiled as she reached the landing. "How are you and Martin today?" She reached out to scratch Martin's head. The docile cat in Helen's arms closed its green eyes at Nora's touch. Helen was a kind lady who had brought them sandwiches and treats while Nora and Bree were moving in up on the fifth floor. The building was old and had no working elevator, so they had to trudge up the stairs past her door every time. Helen lived alone with her cat and was the unofficial gatekeeper of the upper floors. She knew everyone who went past her door.

"My poor boy isn't eating. I don't think he is feeling too well." The older woman, short and stocky, held the cat like a baby in her arms. Nora eyed the fat orange cat; the Garfield lookalike was not starving. Then Nora had an inspiration.

"I'd be more than happy to take Martin and have him looked at. I know a very good veterinarian. Let me go upstairs and see if I can get an appointment." It was time to see *him* again; it had been almost two months since Ben walked away from her. He had not returned her calls. With working crazy hours, moving to a new country, and getting settled in, Nora stopped calling him. But Ben was always on her mind.

"I'm so worried about Martin. Are you sure that won't be any trouble for you?"

"It's no trouble. The vet is outside the city and I've wanted to take a drive now that I have a car." Nora shifted the weight of the grocery bag she was carrying. After her run she had darted into the market for a few things. "Let me put this stuff away, and then I'll make the call."

"Oh, that would be wonderful, dear. Thank you."

Nora continued up the stairs. Helen spoke softly to her cat and closed her door. Nora passed Ashley's apartment on the fourth floor, wondering what she'd say about her going to Ben's clinic. Nora entered the empty apartment. She pulled out her phone and set it on the counter. As she stared skeptically at the phone she told herself, "You can't chicken out now!" She already promised Helen. Once the groceries were put away, she picked up her phone and walked to her laptop. Ashley mentioned Ben's clinic opened a few weeks ago. Nora searched the website and saw his picture. Her heart contracted.

She glanced at the days of operation and the hours. Today was Wednesday; they were open until five. Nora was shocked to read the clinic was closed tomorrow in observance of the American Thanksgiving holiday. After a deep breath in and out, she dialed the clinic's phone number. The phone rang. Suddenly the thought struck her, *What if he answers!* But before panic set in, a woman's voice came on the line.

"Westborough Veterinary Clinic, how may I help you?"

Nora slowed to make the turn into the parking lot. The new sign was simply painted white, with black lettering: WESTBOROUGH VETERINARY CLINIC. A car was pulling onto the street, two large dogs' heads hanging out the windows, their noses lifted to catch the scents on the breeze. Her dashboard clock read 4:25 p.m. Nora had the last appointment of the day. She turned off the engine and regarded herself in the rearview mirror. She smoothed the front of her hair and checked the claw-clip. She hesitated only a moment before she said to Martin in the cat carrier, "Here goes nothing."

Inside, the familiar voice of the receptionist greeted her. Nora explained Martin was her elderly neighbor's cat and she apologized for not having much information to fill out on the form on the clipboard she was given. The woman disappeared into another room with the clipboard and came right back.

"Dr. Westborough can see you now. Right this way." Nora followed her, carrying Martin's heavy carrier. She stepped past the woman, who closed the door behind her.

Ben stood in front of her, his head bent over the form she just filled out. "So we have Martin here. What seems to be the problem with...?" The words died on his lips when he glanced up and saw Nora, shock and disbelief in his eyes.

"Hi, Ben," Nora said, a little too breathily. She felt suddenly shy under his intense gaze.

"It says here Helen Blunt." Clearly he was trying to figure out why she filled in a false name.

"Yes, Helen is my neighbor. Martin is her cat. Martin wasn't eating, and she was worried about him. Ashley said you opened your clinic, and I offered to bring Martin, because Helen is elderly and she doesn't drive, and anyway, that's why I'm here." She fell silent and waited for Ben to say something. She could almost see the gears turning behind his eyes. Finally he spoke.

"Let me take a look at him then." Ben gestured to the stainless steel counter in the center of the small room, and Nora heaved the carrier on to it. Nora retreated as Ben opened the carrier and peeked in. Martin stood up, gave a sniff, and waltzed out. With Ben's hello pat, Martin dropped to the counter top with a satisfied purr.

Ben asked his questions, and Nora answered as best she could. Keeping their conversation professional seemed to be breaking the ice. Ben carried Martin to the scale to get his weight.

Nora noticed the improvements he had made and how his vision of the clinic had really come through. "Ben, this place is great."

He set Martin on the counter, his attention returned to Nora. Their gazes locked. *Do you feel this tension, Ben?*

"Yeah, thanks. I'm happy with the renovations. There are a couple minor things that need some adjustment, but overall everything went well. We've been open almost a month, since the beginning of November." Ben pressed and prodded the cat, which could not have cared less, and Nora continued.

"Ashley mentioned you've had great success so far. I'm really happy for you."

Ben smiled at her praise of his accomplishments. His endearing smile and dimpled cheek made her heart flutter. Nora gazed at his handsome face. She had been angry with him for not letting her explain. Now she just wanted to be in his arms.

"Thanks. I threw myself into getting the clinic open after..." He shrugged. Nora knew the rest of his unsaid statement. *"...after I returned from America, where you were proposed to by another guy."*

He continued his examine, poking around Martin's teeth. "Keegan has taken over at Westborough, but I'm there all the time. I'm only half moved into the cottage." He stretched Martin's ear to have a look inside, and then he continued. "Ashley told me you and Bree have a place in her building. How do you like the city?"

So he knew I was here, but he still didn't want to call me. "I like it." Her happy tone reached her ears as high-pitched; she began to regret coming.

He turned his focus to Martin's other ear. "You can tell your neighbor Martin is fine. Tell her to be sure he's getting plenty of fresh water, to keep things moving through his system." He put Martin into the carrier and latched the door. "And she could cut back a little on his food to maintain a healthy weight. He weighs 8 kilograms."

They both shared a chuckle at Martin's expense. "Yeah, he's Helen's baby. She spoils him." Nora stepped forward to gather up the carrier, her laughter dying away. Nora looked into Ben's eyes, where his conflicted emotions were so clearly expressed to her. She paused, contemplating what to say. She came all this way. "Ben, I just wanted to say…" She hesitated.

"You don't have to say anything. Before–" he started searching her dark eyes for his meaning–"before, I behaved badly. I was just so hurt and confused that I walked away." He rubbed his knuckles under his chin, a gesture she recognized from before when he was frustrated. "I should have stayed and talked everything out, but I couldn't. I messed up." He spoke quietly but intently. "Ashley said you turned that guy down." She could hear the anguish in his voice, and it tore her up inside. She shut her eyes momentarily, and when she opened them they were bright with tears.

"Ben, I'm so sorry about that. I had no idea that was going to happen. I had broken up with him. I never gave him any idea I was interested in marrying him. I was shocked to see him. And he has not contacted me since," she stated emphatically. "I'm sorry I barged in here today, but I couldn't…not ever see you again."

His expression softened and his eyes roved over her face. It looked to Nora like he believed her and believed what Ashley had told him. "I behaved badly, and still, here you are." He shook his head in bewilderment.

There was a knock at the door. "Yes?" Ben called, stepping away from Nora with an apologetic smile.

"Dr. Westborough, everything is finished. Do you need me to process anything for the lab before five o'clock?" the receptionist asked.

"No, there is nothing to process tonight. And this last patient is on the house, for a friend, so you can go. I'll see you on Friday."

The receptionist's face lit up. "Okay then. In that case I'll be on my way. Enjoy your holiday," she said. Nora watched her collect her coat and leave the building.

Nora was composed by the time she stepped into the reception area. She set Martin's carrier on the floor while she collected her coat from a hook and turned to Ben. "Ben, thank you, but I can pay. It's not even my cat."

He waved her comment away and changed the subject. "So you're not traveling to America for Thanksgiving?"

Nora pouted. The moment passed, and they returned to small talk. "I have to fly out on Friday afternoon. There wasn't time to squeeze a visit in. I was thinking about making my own turkey, but Bree's working, and I can never find a small turkey."

"You should come have Thanksgiving with us. The clinic is closed tomorrow. Judy, our American, insisted we celebrate with turkey and all the fixings, as you would say. You should come."

Nora was both touched and hopeful. "Ben, you're sure you want me there?"

He leaned nonchalantly on the doorframe, his arms folded over his chest. "Everyone would love to see you. Corrine will be there. Do you remember Will and Liza?" He continued after her nod. "They are coming to dinner also." He paused and seemed to wrestle with himself. "And yes, I would really like it if you came."

"I'd love to." They stood grinning at each other until it became awkward. Nora broke the silence. "Thank you again for checking Martin over." She lifted the carrier and headed for the door. "I'll see you tomorrow. What time is good?"

"Ah, I think around two would be fine." He smiled, looking more invigorated than when she entered his exam room.

"Okay. Bye, Ben." She slipped out the door, walked to her car, and drove away. Speeding to the city she cranked the radio and sang all the way home. At first, the wide-eyed cat flattened his ears at the loud sound, but he settled in and slept for the rest of the ride. Nora couldn't wait for tomorrow.

Chapter Twenty-Four

The cool, dry November day made it a nice drive into the picturesque English countryside. Nora wore a woven wool skirt, complete with stockings and boots. Her fitted burgundy sweater hugged her curves. She wore long pendent earrings, her hair pinned up. A bracelet hung around her slim wrist.

Judy greeted Nora with an enthusiastic long hug. She held Nora at arm's length admiring her. "It is so wonderful to see you again."

"It's wonderful to see you too. I'm lucky you are celebrating Thanksgiving." Nora inhaled the delicious holiday aromas. "I made some butterscotch cookies." She handed the platter to Judy.

"Thank you! Now come say hello. Corrine's in the family room. You are the first guest," Judy said as they made their way down the hall to the cozy gathering room.

Corrine jumped up and ran over to Nora. She was still wearing pajamas, her hair in a ponytail. As they hugged, Corrine said into her ear, "I'm so happy he invited you. It has been weeks since he's been agreeable, if you know what I mean."

"I'll let Ben know you're here," Judy said. "I'll take these to the kitchen. It's so thoughtful of you to bring homemade cookies." Judy then pinned Corrine with a suggestive gaze and spoke with quiet authority. "Please go up and get dressed."

Corrine's dad, Derek, stood to shake Nora's hand. "How was the drive."

After a few minutes of pleasantries, Ben entered the room dressed in a gray sweater and dark trousers. He clasped Nora in a brief hug, overwhelming her by his nearness.

Corrine, who hadn't yet obeyed Judy, prodded, "How is it you happened to see each other yesterday?"

Nora told her the story about volunteering to bring Martin, her neighbor's cat, to Ben because Martin's owner didn't drive. Nora went on to say how Martin was always escaping into the hallway. When they were moving in, he ended up asleep in a box in their apartment. After listening to a couple more stories about Martin's antics, Corrine left to get dressed before the rest of the guests arrived. Derek returned to his chair to continue reading. Nora heard Judy working in the kitchen.

"Am I too early? You said two, right?" Nora asked Ben quietly.

A guilty smile played on his lips. "Yeah, well... I thought if you came early you might want to visit Grand Duke and Duchess in the stables."

"*Yes,* of course! I'd love to," She would never forget witnessing Grand Duke's birth. The horse would always be special to her.

"Let's go." They ducked out the door, shrugging on their coats.

When they entered the stable, it took their eyes a minute to adjust. Ben gave a low whistle, and a dark nose protruded out of the stall.

"This is Grand Duke? He's so big!" Nora exclaimed. Ben talked quietly about the horses, and Nora listened, relaxed, as she leaned against the side of the stall, stroking Grand Duke's neck. They visited Duchess, a couple stalls down, chatting easily, like there had never been any tension between them.

"There is something peaceful about these animals." Nora looked in at Duchess, studying her strong, fine lines. The horse's large dark eyes curiously regarded Nora. The soft blowing sounds of her breath were calming.

Ben became quiet. Nora was aware he studied her. She felt his eyes caress her sable-colored hair, piled up on her head, exposing her long, slender neck before it disappeared into the collar of her jacket. She met his gaze over her shoulder, unable to take his scrutiny any longer.

"What is it?" she asked, sensing his sudden discomfort at being apprehended.

He glanced around to be sure they were alone before he pulled a box out of his pocket. "It's nothing. It's just I never got a chance to give you your birthday gift. I thought I could give it to you now."

"Oh." Speechless, she stared at the small box he held out to her. She took it and opened the top.

"Oh, Ben!" She examined the necklace with a horseshoe charm, reading the engraving: Grand Duke. Her hand flew to her mouth to stifle her emotions. "Ben, I love it!" She rushed into his arms. Closing her eyes, she thanked him over and over.

He squeezed her close to his chest, nuzzling his nose along her neck. He murmured into her hair, "Nora, I wanted to pick up the phone so many times and call you. I wanted to tell you about every detail as my business came to life. I couldn't stop thinking about when I took you there and how I imagined you'd be a part of it. Nora, you are an amazing person, and I'm such an ass for running away. I will never make that mistake again."

She lifted her chin, and they gazed into each other's eyes. Their lips brushed. A moment later they were locked together in a passionate kiss.

Ben cradled Nora's head in his hands and whispered, "You are the girl of my dreams, Nora. I was going crazy without you. You are all I can think about."

They kissed again and again.

Finally Ben rested his forehead against hers and whispered with regret. "I am so sorry I didn't call you. I'm sorry I did that to you...to us. When I thought there was someone else..." His eyes roamed her face. "It killed me, because I knew...I know I'm in love with you."

Nora felt taut with emotion. Ben, the man she had wanted all along, loved her. "Ben, you snared me the moment I met you. *You* are all *I* think about. I told you I had to see you again. I just had to, because I feel the same way. I love you too."

They didn't know how long they stood in front of the stall, entranced, locked together in a passionate embrace, before they heard car doors slam in the distant yard and the loud shouts of jovial greeters.

"We should go inside." His voice was hoarse, and she was touched by his emotion.

"It sounds like some guests have arrived," she agreed, reluctantly stepping out of his embrace.

Before they left the stables, Ben slipped the necklace around Nora's neck and fastened it; the horseshoe rested just below the hollow of her throat. Nora caressed it between her fingers. *Ben is a thoughtful and romantic man, and I love him.*

Apparently Corrine noticed their handholding and intimate exchanges. In a shallow whisper only the two of them could hear, she said, "It's good to see you together again."

"I couldn't be happier," Ben murmured, and he caressed Nora's face with loving eyes.

"Good," Corrine emphasized, "because we all love Nora, and we want her sticking around."

Nora felt her throat swell with emotion when she heard Corrine's response.

"What's going on over here?" Liza asked, her husband Will in tow. Nora hugged her warmly, remembering she had really enjoyed meeting Liza and Will at the Atlas.

Nora fit right in, talking to everyone with ease, just like when she visited the Westborough household before. She felt comfortable there. Judy had bonded with her instantly. Derek had given his son a wink of approval. Corrine thought very highly of Bree's friend. Will, a quiet kind of guy, went out of his way to comment Nora was great for Ben. Liza was already making plans for them to hang out again. Nora glanced around at her new family in this home away from home.

After dinner Nora caught Ben glancing her way and their eyes locked. The way he made her feel with one look told her she made the right choice long ago when she took action to change her dull life. *This is what true love feels like.*

Epilogue

A warm August day, tents were set up in the backyard of the Clark's home. Beneath them, several tables were covered in pale pink linens. Each floral centerpiece carefully and individually constructed from an array of flowers, pink ribbons, and baby rattles. Heidi oversaw every detail of her granddaughter's christening celebration. Victoria and Perry were the proud parents of a daughter, Lana Lillian Reynolds. When Victoria stopped the fertility treatments after the loss of her son, she soon became pregnant naturally.

Since Nora and Ben planned to come for the christening, Ben suggested they extend their stay and spend some quality time visiting Nora's parents, who had met Ben on a few occasions before, but he thought this would give them the opportunity to get to know one another better. Nora didn't know Ben had an important question to ask her father.

Nora lived in London for over a year and a half. She explored a vast number of cities with both Bree and Ben. Bree and Evan became engaged in February, on Valentine's Day, and were planning a spring wedding in Italy the following year. From time to time Bree's parents visited, separately of course; they both promised Bree her wedding day was *her* special day, and they wouldn't cause any drama.

Nora thought it remarkable how people came and went in life. She lost touch with her flight attendant friends in the states: Jackie, Miguel, and Rebecca. She regretted not speaking to Sergei but knew it was right to let that relationship go silent. When she wasn't flying, she was with Ben. He had the cottage modernized, and his clinic was doing well. They took time to ride the horses and spent time with friends like Liza and Will and others Ben introduced Nora to.

Nora didn't regret any of the things she'd done that brought her to this very day, this very moment. Even though at times she felt like she stumbled through indecisions or bad decisions, they made her grow. Each memory was like a compass, keeping her true to herself.

Finished eating a delicious luncheon, Nora sat at the edge of a tent, feeling the warm sun on her bare legs. She watched her mom gather her granddaughter in her arms. Dad looked over Heidi's shoulder, offering baby Lana a finger to grab. Heidi was ready to parade Lana past the gaggle of her friends waiting nearby.

Nora's gaze drifted and followed Lizzy. Lizzy, barefoot and in a dress, corralled the younger kids at the party to play soccer. Tyler, now Lizzy's official boyfriend, jogged over with another soccer ball to join her. Always one to love sports, her little sister had straightened out and found her niche, a coaching job she held more than a year now. Also, she focused on finishing up her degree. Nora relaxed, observing her family, until she was distracted.

She shielded her eyes from the sun as she watched the man she loved stroll toward her with two ice-filled glasses of lemonade. *Yum,* she thought—not about the sweating glasses of golden liquid but the smoldering look she was getting. He paused in front of her, his eyes flashing over her with approval, before he bent to give her a lingering kiss. He backed away slowly, and she sighed with happiness.

After passing the cold glass to Nora, Ben sat across from her and stretched out his legs before he drew in a long, thirsty swallow. Nora took a small sip, savoring the pungent flavor of lemon. The ice chips rolled over her tongue as she peeked at him under her lashes. *Life is good.* She finally felt the feeling she had been missing all her life—*contentment.*

Have you read the Landing in Love Series?

Defying Gravity

Jacob Dodge made mistakes in the past, almost destroying his life. Moving to Massachusetts is the only way to start over. Hellbent to not make the same mistakes again he starts living by new rules put in place to protect himself, especially when it comes to women. While volunteering as a coach and mentor for the youth basketball league he's paired with Olivia, the assistant coach who manages to push all his buttons. The energetic, wide-eyed brunette has the natural talent to get herself in some precarious situations—situations he always seems to get involved in. No matter how hard he tries to stay away from her it's as if fate keeps on pushing them in the same direction. And the more he fights it, the more he seems to fall for her.

When flight attendant Olivia Ward is off duty you can find her in the kitchen, usually dusted in flour. However eating too many sweets has caused her waistline to expand. She joins the Athletic Club where awkward run-ins with a handsome new guy only gets more complicated when they begin volunteering together. Tension burns hotter between them as they bring their team to the championship game. Olivia can't deny the magnetism between them but is it even possible her awkward charm can win him over and melt his steely resolve?

LANDING IN LOVE novels are aviation-inspired standalone titles. These are fresh, flirty stories of modern women and every-day men, finding their happily-ever-after in small New England towns.

Look for more titles in the Landing in Love Series!

Holiday Special

Falling in Love at Christmas
Landing in Love Holiday Special I

Airline pilot Trevor West—survives a plane crash. That one death defying moment sets off an avalanche of life-altering events. He unexpectedly becomes a single dad and leaves the airline. Needing a fresh start, he heads to Evergreen, a sleepy Connecticut town. But finding a suitable home proves impossible. He temporarily rents an apartment on the grounds of a Victorian mansion. The introverted owner, Prudence, piques his interest, especially when she bonds with his five-year-old daughter. As the holiday season approaches, he helps decorate the grand house for the annual Holiday Home Tour but despite their growing, mutual attraction, Pru seems to avoid the mistletoe—at all costs.

Prudence Nightingale has a secret. The locals have kept it hush-hush. Writing under a penname has kept this bestselling novelist out of the spotlight. Helping a friend, she begrudgingly rents the apartment over the garage to strangers. Pru plans to avoid this handsome newcomer and his inquisitive daughter, eager to finish her latest book. But her plans evaporate when her meddling sister enlists their help in decorating the stately home for the tour. The little girl brings Christmas alive, but with a deadline looming, she cannot spare time to get involved. And a distraction, such as the extraordinary Trevor West, is the last thing she needs.

This sweet, small-town romance is packed with Christmas chaos and cheer when a handsome stranger comes to town.

About the Author

Jennifer W. Smith is the author of the Landing in Love series. Her contemporary small-town romances are both sweet and heartwarming with happily-ever-afters. These opposites-attract love connections always have something to do with aviation because this former flight attendant turned novelist has a flare for travel and adventure.

For adventure in an alternative reality, check out her paranormal romances in the Broken Water series where these stories are laced with mystery, intrigue, and sacrifice.

When not writing, Jennifer loves reading, cooking, and hanging out with friends. She lives in a quaint New England town with her family. An early morning riser, she loves sunrises and sipping mocha lattes.

Social Media Links

I'm always happy to hear from readers. Please let others know how much you enjoyed the book by leaving a review on Amazon.com and/or Goodreads.com (or other places you hangout on social media). A kind review goes a long way and is greatly appreciated.

WEBSITE jenniferwsmith.com
*Sign-up for my *newsletter*

FACEBOOK authorjenniferwsmith

AMAZON AUTHOR PAGE Jennifer W. Smith

GOODREADS Jennifer W. Smith

BOOKBUB AUTHOR PAGE_Jennifer W. Smith

PINTEREST authorjensmith

Thanks for your support!